MARVEL

ULTIMATE SPIDER-MAN WEB-WARRIORS

SPIDER-VERSE

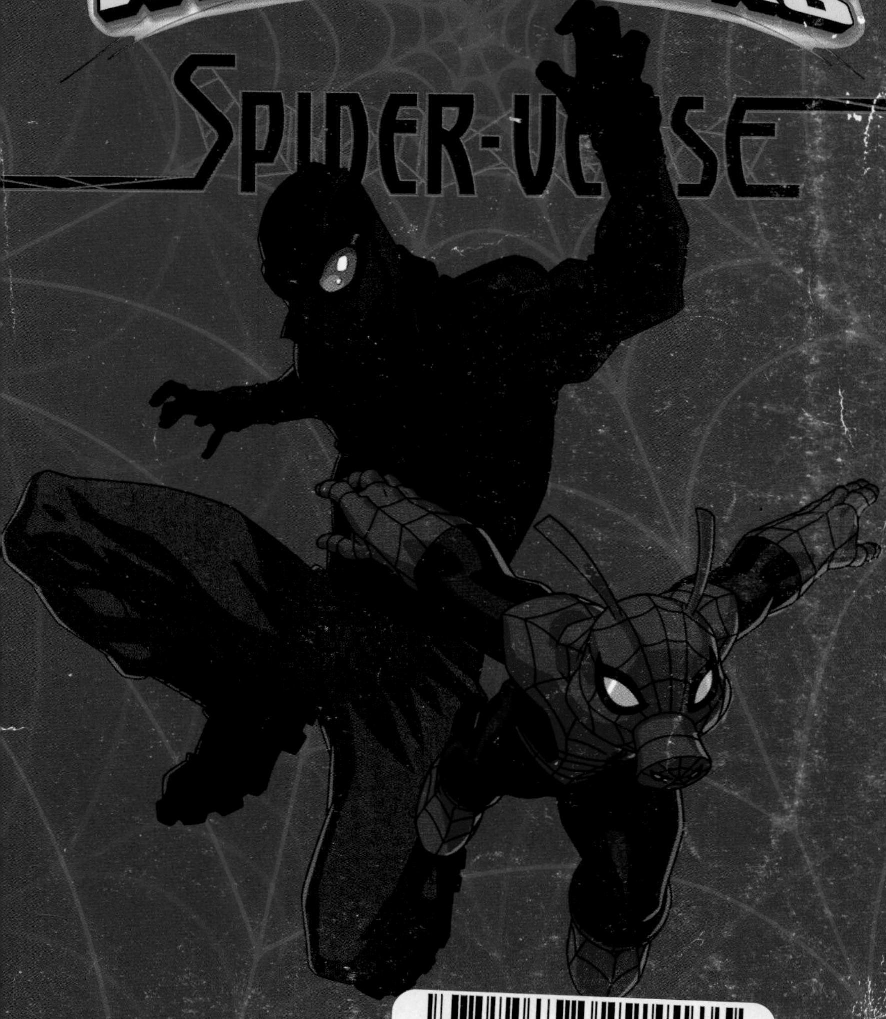

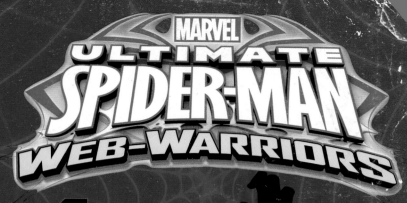

MARVEL UNIVERSE ULTIMATE SPIDER-MAN: SPIDER-VERSE. Contains material originally published in magazine form as MARVEL UNIVERSE ULTIMATE SPIDER-MAN SPIDER-VERSE #1-4. First printing 2016. ISBN# 978-0-7851-9442-2. Published by MARVEL WORLDWIDE, INC., a subsidiary of MARVEL ENTERTAINMENT, LLC. OFFICE OF PUBLICATION: 135 West 50th Street, New York, NY 10020. Copyright © 2016 MARVEL. No similarity between any of the names, characters, persons, and/or institutions in this magazine with those of any living or dead person or institution is intended, and any such similarity which may exist is purely coincidental. **Printed in the U.S.A.** ALAN FINE, President, Marvel Entertainment; DAN BUCKLEY, President, TV, Publishing & Brand Management; JOE QUESADA, Chief Creative Officer; TOM BREVOORT, SVP of Publishing; DAVID BOGART, SVP of Business Affairs & Operations, Publishing & Partnership; C.B. CEBULSKI, VP of Brand Management & Development, Asia; DAVID GABRIEL, SVP of Sales & Marketing, Publishing; JEFF YOUNGQUIST, VP of Production & Special Projects; DAN CARR, Executive Director of Publishing Technology; ALEX MORALES, Director of Publishing Operations; SUSAN CRESPI, Production Manager; STAN LEE, Chairman Emeritus. For information regarding advertising in Marvel Comics or on Marvel.com, please contact Vit DeBellis, Integrated Sales Manager, at vdebellis@marvel.com. For Marvel subscription inquiries, please call 888-511-5480. **Manufactured between 2/19/2016 and 3/28/2016 by SHERIDAN, CHELSEA, MI, USA.**

10 9 8 7 6 5 4 3 2 1

MARVEL ULTIMATE SPIDER-MAN WEB-WARRIORS

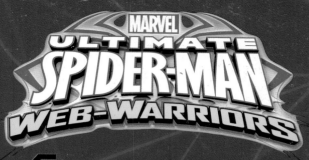

SPIDER-VERSE

BASED ON THE TV SERIES WRITTEN BY
DANIELLE WOLFF, PAUL DINI, KEVIN BURKE, CHRIS "DOC" WYATT & EUGENE SON

DIRECTED BY
KALVIN LEE, ROY BURDINE & TIM MALTBY

ANIMATION PRODUCED BY
MARVEL ANIMATION STUDIOS WITH FILM ROMAN

ADAPTED BY
JOE CARAMAGNA

EDITOR
SEBASTIAN GIRNER

CONSULTING EDITOR
MARK BASSO

SENIOR EDITOR
MARK PANICCIA

SPIDER-MAN CREATED BY STAN LEE & STEVE DITKO

Collection Editor: Alex Starbuck
Associate Editor: Sarah Brunstad
Editors, Special Projects: Jennifer Grünwald & Mark D. Beazley
VP, Production & Special Projects: Jeff Youngquist
SVP Print, Sales & Marketing: David Gabriel
Book Designer: Adam Del Re

Editor In Chief: Axel Alonso
Chief Creative Officer: Joe Quesada
Publisher: Dan Buckley
Executive Producer: Alan Fine

SPECIAL THANKS TO HANNAH MACDONALD & PRODUCT FACTORY

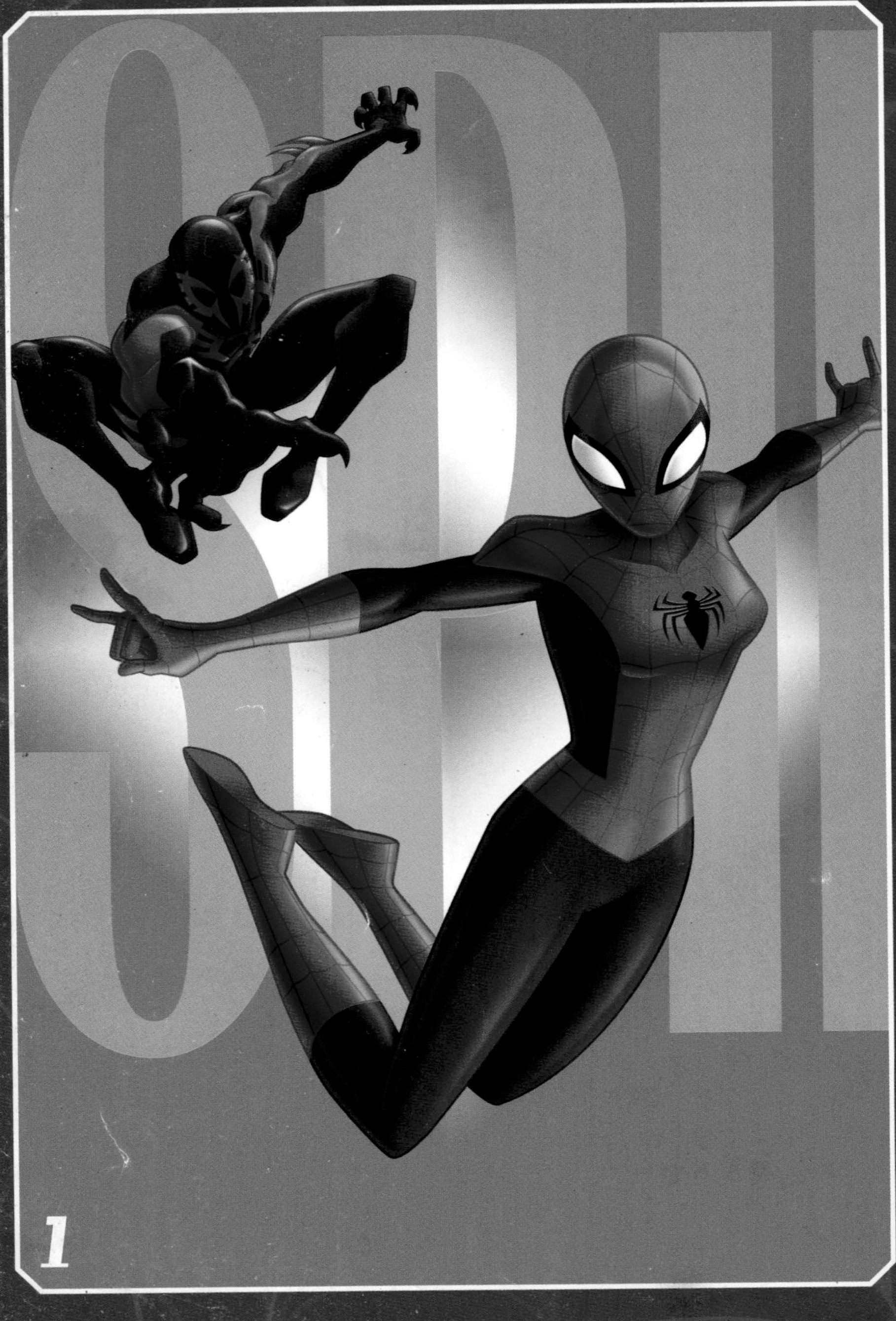
1

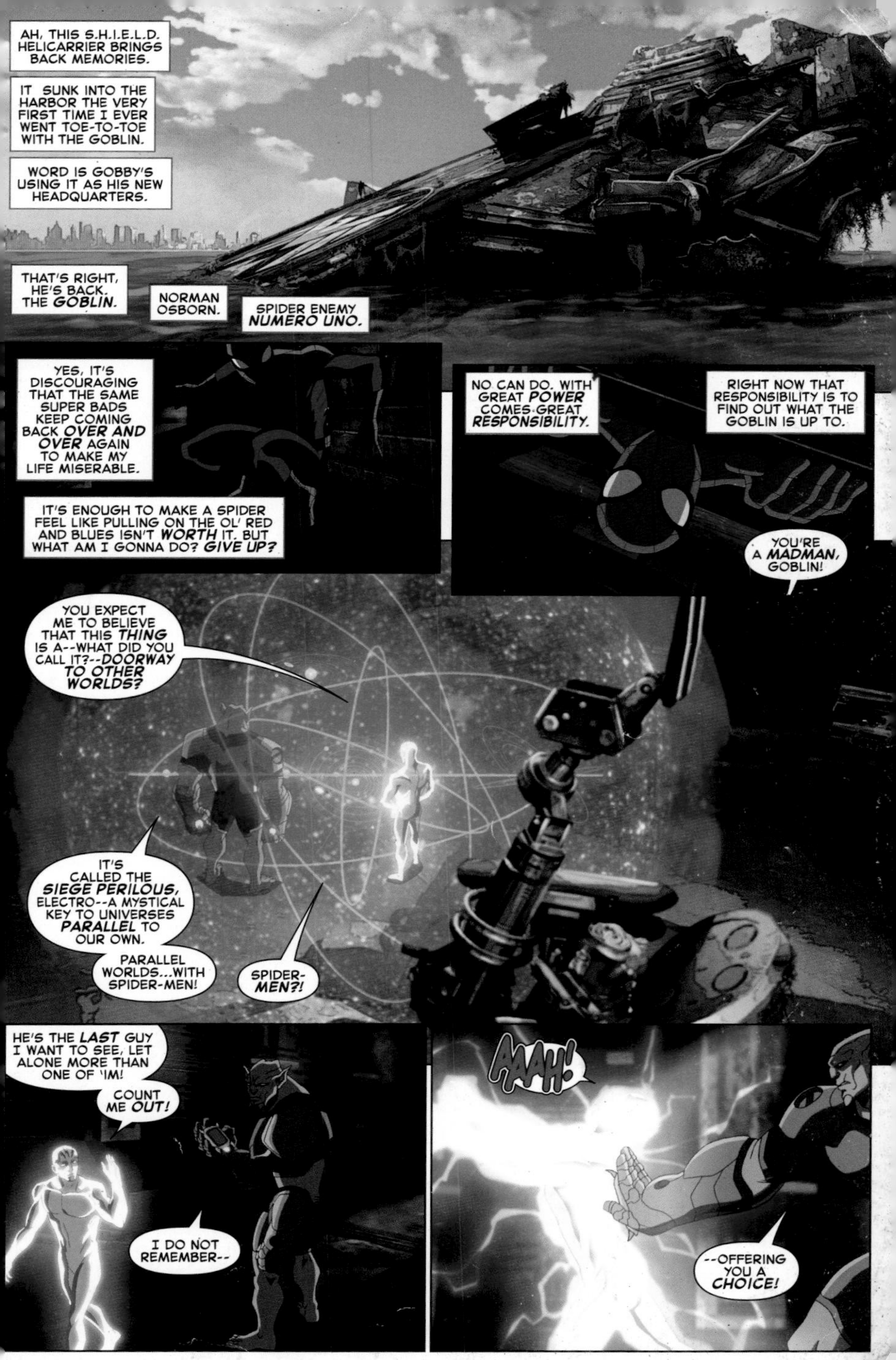
AH, THIS S.H.I.E.L.D. HELICARRIER BRINGS BACK MEMORIES.
IT SUNK INTO THE HARBOR THE VERY FIRST TIME I EVER WENT TOE-TO-TOE WITH THE GOBLIN.
WORD IS GOBBY'S USING IT AS HIS NEW HEADQUARTERS.
THAT'S RIGHT, HE'S BACK. THE GOBLIN.
NORMAN OSBORN.
SPIDER ENEMY NUMERO UNO.
YES, IT'S DISCOURAGING THAT THE SAME SUPER BADS KEEP COMING BACK OVER AND OVER AGAIN TO MAKE MY LIFE MISERABLE.
IT'S ENOUGH TO MAKE A SPIDER FEEL LIKE PULLING ON THE OL' RED AND BLUES ISN'T WORTH IT. BUT WHAT AM I GONNA DO? GIVE UP?
NO CAN DO. WITH GREAT POWER COMES GREAT RESPONSIBILITY.
RIGHT NOW THAT RESPONSIBILITY IS TO FIND OUT WHAT THE GOBLIN IS UP TO.
YOU'RE A MADMAN, GOBLIN!
YOU EXPECT ME TO BELIEVE THAT THIS THING IS A--WHAT DID YOU CALL IT?--DOORWAY TO OTHER WORLDS?
IT'S CALLED THE SIEGE PERILOUS, ELECTRO--A MYSTICAL KEY TO UNIVERSES PARALLEL TO OUR OWN.
PARALLEL WORLDS...WITH SPIDER-MEN!
SPIDER-MEN?!
HE'S THE LAST GUY I WANT TO SEE, LET ALONE MORE THAN ONE OF 'IM!
COUNT ME OUT!
I DO NOT REMEMBER--
AAAH!
--OFFERING YOU A CHOICE!

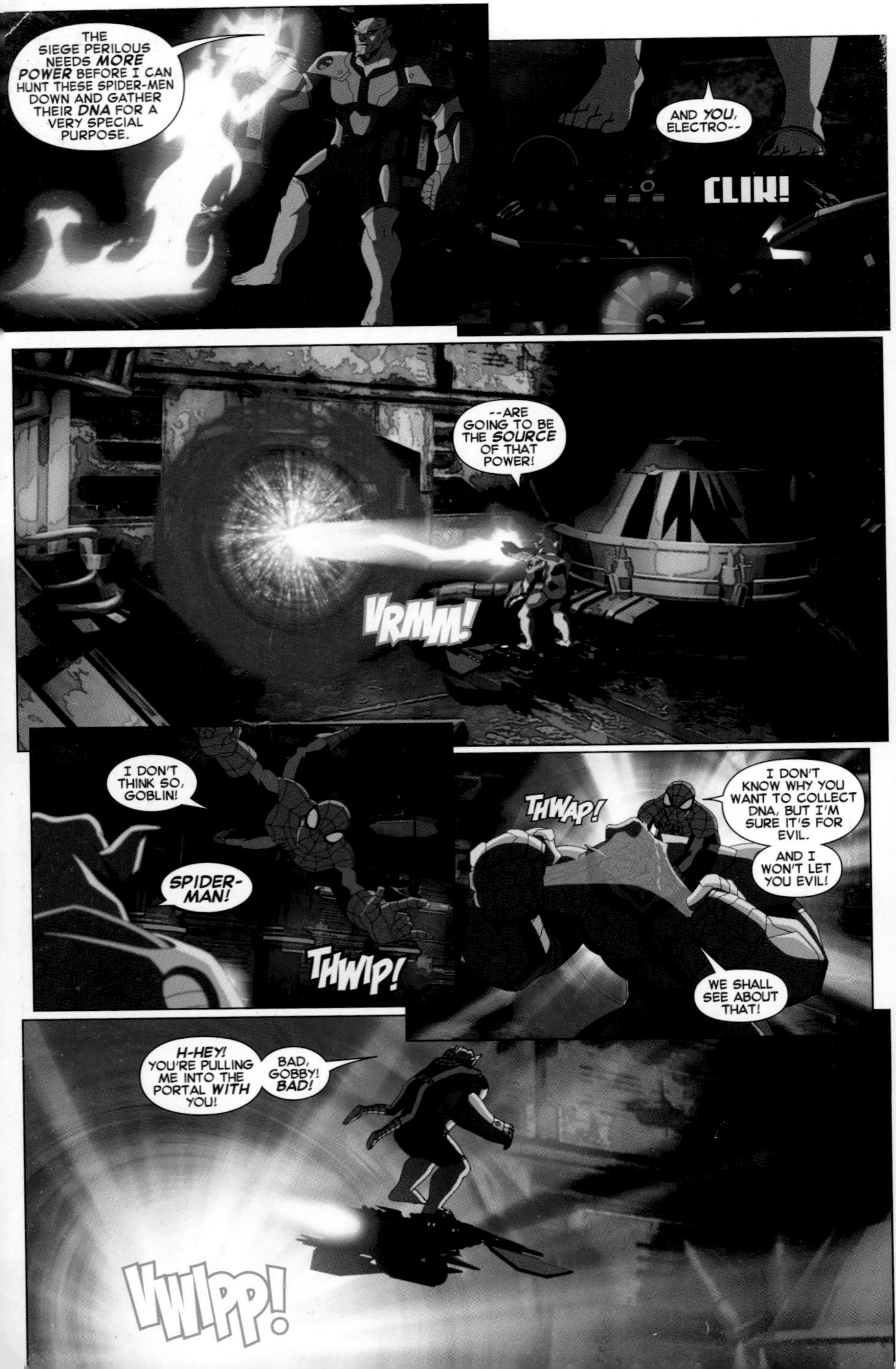

THE SIEGE PERILOUS NEEDS MORE POWER BEFORE I CAN HUNT THESE SPIDER-MEN DOWN AND GATHER THEIR DNA FOR A VERY SPECIAL PURPOSE.
AND YOU, ELECTRO--
CLIK!
--ARE GOING TO BE THE SOURCE OF THAT POWER!
VRMM!
I DON'T THINK SO, GOBLIN!
SPIDER-MAN!
THWIP!
THWAP!
I DON'T KNOW WHY YOU WANT TO COLLECT DNA, BUT I'M SURE IT'S FOR EVIL.
AND I WON'T LET YOU EVIL!
WE SHALL SEE ABOUT THAT!
H-HEY! YOU'RE PULLING ME INTO THE PORTAL WITH YOU!
BAD, GOBBY! BAD!
VWIPP!

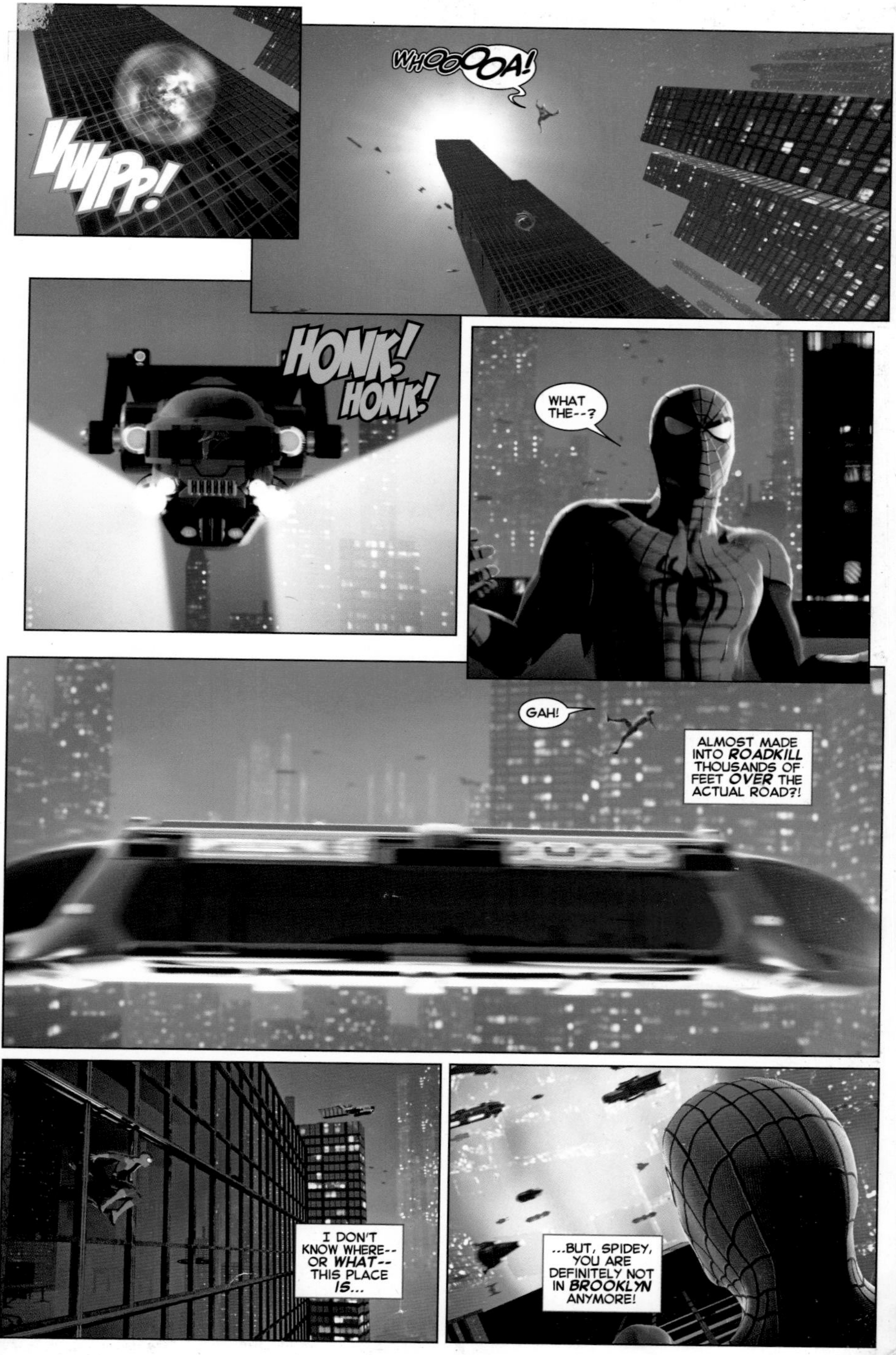
VWIPP!
WHOOOOOA!
HONK! HONK!
WHAT THE--?
GAH!
ALMOST MADE INTO ROADKILL THOUSANDS OF FEET OVER THE ACTUAL ROAD?!
I DON'T KNOW WHERE-- OR WHAT-- THIS PLACE IS...
...BUT, SPIDEY, YOU ARE DEFINITELY NOT IN BROOKLYN ANYMORE!

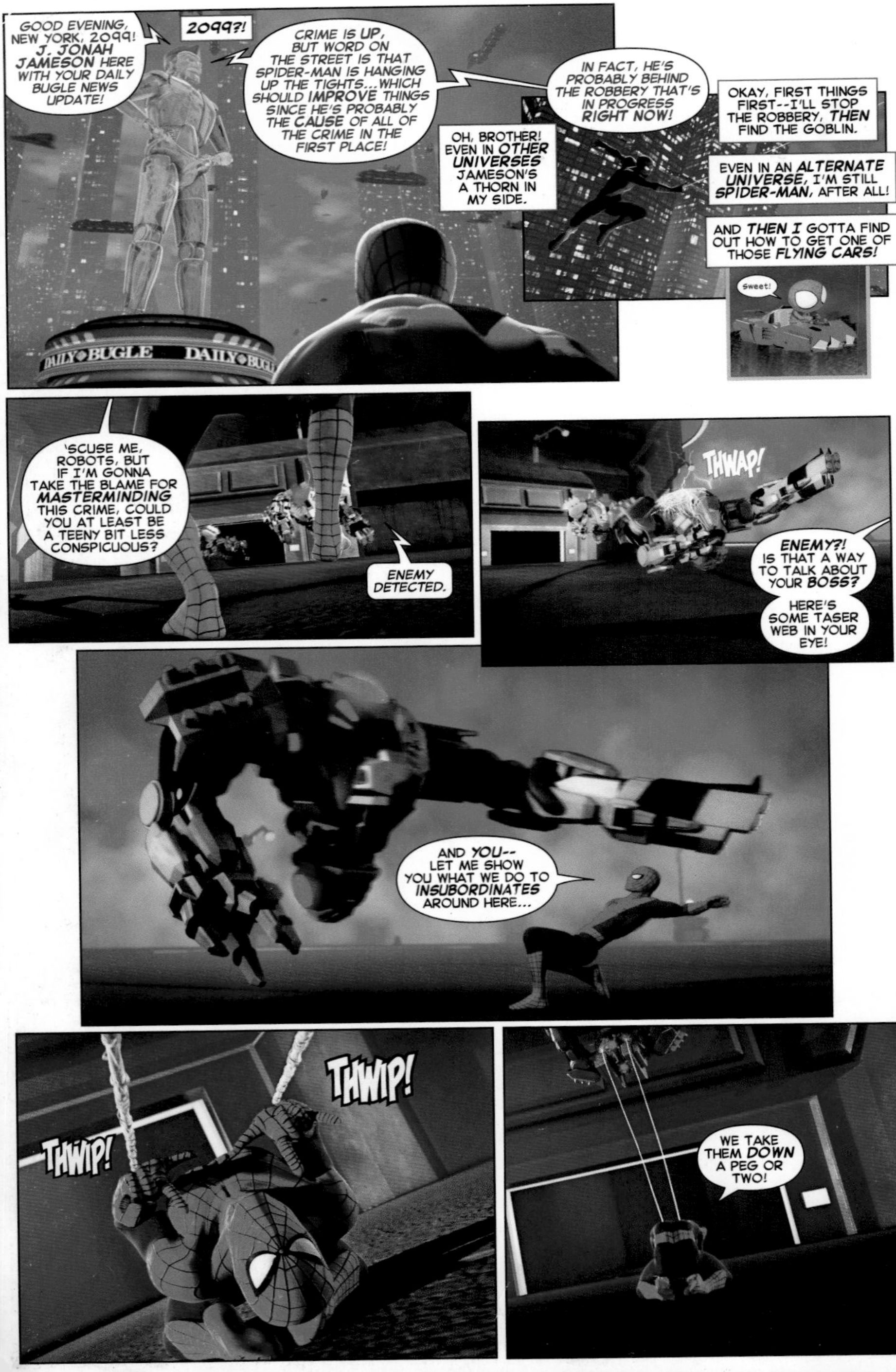
GOOD EVENING, NEW YORK, 2099! J. JONAH JAMESON HERE WITH YOUR DAILY BUGLE NEWS UPDATE!
2099?!
CRIME IS UP, BUT WORD ON THE STREET IS THAT SPIDER-MAN IS HANGING UP THE TIGHTS...WHICH SHOULD IMPROVE THINGS SINCE HE'S PROBABLY THE CAUSE OF ALL OF THE CRIME IN THE FIRST PLACE!
IN FACT, HE'S PROBABLY BEHIND THE ROBBERY THAT'S IN PROGRESS RIGHT NOW!
DAILY BUGLE DAILY BUGLE
OH, BROTHER! EVEN IN OTHER UNIVERSES JAMESON'S A THORN IN MY SIDE.
OKAY, FIRST THINGS FIRST--I'LL STOP THE ROBBERY, THEN FIND THE GOBLIN.
EVEN IN AN ALTERNATE UNIVERSE, I'M STILL SPIDER-MAN, AFTER ALL!
AND THEN I GOTTA FIND OUT HOW TO GET ONE OF THOSE FLYING CARS!
Sweet!
'SCUSE ME, ROBOTS, BUT IF I'M GONNA TAKE THE BLAME FOR MASTERMINDING THIS CRIME, COULD YOU AT LEAST BE A TEENY BIT LESS CONSPICUOUS?
ENEMY DETECTED.
THWAP!
ENEMY?! IS THAT A WAY TO TALK ABOUT YOUR BOSS?
HERE'S SOME TASER WEB IN YOUR EYE!
AND YOU-- LET ME SHOW YOU WHAT WE DO TO INSUBORDINATES AROUND HERE...
THWIP!
THWIP!
WE TAKE THEM DOWN A PEG OR TWO!

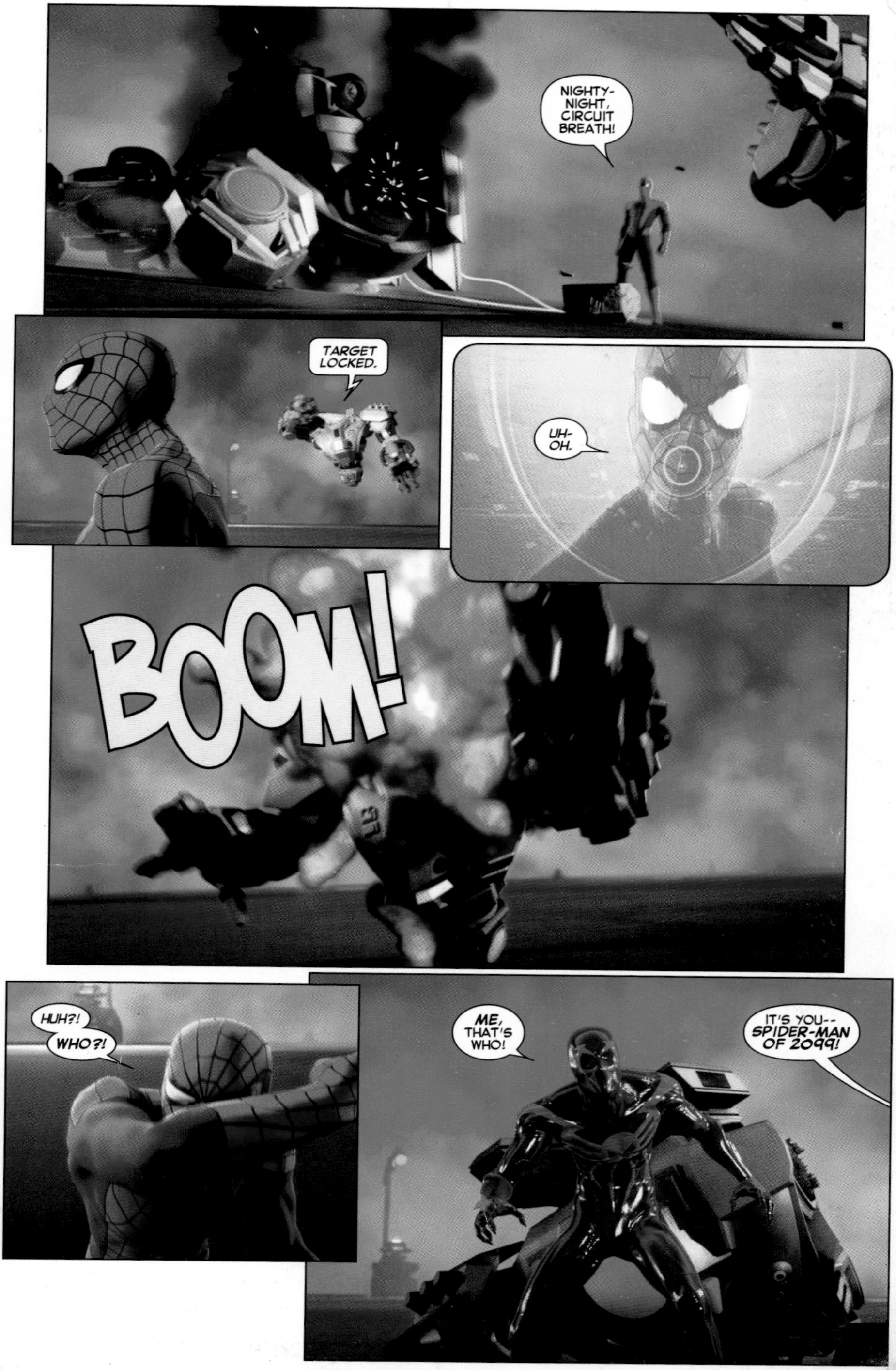
NIGHTY-NIGHT, CIRCUIT BREATH!
TARGET LOCKED.
UH-OH.
BOOM!
HUH?!
WHO?!
ME, THAT'S WHO!
IT'S YOU-- SPIDER-MAN OF 2099!

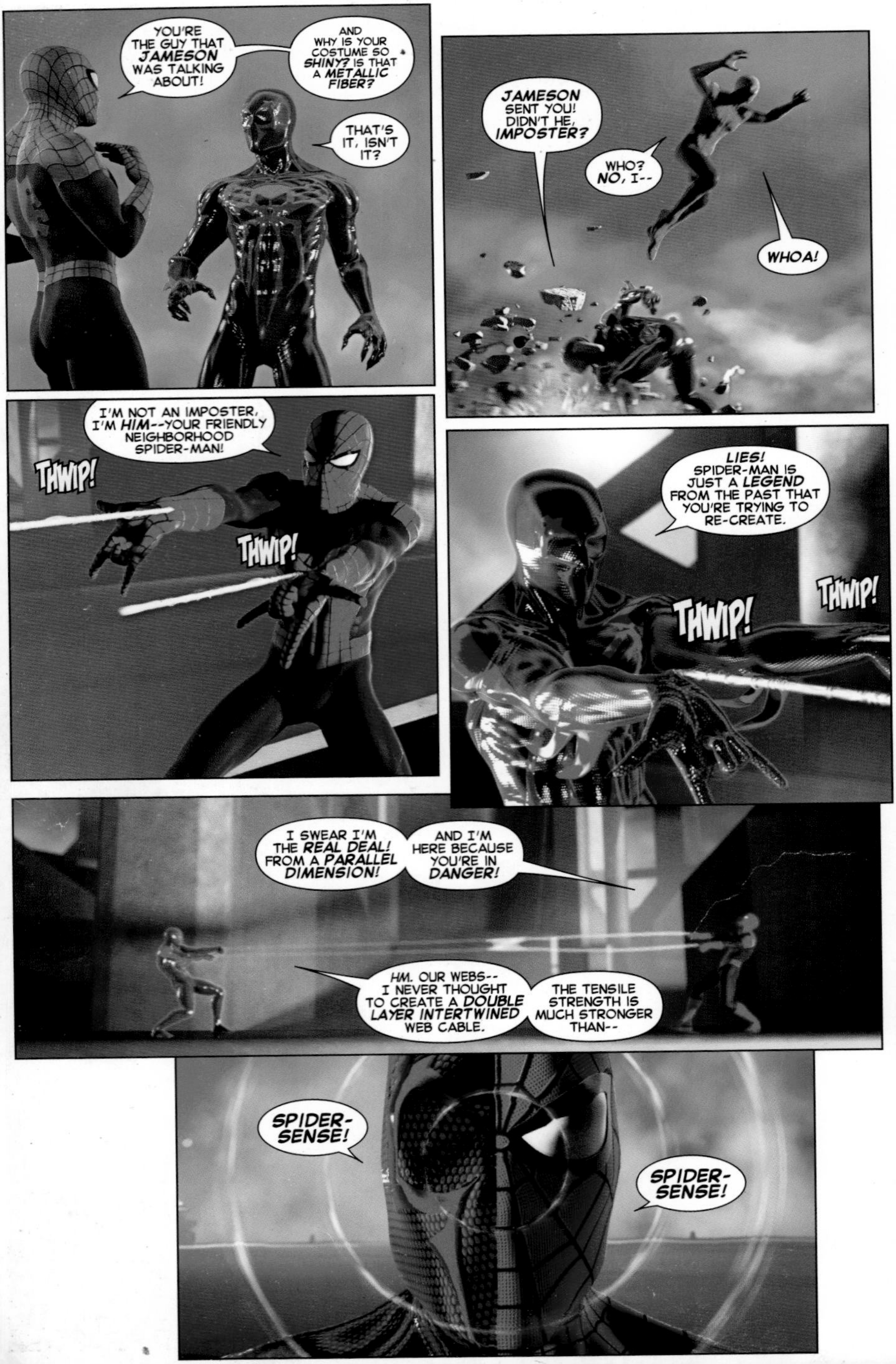
YOU'RE THE GUY THAT JAMESON WAS TALKING ABOUT!
AND WHY IS YOUR COSTUME SO SHINY? IS THAT A METALLIC FIBER?
THAT'S IT, ISN'T IT?
JAMESON SENT YOU! DIDN'T HE, IMPOSTER?
WHO? NO, I--
WHOA!
I'M NOT AN IMPOSTER, I'M HIM--YOUR FRIENDLY NEIGHBORHOOD SPIDER-MAN!
THWIP!
THWIP!
LIES! SPIDER-MAN IS JUST A LEGEND FROM THE PAST THAT YOU'RE TRYING TO RE-CREATE.
THWIP!
THWIP!
I SWEAR I'M THE REAL DEAL! FROM A PARALLEL DIMENSION!
AND I'M HERE BECAUSE YOU'RE IN DANGER!
HM. OUR WEBS-- I NEVER THOUGHT TO CREATE A DOUBLE LAYER INTERTWINED WEB CABLE.
THE TENSILE STRENGTH IS MUCH STRONGER THAN--
SPIDER-SENSE!
SPIDER-SENSE!

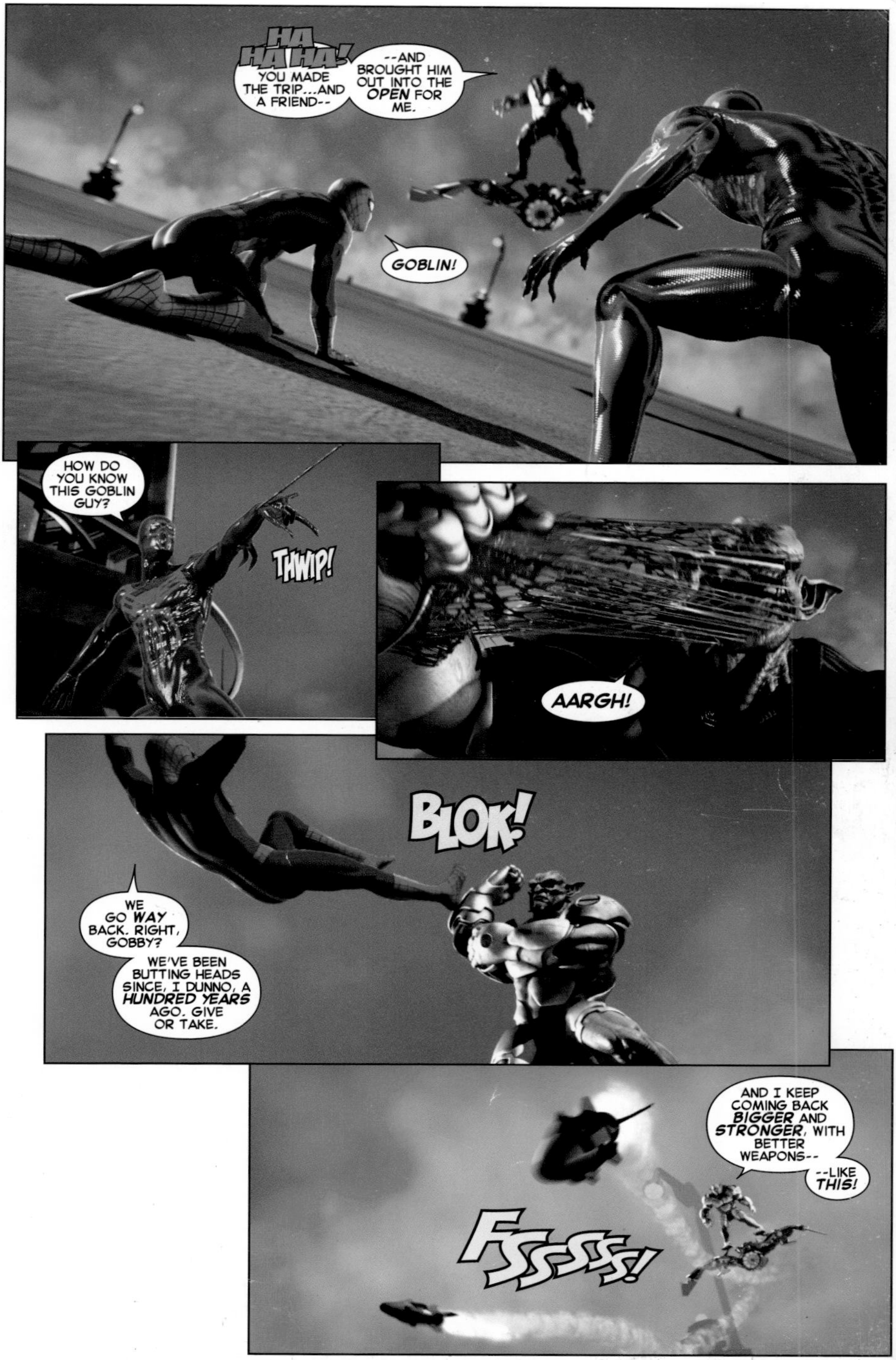
HA HA HA! YOU MADE THE TRIP...AND A FRIEND--
--AND BROUGHT HIM OUT INTO THE OPEN FOR ME.
GOBLIN!
HOW DO YOU KNOW THIS GOBLIN GUY?
THWIP!
AARGH!
BLOK!
WE GO WAY BACK. RIGHT, GOBBY?
WE'VE BEEN BUTTING HEADS SINCE, I DUNNO, A HUNDRED YEARS AGO. GIVE OR TAKE.
AND I KEEP COMING BACK BIGGER AND STRONGER, WITH BETTER WEAPONS--
--LIKE THIS!
FSSSSS!

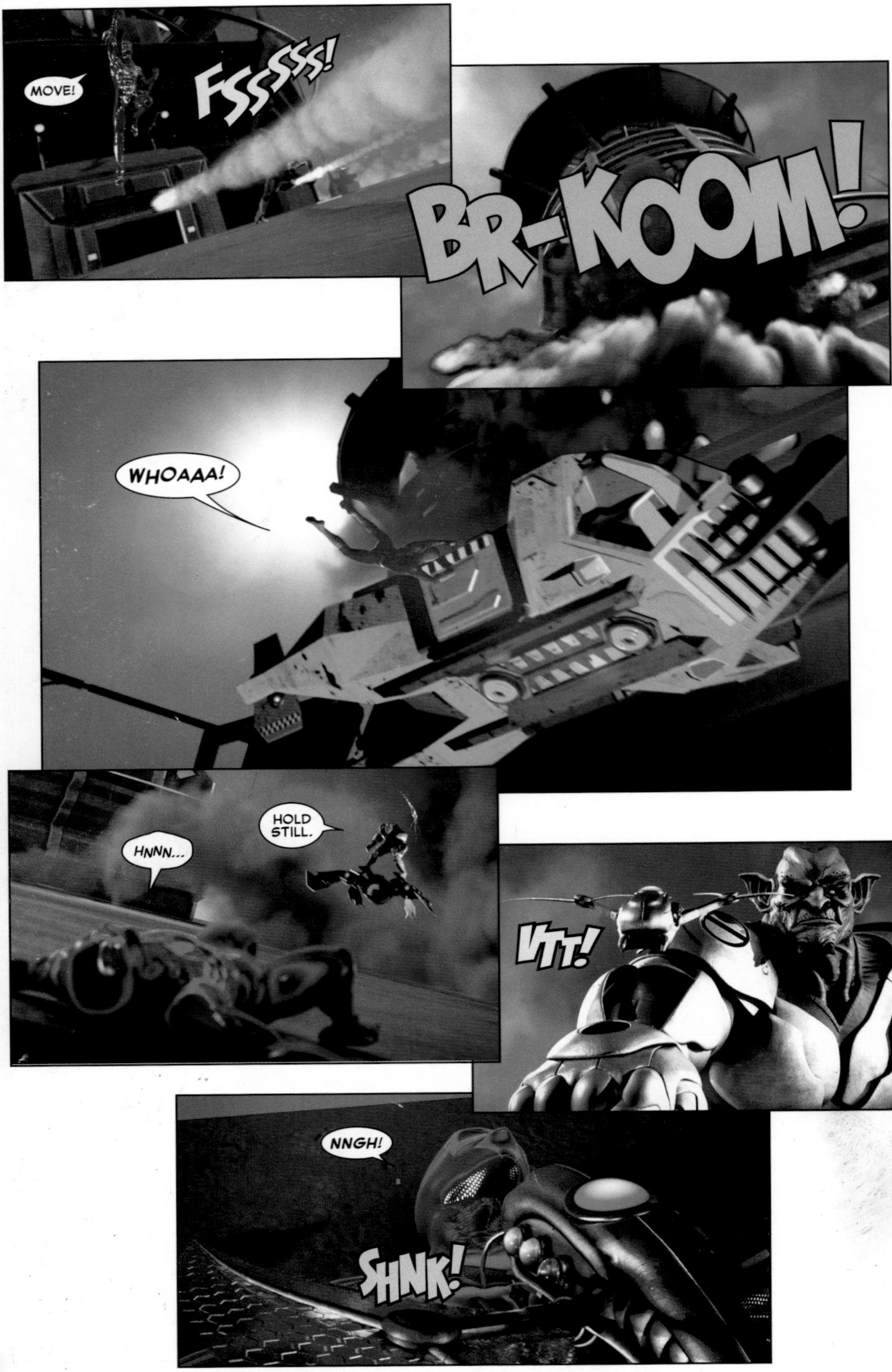
MOVE!
FSSSSS!
BR-KOOM!
WHOAAA!
HNNN...
HOLD STILL.
VTT!
NNGH!
SHNK!

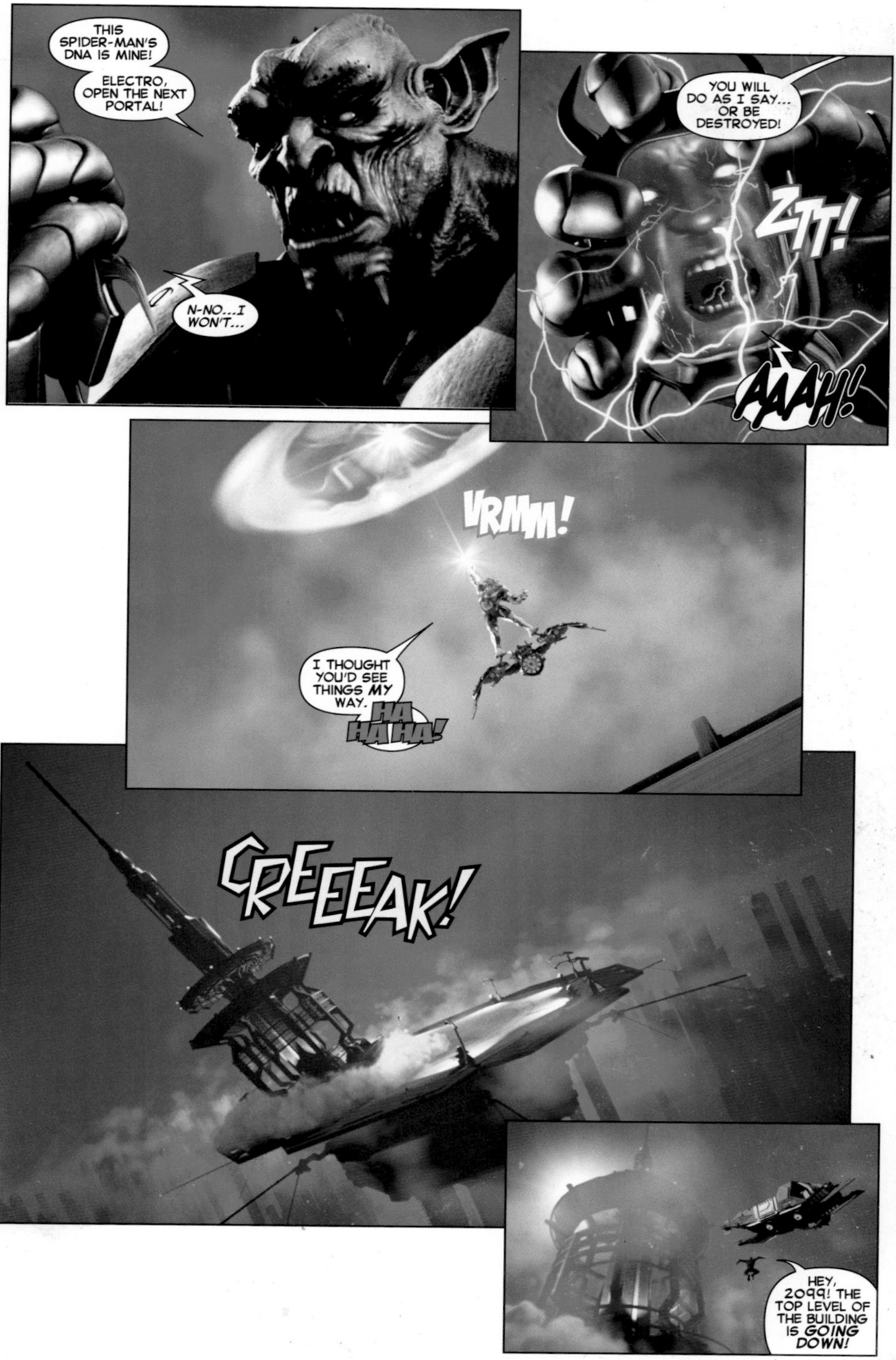
THIS SPIDER-MAN'S DNA IS MINE!
ELECTRO, OPEN THE NEXT PORTAL!
N-NO...I WON'T...
YOU WILL DO AS I SAY... OR BE DESTROYED!
ZTT!
AAAH!
VRMMM!
I THOUGHT YOU'D SEE THINGS MY WAY.
HA HA HA!
CREEEAK!
HEY, 2099! THE TOP LEVEL OF THE BUILDING IS GOING DOWN!

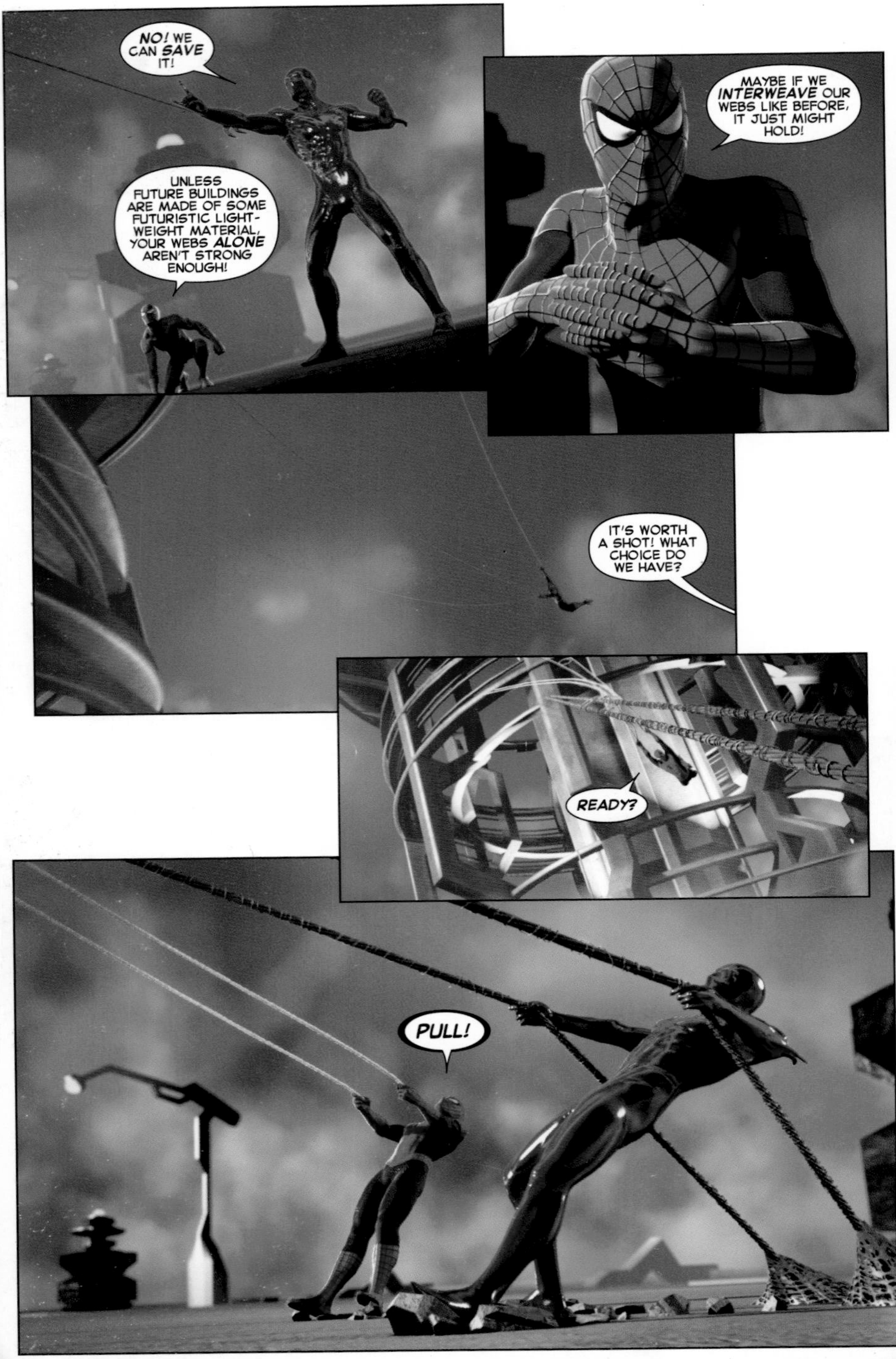
NO! WE CAN SAVE IT!
UNLESS FUTURE BUILDINGS ARE MADE OF SOME FUTURISTIC LIGHT-WEIGHT MATERIAL, YOUR WEBS ALONE AREN'T STRONG ENOUGH!
MAYBE IF WE INTERWEAVE OUR WEBS LIKE BEFORE, IT JUST MIGHT HOLD!
IT'S WORTH A SHOT! WHAT CHOICE DO WE HAVE?
READY?
PULL!

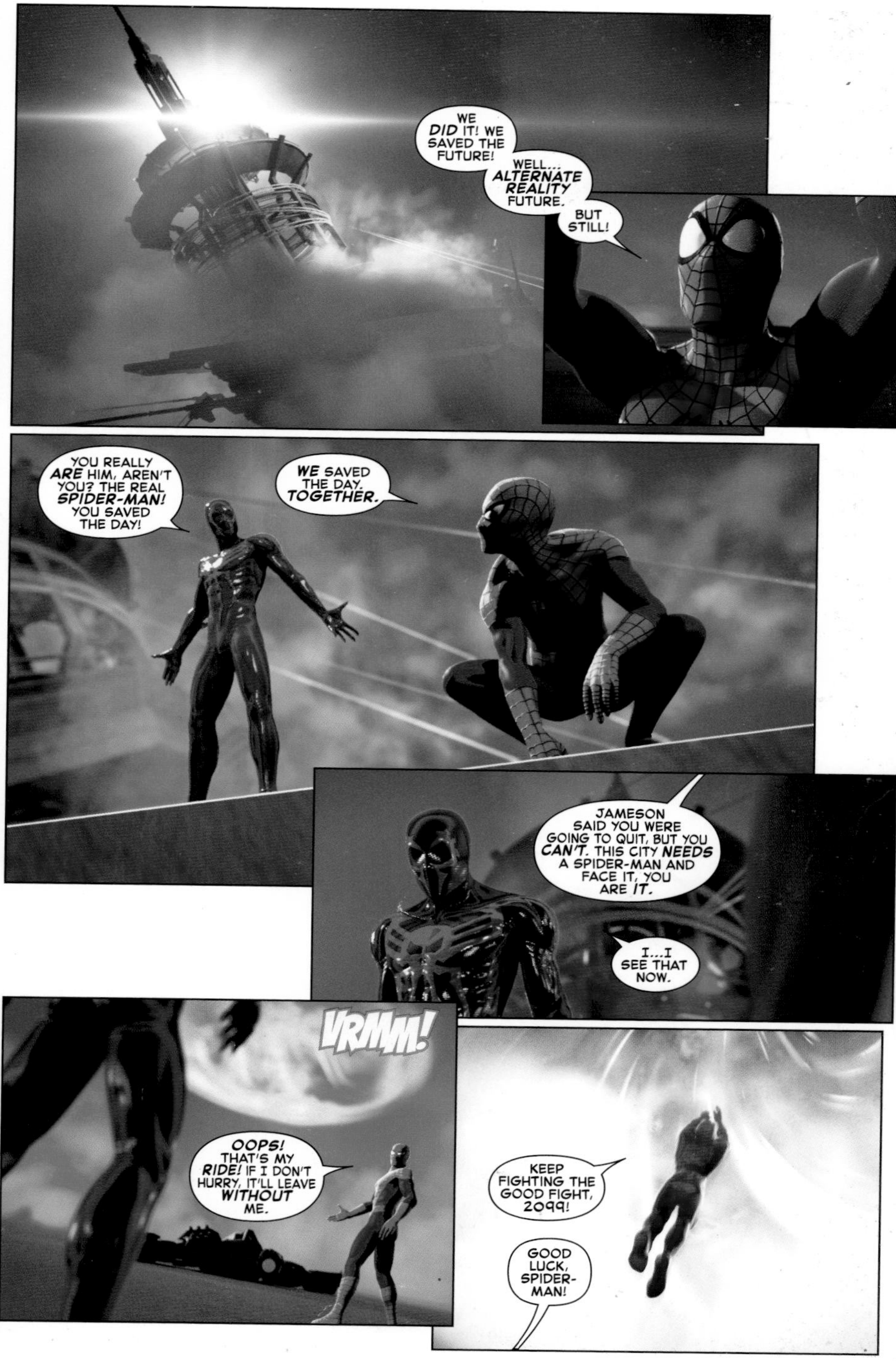

WE DID IT! WE SAVED THE FUTURE!
WELL... ALTERNATE REALITY FUTURE.
BUT STILL!
YOU REALLY ARE HIM, AREN'T YOU? THE REAL SPIDER-MAN! YOU SAVED THE DAY!
WE SAVED THE DAY. TOGETHER.
JAMESON SAID YOU WERE GOING TO QUIT, BUT YOU CAN'T. THIS CITY NEEDS A SPIDER-MAN AND FACE IT, YOU ARE IT.
I...I SEE THAT NOW.
VRMM!
OOPS! THAT'S MY RIDE! IF I DON'T HURRY, IT'LL LEAVE WITHOUT ME.
KEEP FIGHTING THE GOOD FIGHT, 2099!
GOOD LUCK, SPIDER-MAN!

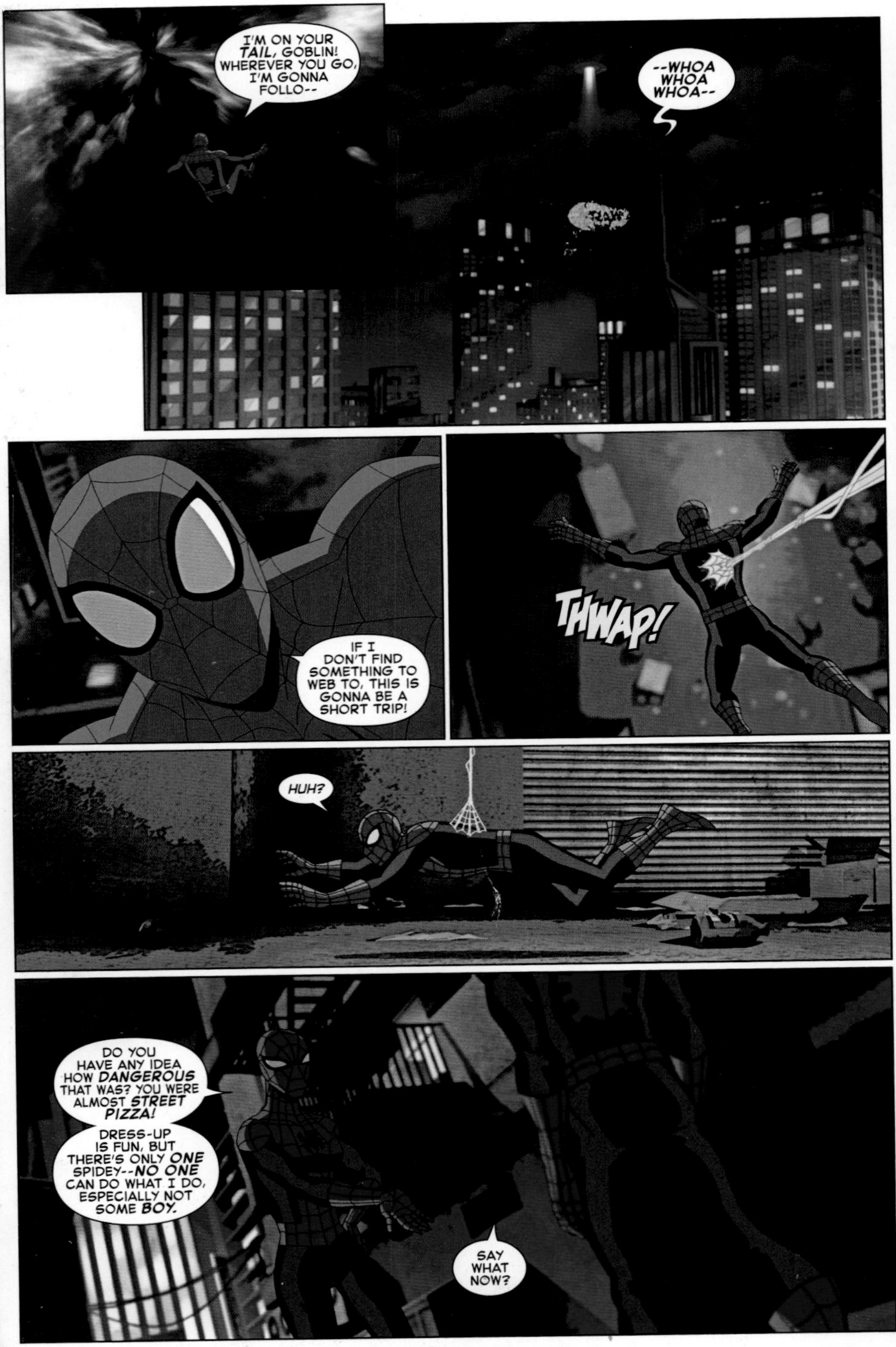
I'M ON YOUR TAIL, GOBLIN! WHEREVER YOU GO, I'M GONNA FOLLO--
--WHOA WHOA WHOA--
IF I DON'T FIND SOMETHING TO WEB TO, THIS IS GONNA BE A SHORT TRIP!
THWAP!
HUH?
DO YOU HAVE ANY IDEA HOW DANGEROUS THAT WAS? YOU WERE ALMOST STREET PIZZA!
DRESS-UP IS FUN, BUT THERE'S ONLY ONE SPIDEY--NO ONE CAN DO WHAT I DO, ESPECIALLY NOT SOME BOY.
SAY WHAT NOW?

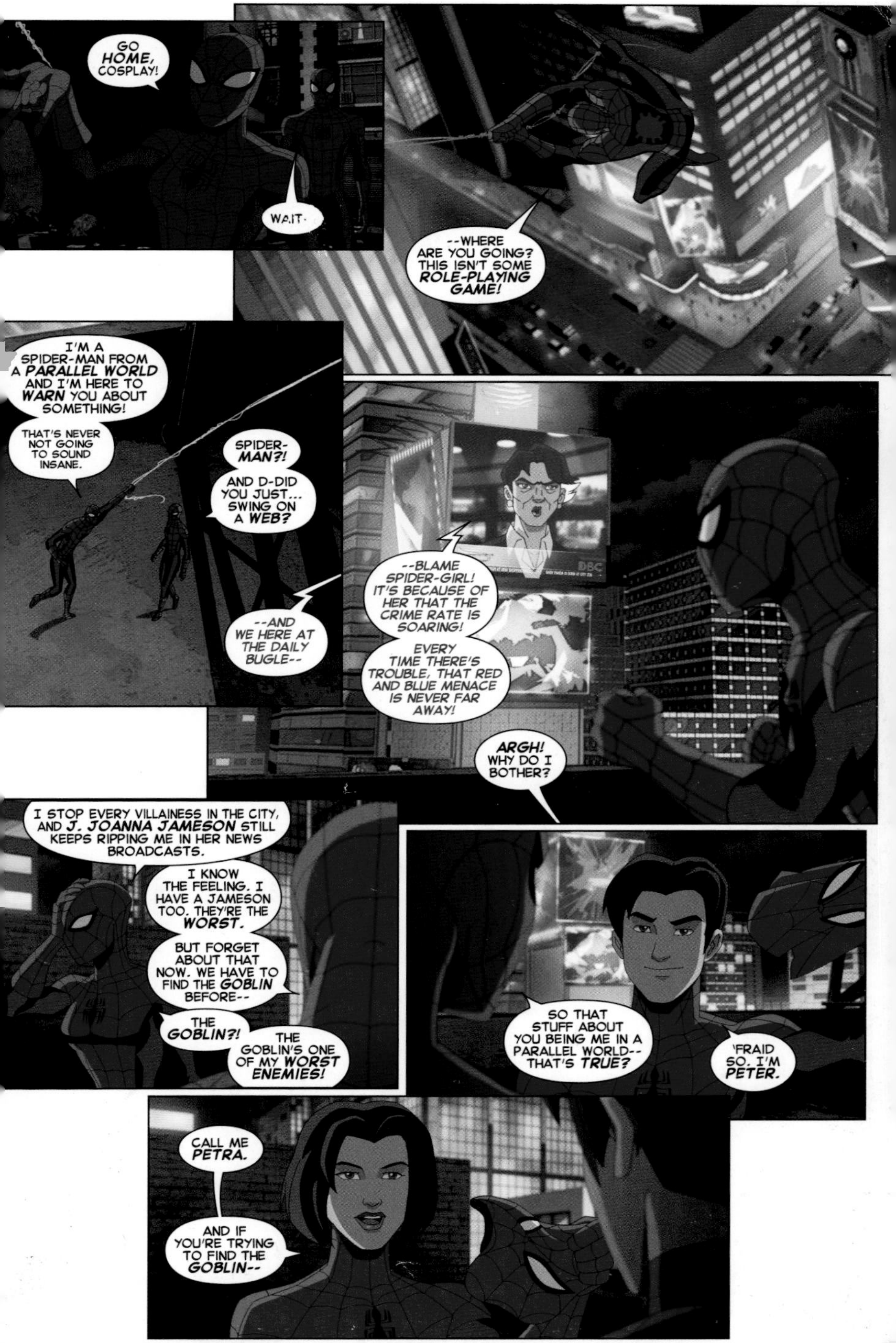
GO HOME, COSPLAY!
WAIT-
--WHERE ARE YOU GOING? THIS ISN'T SOME ROLE-PLAYING GAME!
I'M A SPIDER-MAN FROM A PARALLEL WORLD AND I'M HERE TO WARN YOU ABOUT SOMETHING!
THAT'S NEVER NOT GOING TO SOUND INSANE.
SPIDER-MAN?!
AND D-DID YOU JUST... SWING ON A WEB?
--AND WE HERE AT THE DAILY BUGLE--
--BLAME SPIDER-GIRL! IT'S BECAUSE OF HER THAT THE CRIME RATE IS SOARING!
EVERY TIME THERE'S TROUBLE, THAT RED AND BLUE MENACE IS NEVER FAR AWAY!
DBC
ARGH! WHY DO I BOTHER?
I STOP EVERY VILLAINESS IN THE CITY, AND J. JOANNA JAMESON STILL KEEPS RIPPING ME IN HER NEWS BROADCASTS.
I KNOW THE FEELING. I HAVE A JAMESON TOO. THEY'RE THE WORST.
BUT FORGET ABOUT THAT NOW. WE HAVE TO FIND THE GOBLIN BEFORE--
THE GOBLIN?!
THE GOBLIN'S ONE OF MY WORST ENEMIES!
SO THAT STUFF ABOUT YOU BEING ME IN A PARALLEL WORLD-- THAT'S TRUE?
'FRAID SO. I'M PETER.
CALL ME PETRA.
AND IF YOU'RE TRYING TO FIND THE GOBLIN--

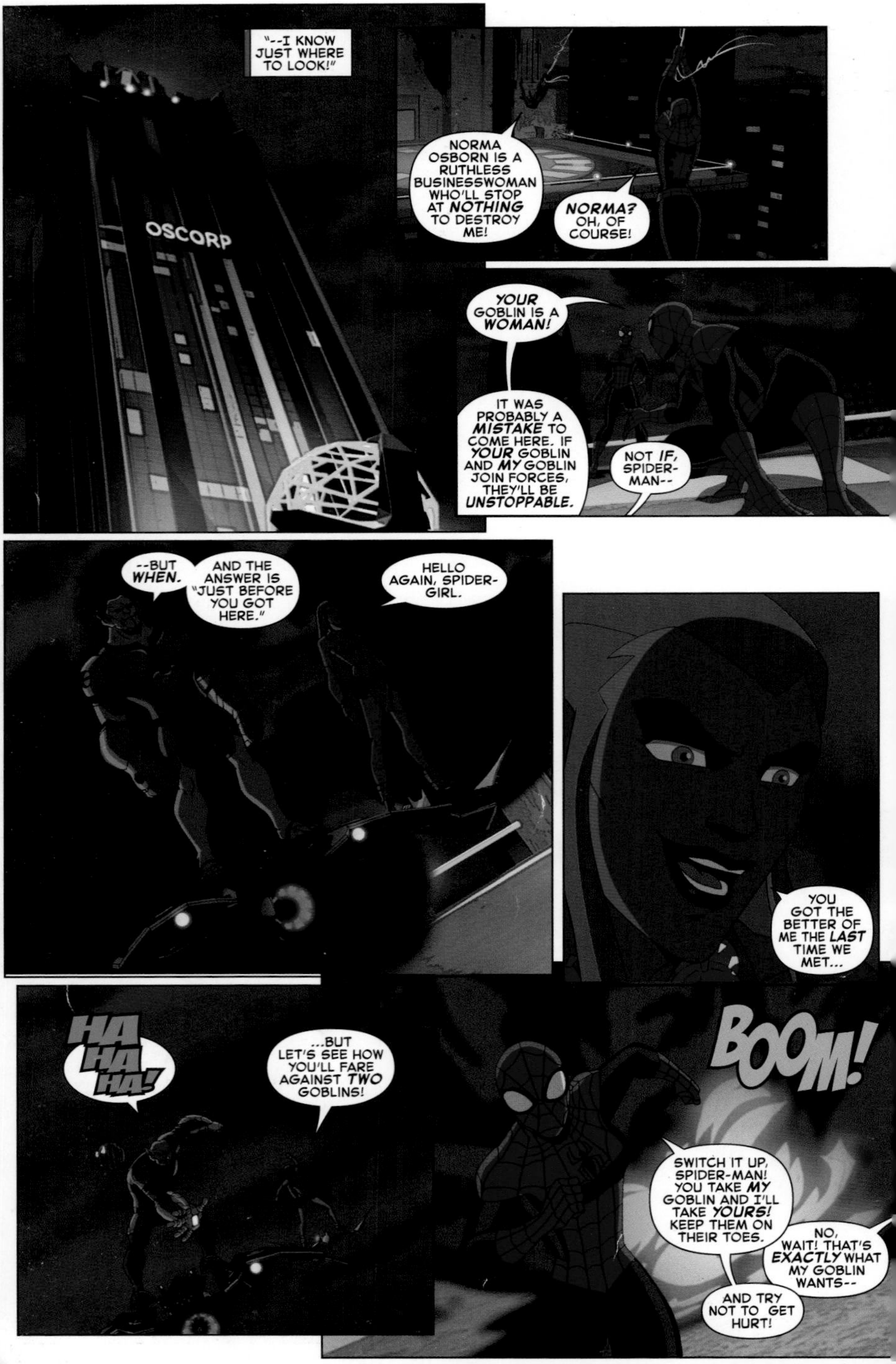

"--I KNOW JUST WHERE TO LOOK!"
OSCORP
NORMA OSBORN IS A RUTHLESS BUSINESSWOMAN WHO'LL STOP AT NOTHING TO DESTROY ME!
NORMA? OH, OF COURSE!
YOUR GOBLIN IS A WOMAN!
IT WAS PROBABLY A MISTAKE TO COME HERE. IF YOUR GOBLIN AND MY GOBLIN JOIN FORCES, THEY'LL BE UNSTOPPABLE.
NOT IF, SPIDER-MAN--
--BUT WHEN.
AND THE ANSWER IS "JUST BEFORE YOU GOT HERE."
HELLO AGAIN, SPIDER-GIRL.
YOU GOT THE BETTER OF ME THE LAST TIME WE MET...
HA HA HA!
...BUT LET'S SEE HOW YOU'LL FARE AGAINST TWO GOBLINS!
BOOM!
SWITCH IT UP, SPIDER-MAN! YOU TAKE MY GOBLIN AND I'LL TAKE YOURS! KEEP THEM ON THEIR TOES.
AND TRY NOT TO GET HURT!
NO, WAIT! THAT'S EXACTLY WHAT MY GOBLIN WANTS--

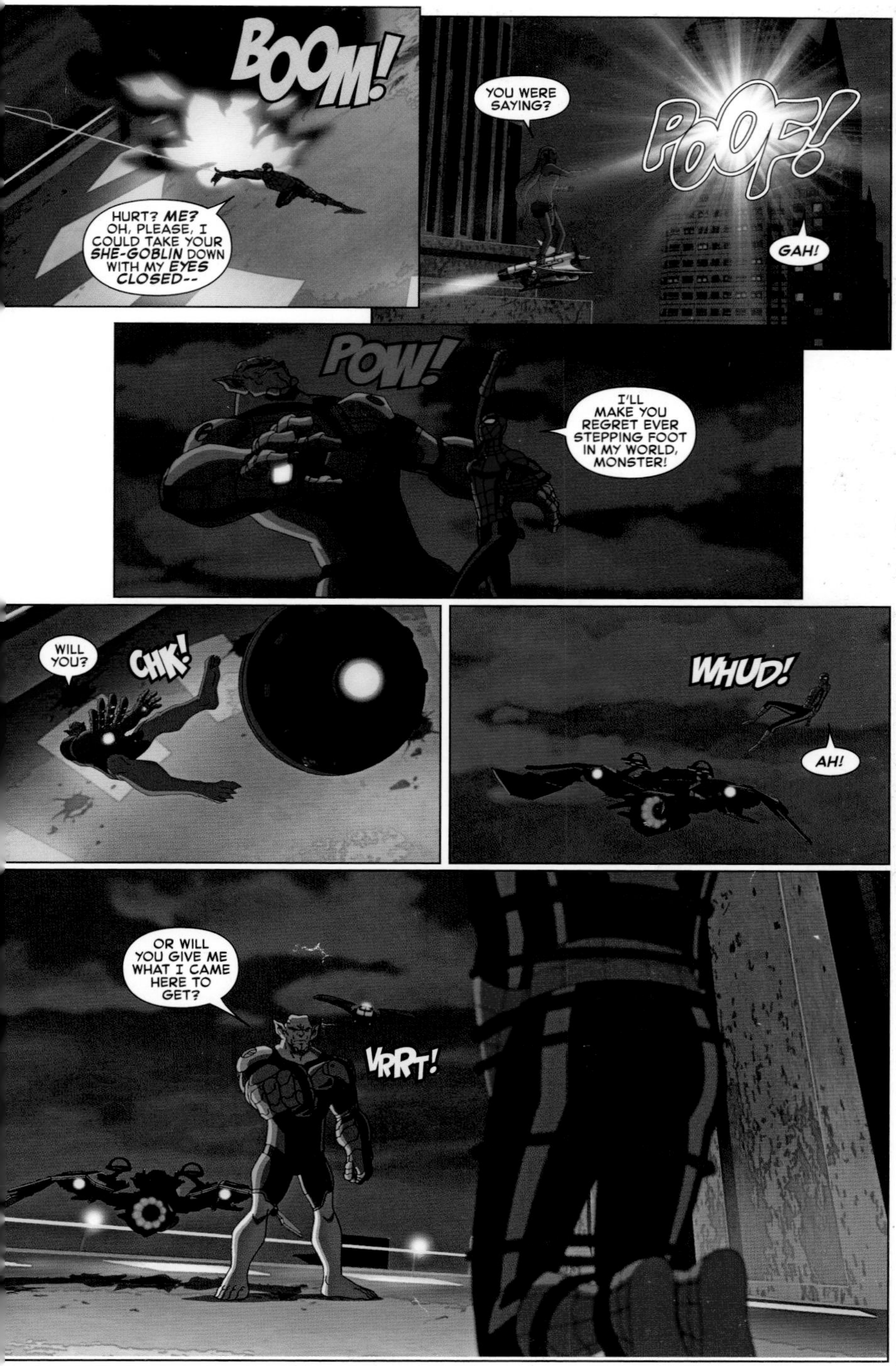
BOOM!
HURT? ME? OH, PLEASE, I COULD TAKE YOUR SHE-GOBLIN DOWN WITH MY EYES CLOSED--
YOU WERE SAYING?
POOF!
GAH!
POW!
I'LL MAKE YOU REGRET EVER STEPPING FOOT IN MY WORLD, MONSTER!
WILL YOU?
CHK!
WHUD!
AH!
OR WILL YOU GIVE ME WHAT I CAME HERE TO GET?
VRRT!

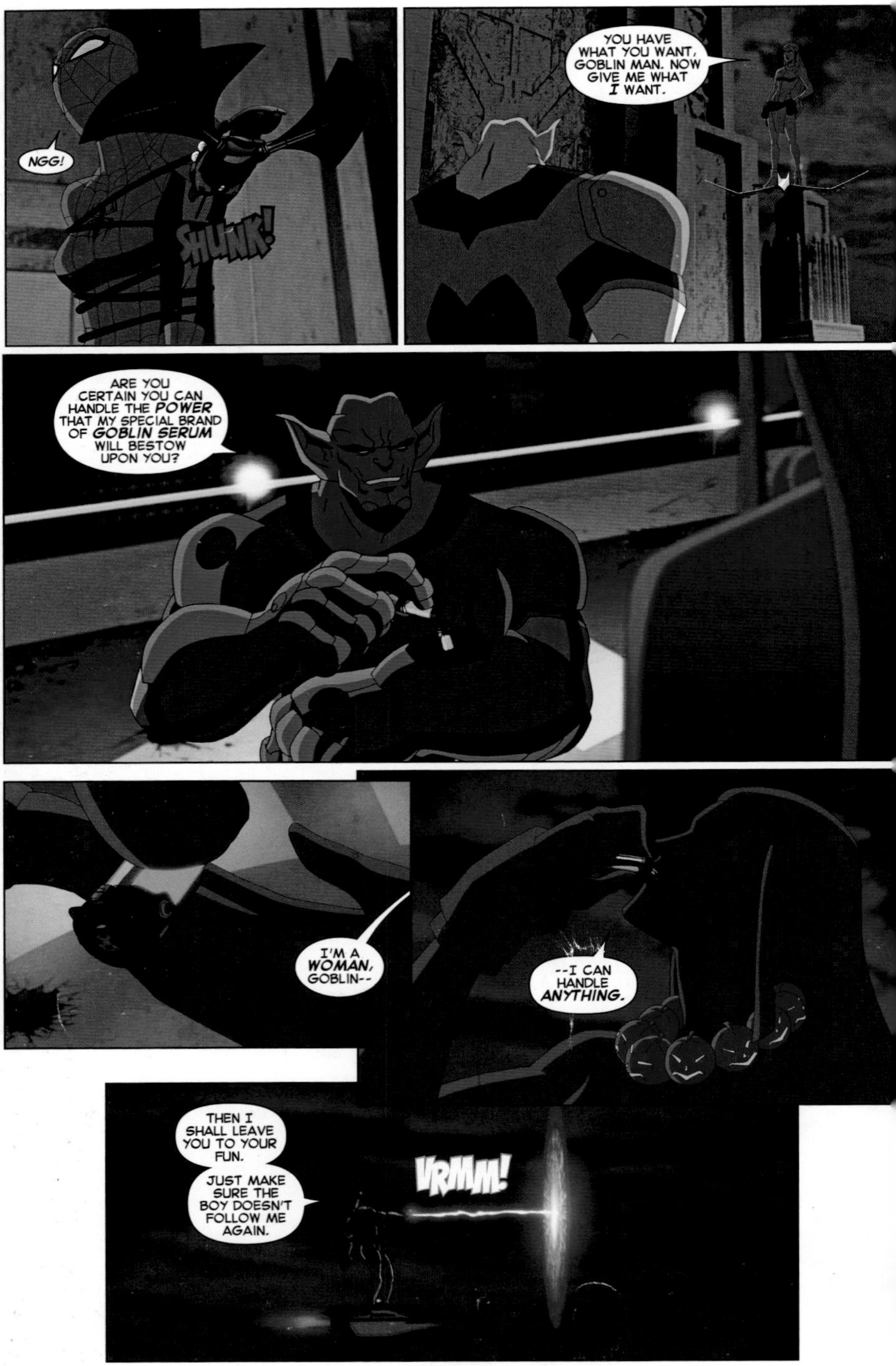
NGG!
SHUNK!
YOU HAVE WHAT YOU WANT, GOBLIN MAN. NOW GIVE ME WHAT I WANT.
ARE YOU CERTAIN YOU CAN HANDLE THE POWER THAT MY SPECIAL BRAND OF GOBLIN SERUM WILL BESTOW UPON YOU?
I'M A WOMAN, GOBLIN--
--I CAN HANDLE ANYTHING.
THEN I SHALL LEAVE YOU TO YOUR FUN.
JUST MAKE SURE THE BOY DOESN'T FOLLOW ME AGAIN.
VRMM!

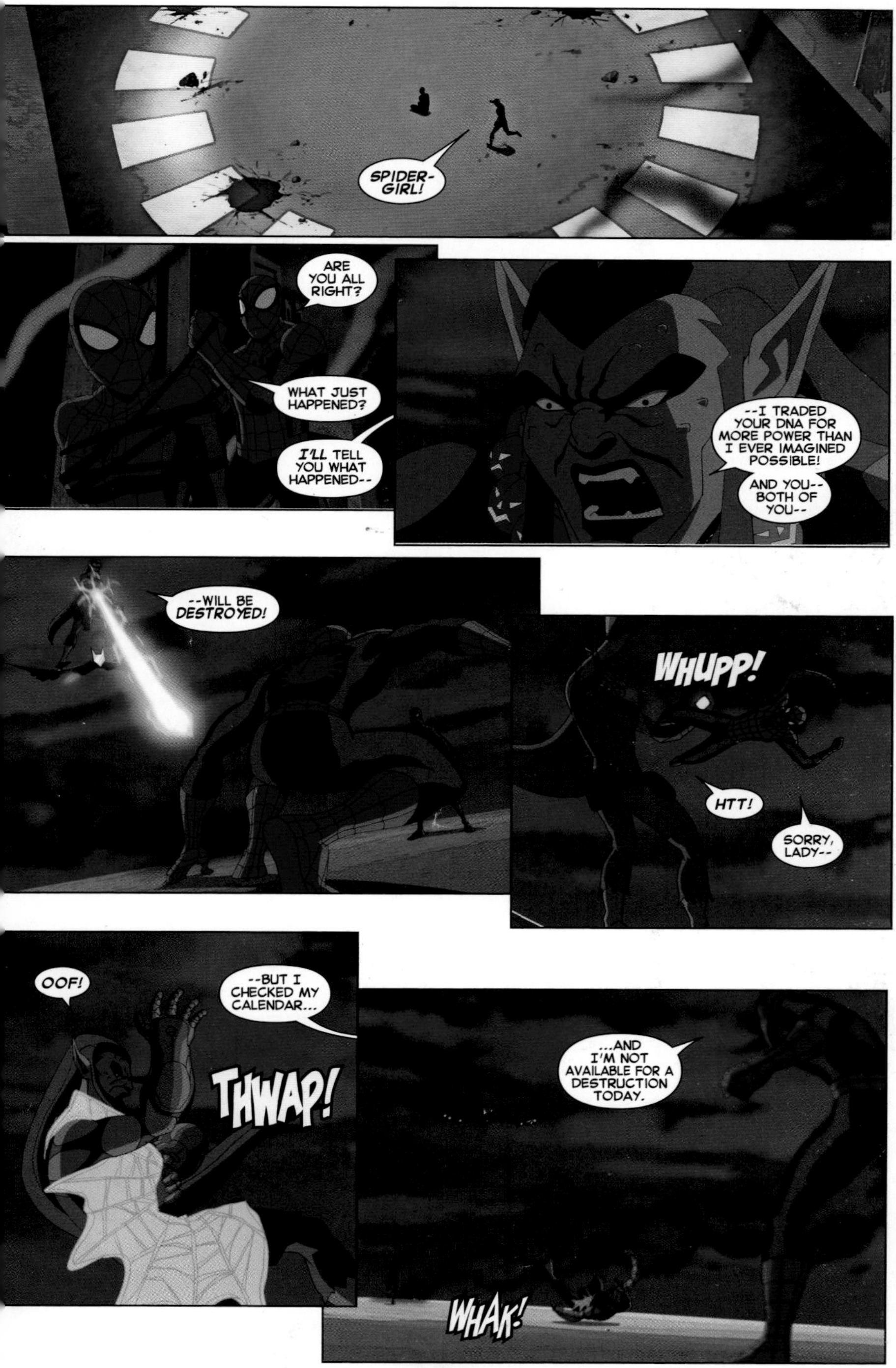
SPIDER-GIRL!
ARE YOU ALL RIGHT?
WHAT JUST HAPPENED?
I'LL TELL YOU WHAT HAPPENED--
--I TRADED YOUR DNA FOR MORE POWER THAN I EVER IMAGINED POSSIBLE!
AND YOU--BOTH OF YOU--
--WILL BE DESTROYED!
WHUPP!
HTT!
SORRY, LADY--
OOF!
--BUT I CHECKED MY CALENDAR...
THWAP!
...AND I'M NOT AVAILABLE FOR A DESTRUCTION TODAY.
WHAK!

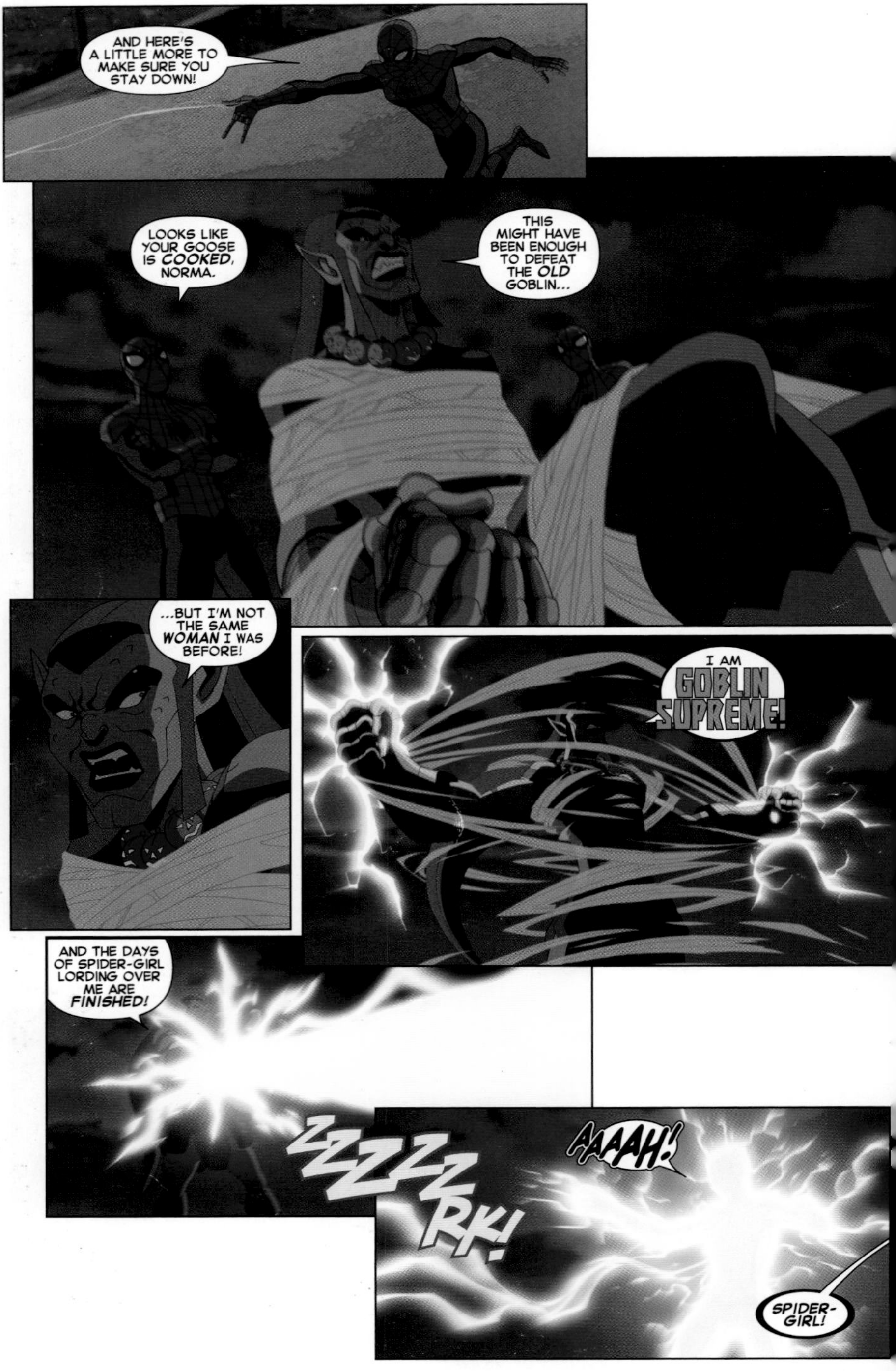
AND HERE'S A LITTLE MORE TO MAKE SURE YOU STAY DOWN!
LOOKS LIKE YOUR GOOSE IS COOKED, NORMA.
THIS MIGHT HAVE BEEN ENOUGH TO DEFEAT THE OLD GOBLIN...
...BUT I'M NOT THE SAME WOMAN I WAS BEFORE!
I AM GOBLIN SUPREME!
AND THE DAYS OF SPIDER-GIRL LORDING OVER ME ARE FINISHED!
ZZZZZZRK!
AAAAH!
SPIDER-GIRL!

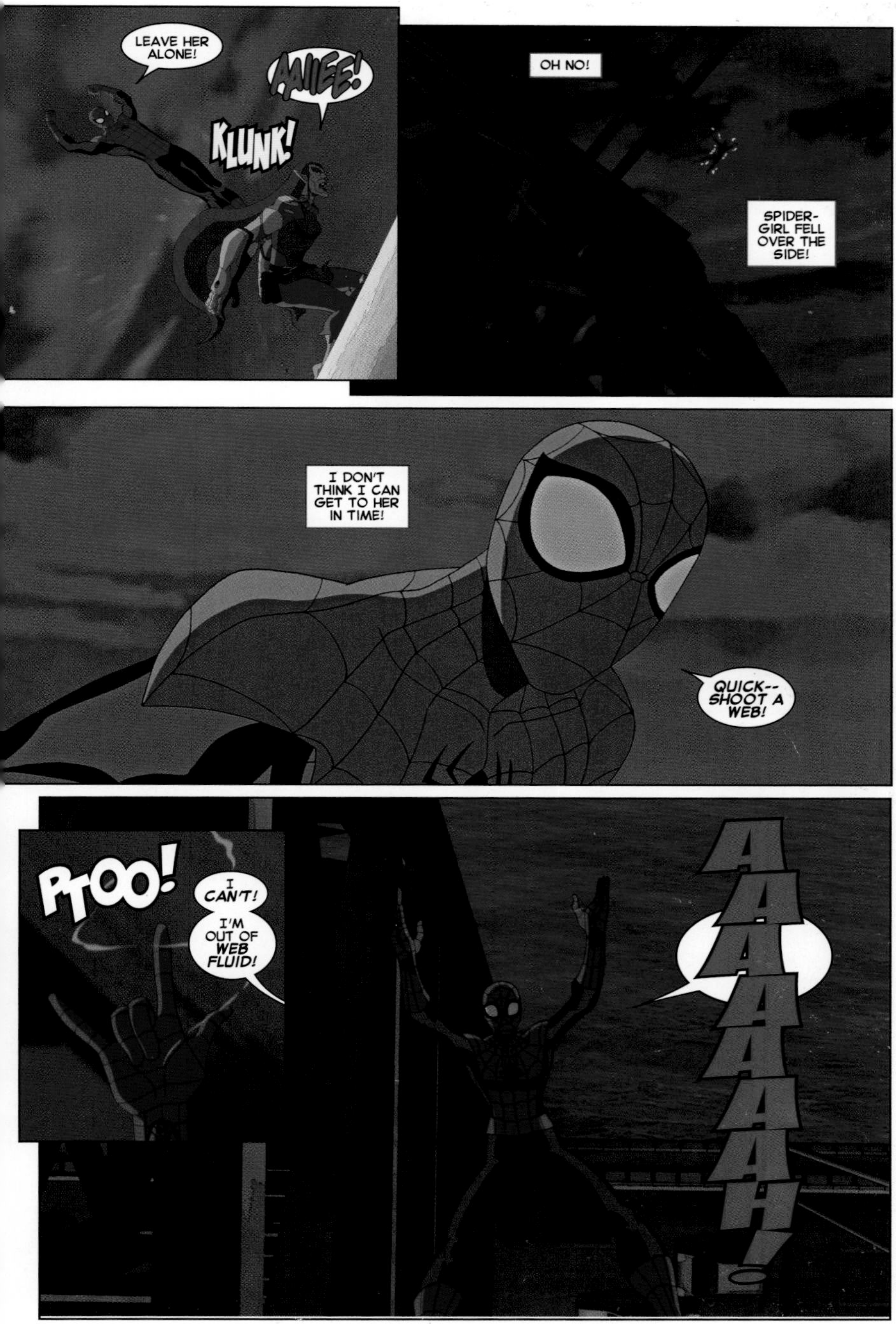
LEAVE HER ALONE!
AAIIEE!
KLUNK!
OH NO!
SPIDER-GIRL FELL OVER THE SIDE!
I DON'T THINK I CAN GET TO HER IN TIME!
QUICK--SHOOT A WEB!
PTOO!
I CAN'T! I'M OUT OF WEB FLUID!
AAAAAAAH!

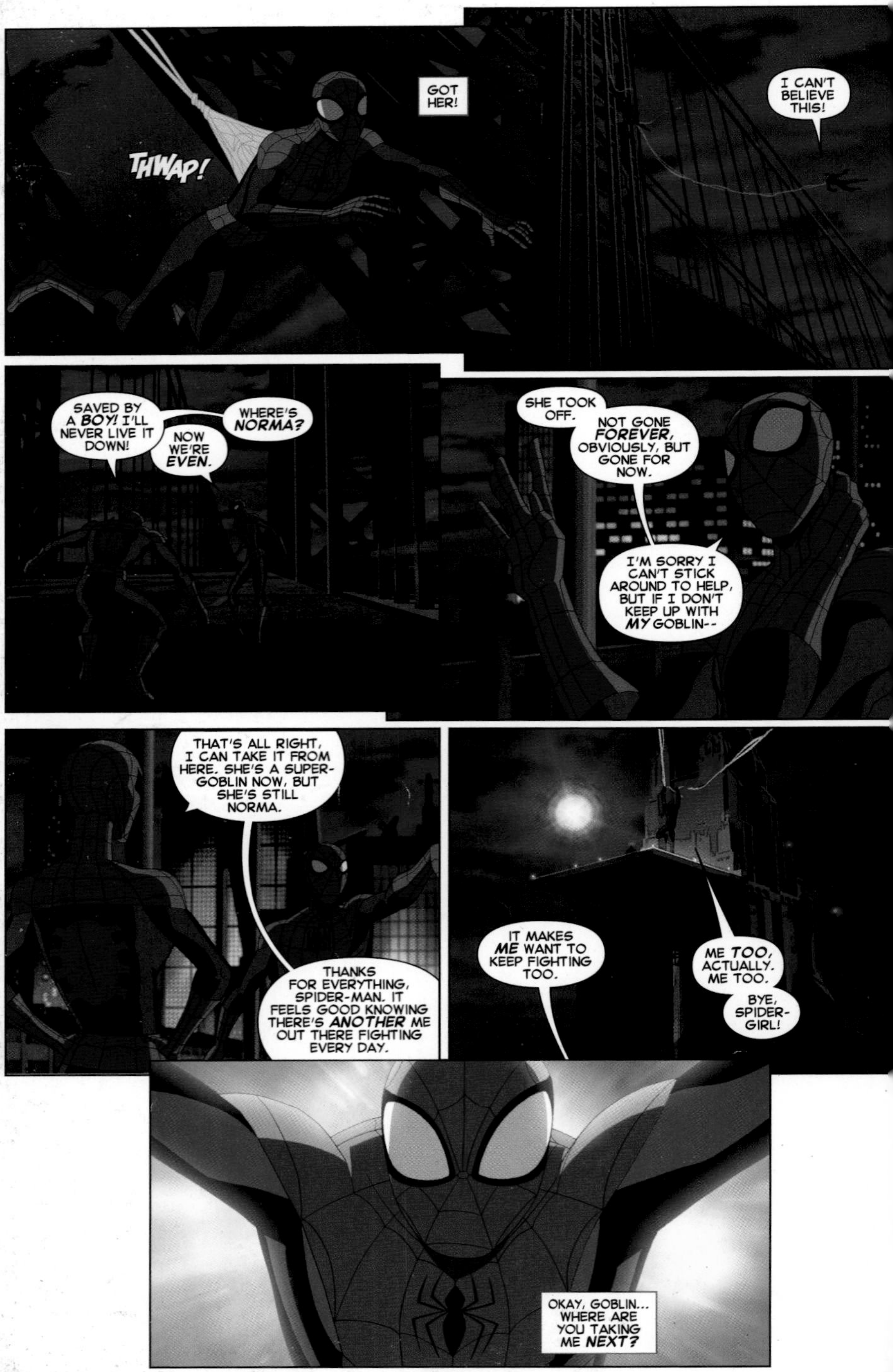
GOT HER!
THWAP!
I CAN'T BELIEVE THIS!
SAVED BY A BOY! I'LL NEVER LIVE IT DOWN!
WHERE'S NORMA?
NOW WE'RE EVEN.
SHE TOOK OFF.
NOT GONE FOREVER, OBVIOUSLY, BUT GONE FOR NOW.
I'M SORRY I CAN'T STICK AROUND TO HELP, BUT IF I DON'T KEEP UP WITH MY GOBLIN--
THAT'S ALL RIGHT, I CAN TAKE IT FROM HERE. SHE'S A SUPER-GOBLIN NOW, BUT SHE'S STILL NORMA.
THANKS FOR EVERYTHING, SPIDER-MAN. IT FEELS GOOD KNOWING THERE'S ANOTHER ME OUT THERE FIGHTING EVERY DAY.
IT MAKES ME WANT TO KEEP FIGHTING TOO.
ME TOO, ACTUALLY. ME TOO.
BYE, SPIDER-GIRL!
OKAY, GOBLIN... WHERE ARE YOU TAKING ME NEXT?

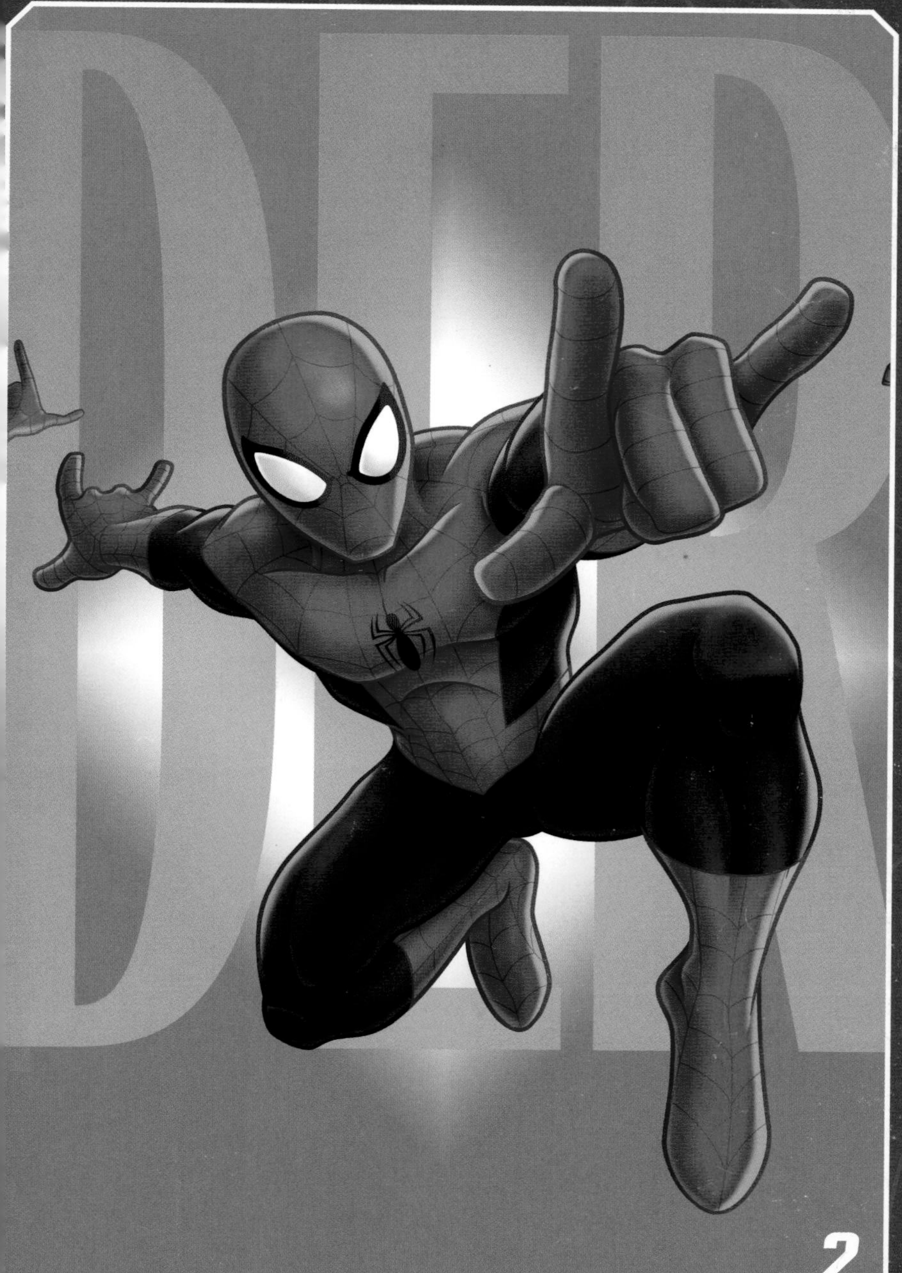

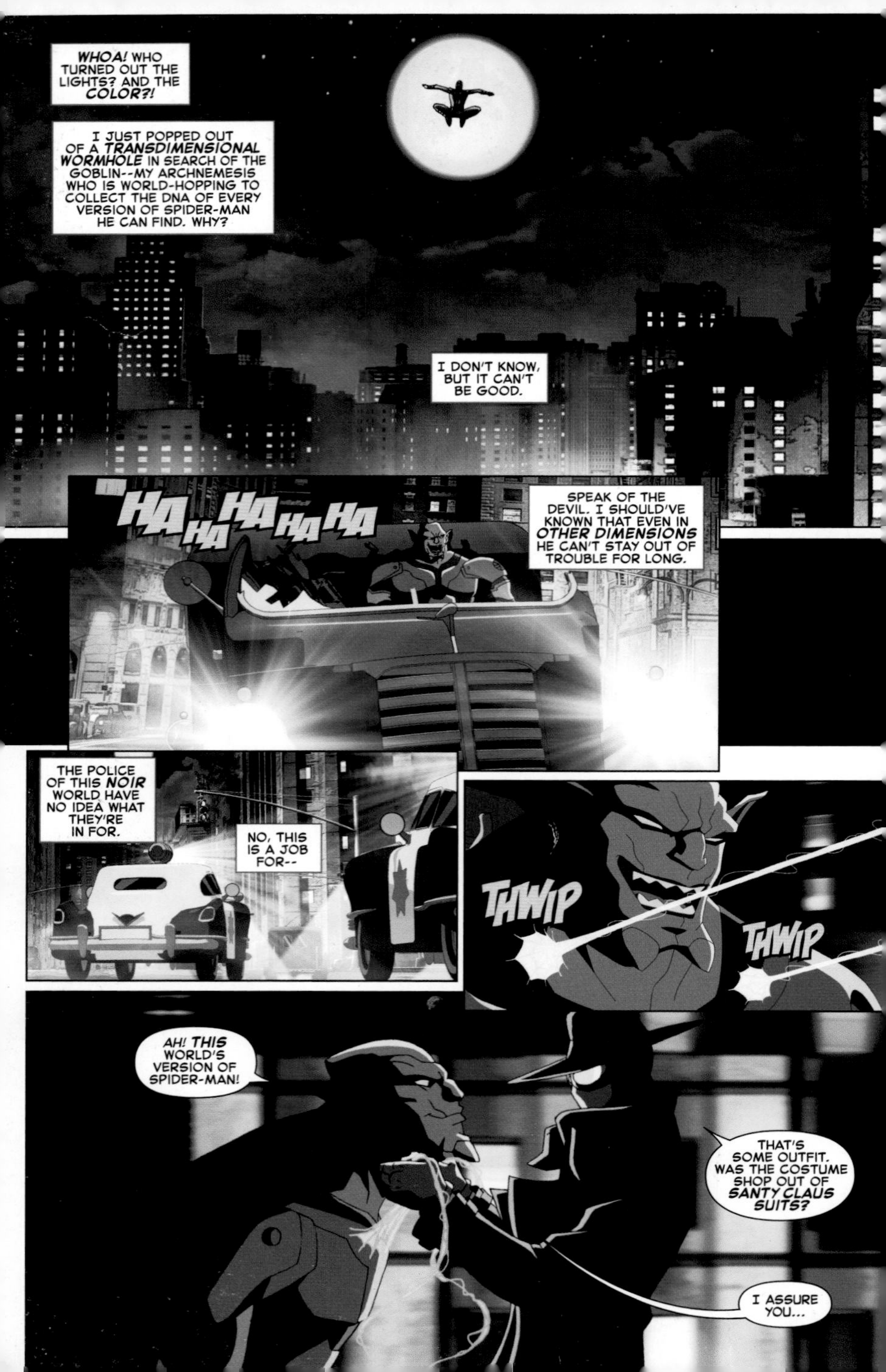
WHOA! WHO TURNED OUT THE LIGHTS? AND THE COLOR?!
I JUST POPPED OUT OF A TRANSDIMENSIONAL WORMHOLE IN SEARCH OF THE GOBLIN--MY ARCHNEMESIS WHO IS WORLD-HOPPING TO COLLECT THE DNA OF EVERY VERSION OF SPIDER-MAN HE CAN FIND. WHY?
I DON'T KNOW, BUT IT CAN'T BE GOOD.
HA HA HA HA HA
SPEAK OF THE DEVIL. I SHOULD'VE KNOWN THAT EVEN IN OTHER DIMENSIONS HE CAN'T STAY OUT OF TROUBLE FOR LONG.
THE POLICE OF THIS NOIR WORLD HAVE NO IDEA WHAT THEY'RE IN FOR.
NO, THIS IS A JOB FOR--
THWIP
THWIP
AH! THIS WORLD'S VERSION OF SPIDER-MAN!
THAT'S SOME OUTFIT. WAS THE COSTUME SHOP OUT OF SANTY CLAUS SUITS?
I ASSURE YOU...

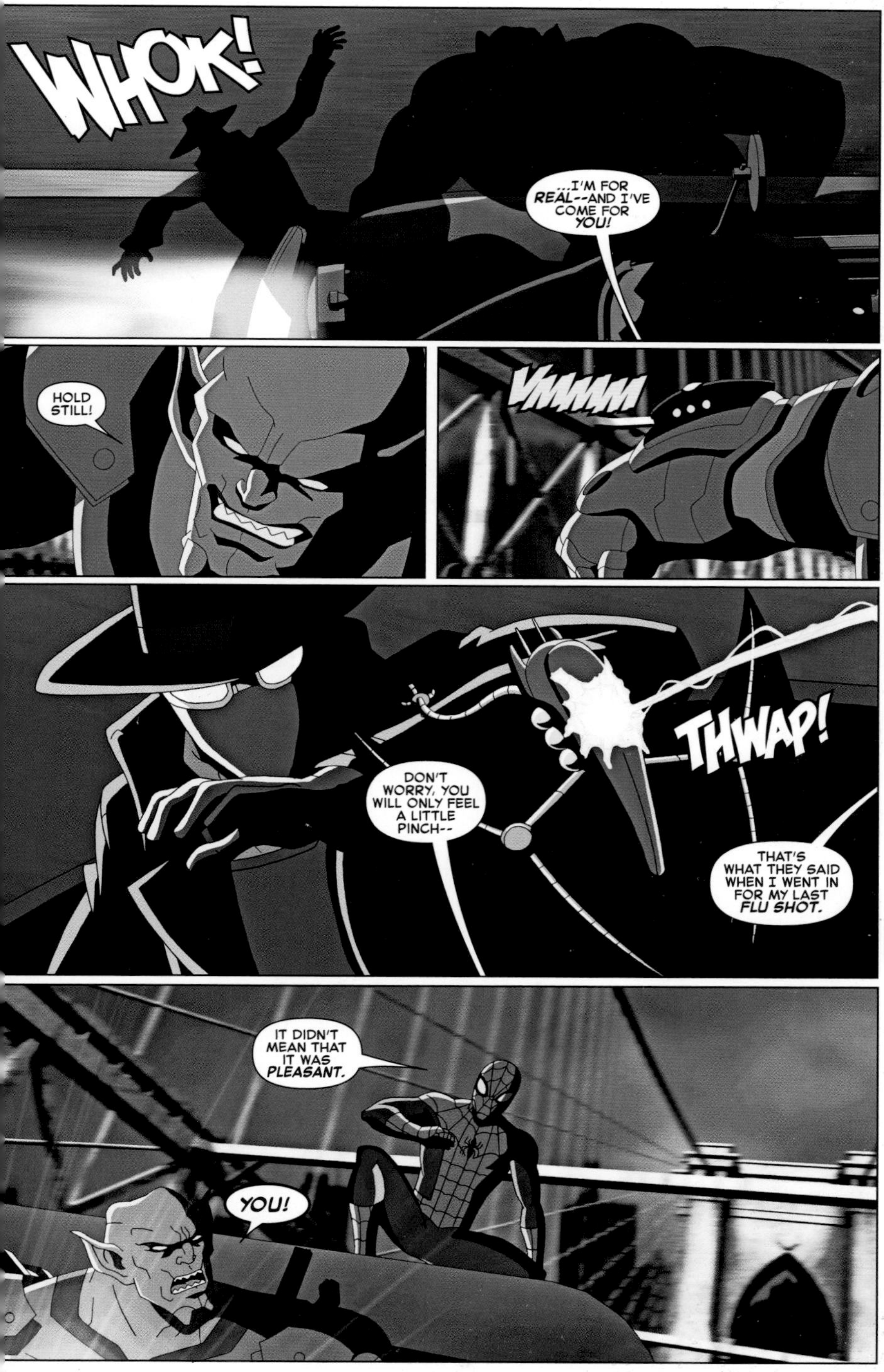
WHOK!
...I'M FOR REAL--AND I'VE COME FOR YOU!
HOLD STILL!
VMMMM
DON'T WORRY, YOU WILL ONLY FEEL A LITTLE PINCH--
THWAP!
THAT'S WHAT THEY SAID WHEN I WENT IN FOR MY LAST FLU SHOT.
IT DIDN'T MEAN THAT IT WAS PLEASANT.
YOU!

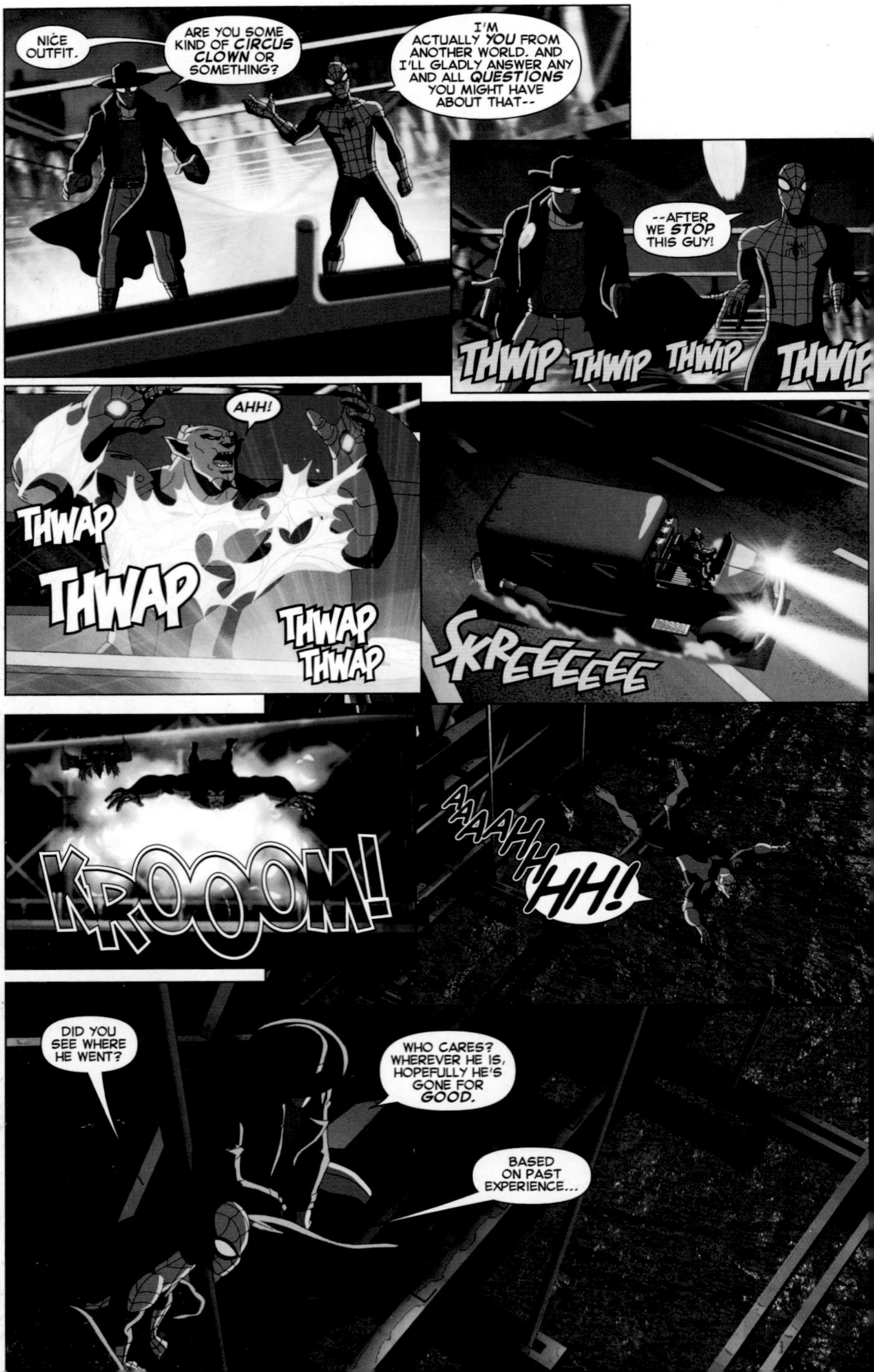
NICE OUTFIT.
ARE YOU SOME KIND OF CIRCUS CLOWN OR SOMETHING?
I'M ACTUALLY YOU FROM ANOTHER WORLD. AND I'LL GLADLY ANSWER ANY AND ALL QUESTIONS YOU MIGHT HAVE ABOUT THAT--
--AFTER WE STOP THIS GUY!
THWIP THWIP THWIP THWIP
AHH!
THWAP
THWAP
THWAP THWAP
SKREEEEEEE
KROOOM!
AAAAHHHHH!
DID YOU SEE WHERE HE WENT?
WHO CARES? WHEREVER HE IS, HOPEFULLY HE'S GONE FOR GOOD.
BASED ON PAST EXPERIENCE...

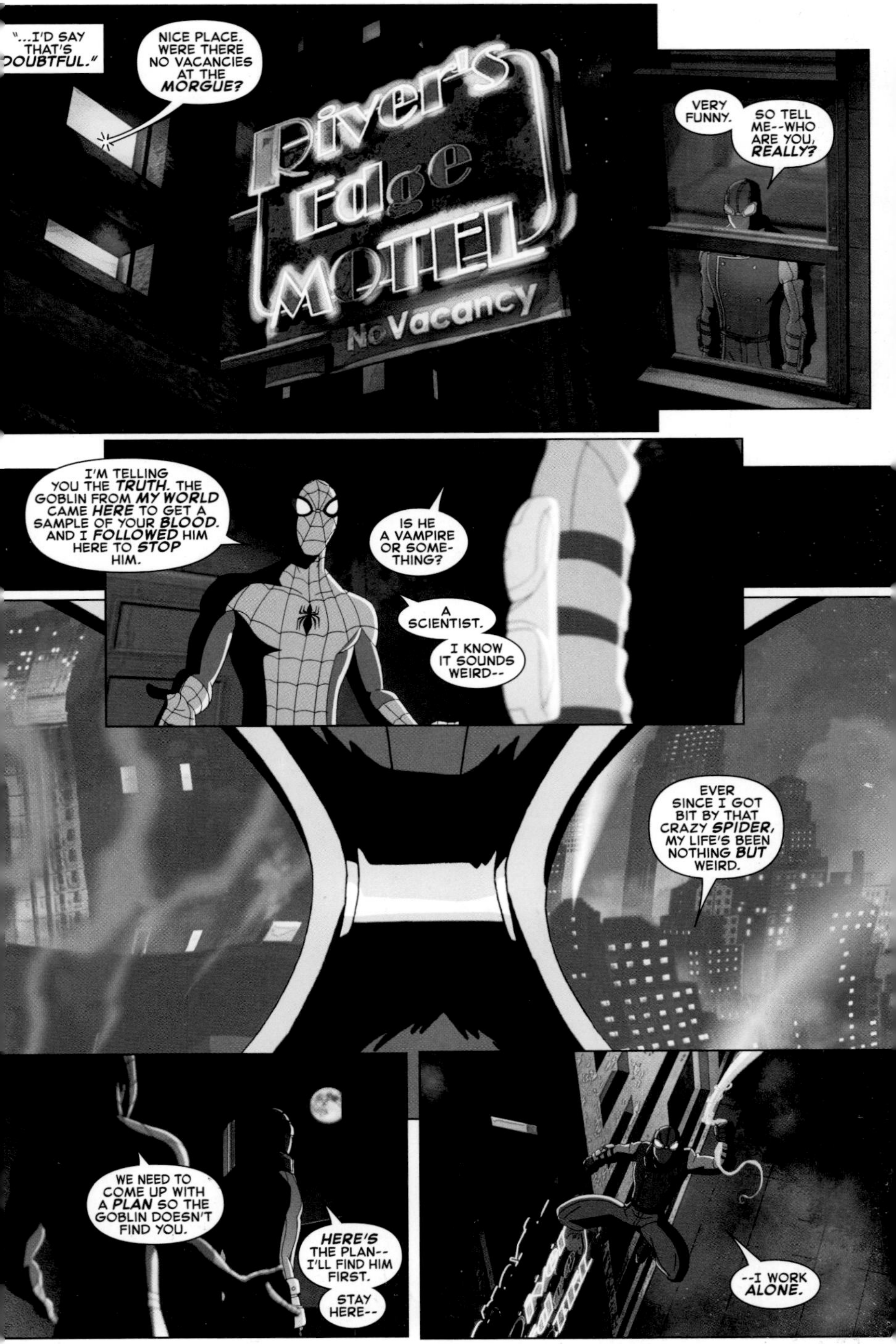
"...I'D SAY THAT'S DOUBTFUL."
NICE PLACE. WERE THERE NO VACANCIES AT THE MORGUE?
River's Edge MOTEL
No Vacancy
VERY FUNNY.
SO TELL ME--WHO ARE YOU, REALLY?
I'M TELLING YOU THE TRUTH. THE GOBLIN FROM MY WORLD CAME HERE TO GET A SAMPLE OF YOUR BLOOD. AND I FOLLOWED HIM HERE TO STOP HIM.
IS HE A VAMPIRE OR SOMETHING?
A SCIENTIST.
I KNOW IT SOUNDS WEIRD--
EVER SINCE I GOT BIT BY THAT CRAZY SPIDER, MY LIFE'S BEEN NOTHING BUT WEIRD.
WE NEED TO COME UP WITH A PLAN SO THE GOBLIN DOESN'T FIND YOU.
HERE'S THE PLAN--I'LL FIND HIM FIRST.
STAY HERE--
--I WORK ALONE.

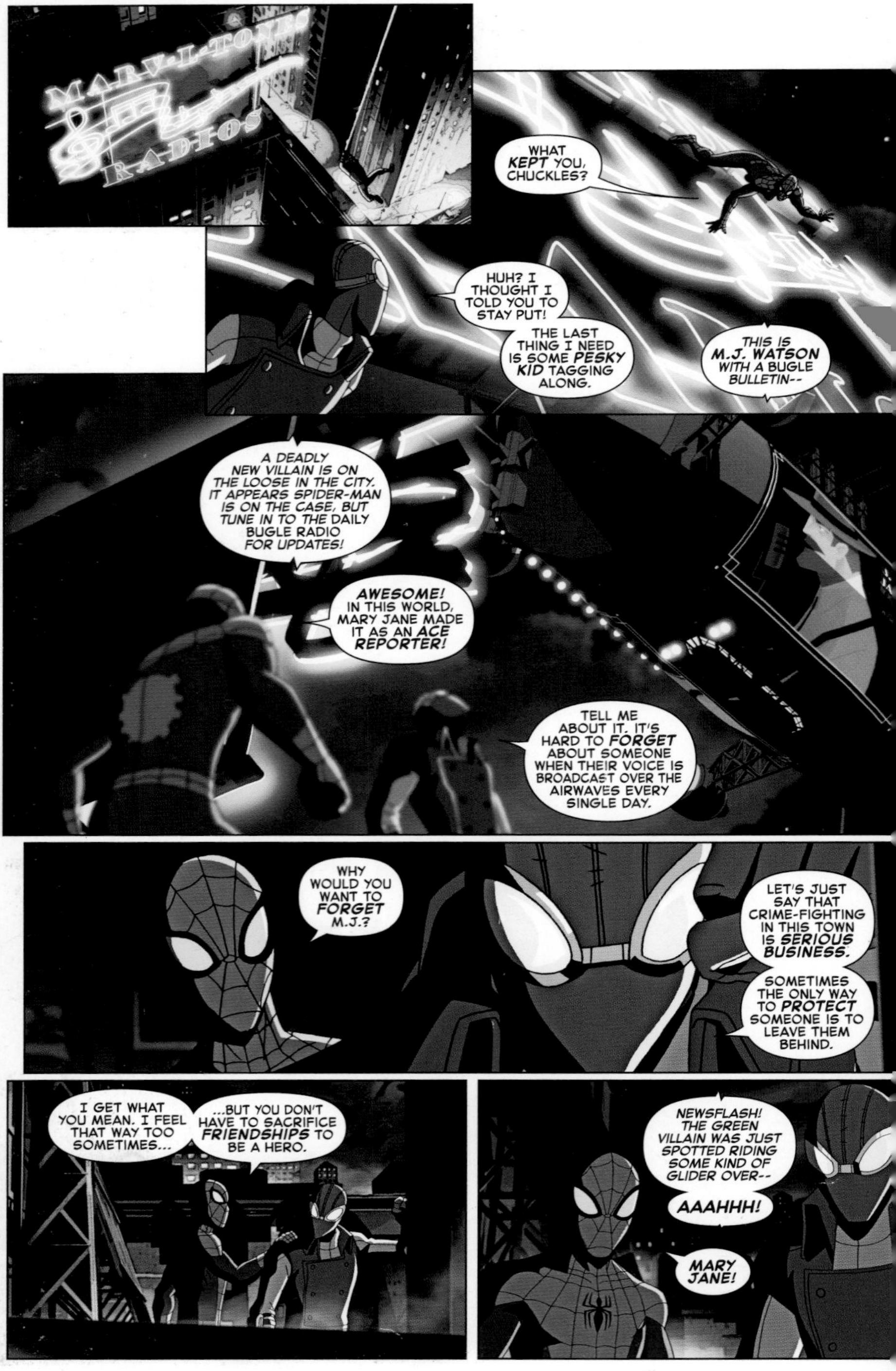
MARV-L-TONES RADIOS
WHAT KEPT YOU, CHUCKLES?
HUH? I THOUGHT I TOLD YOU TO STAY PUT!
THE LAST THING I NEED IS SOME PESKY KID TAGGING ALONG.
THIS IS M.J. WATSON WITH A BUGLE BULLETIN--
A DEADLY NEW VILLAIN IS ON THE LOOSE IN THE CITY. IT APPEARS SPIDER-MAN IS ON THE CASE, BUT TUNE IN TO THE DAILY BUGLE RADIO FOR UPDATES!
AWESOME! IN THIS WORLD, MARY JANE MADE IT AS AN ACE REPORTER!
TELL ME ABOUT IT. IT'S HARD TO FORGET ABOUT SOMEONE WHEN THEIR VOICE IS BROADCAST OVER THE AIRWAVES EVERY SINGLE DAY.
WHY WOULD YOU WANT TO FORGET M.J.?
LET'S JUST SAY THAT CRIME-FIGHTING IN THIS TOWN IS SERIOUS BUSINESS.
SOMETIMES THE ONLY WAY TO PROTECT SOMEONE IS TO LEAVE THEM BEHIND.
I GET WHAT YOU MEAN. I FEEL THAT WAY TOO SOMETIMES...
...BUT YOU DON'T HAVE TO SACRIFICE FRIENDSHIPS TO BE A HERO.
NEWSFLASH! THE GREEN VILLAIN WAS JUST SPOTTED RIDING SOME KIND OF GLIDER OVER--
AAAHHH!
MARY JANE!

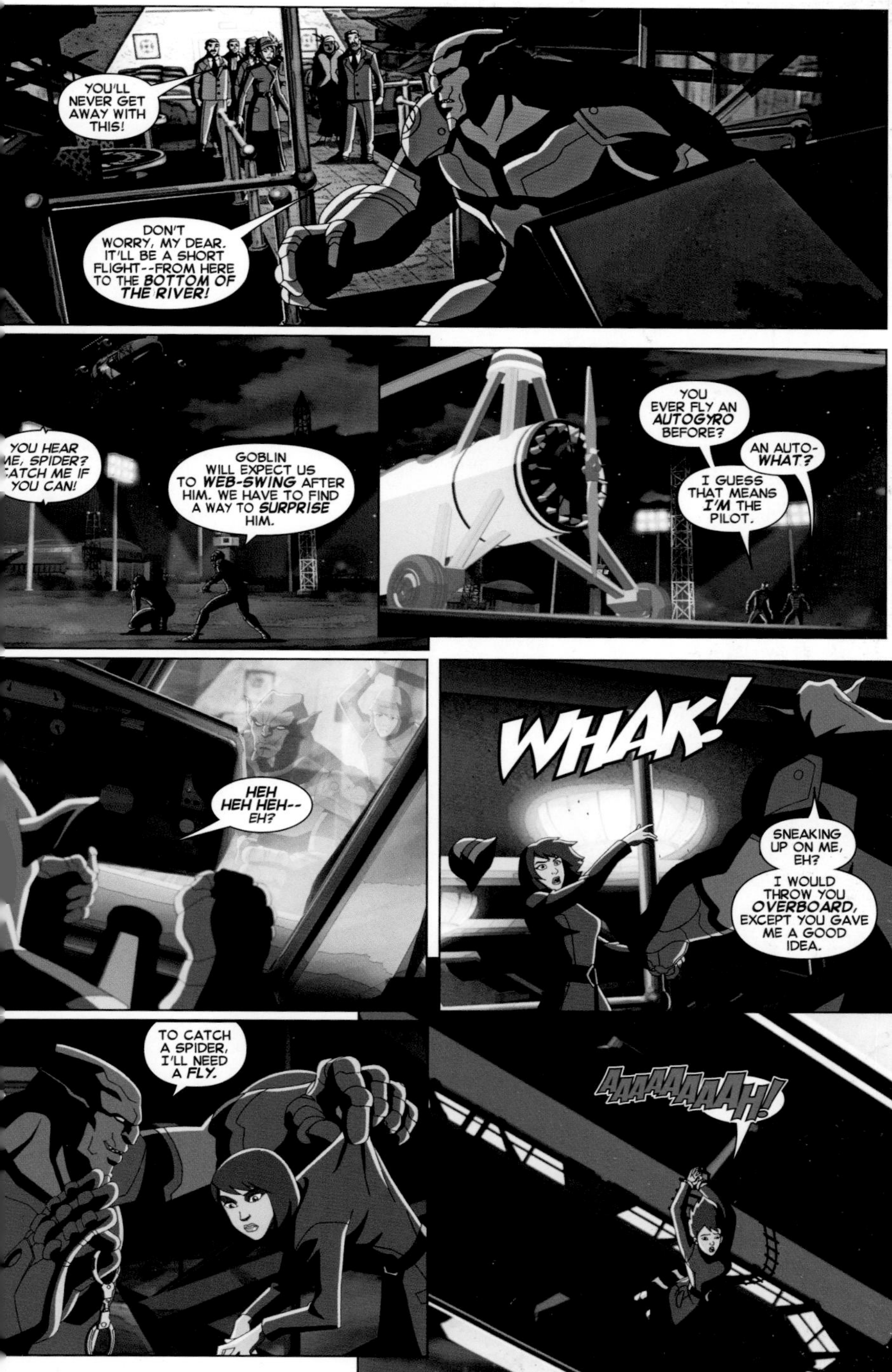

YOU'LL NEVER GET AWAY WITH THIS!
DON'T WORRY, MY DEAR. IT'LL BE A SHORT FLIGHT--FROM HERE TO THE BOTTOM OF THE RIVER!
YOU HEAR ME, SPIDER? CATCH ME IF YOU CAN!
GOBLIN WILL EXPECT US TO WEB-SWING AFTER HIM. WE HAVE TO FIND A WAY TO SURPRISE HIM.
YOU EVER FLY AN AUTOGYRO BEFORE?
AN AUTO-WHAT?
I GUESS THAT MEANS I'M THE PILOT.
HEH HEH HEH--EH?
WHAK!
SNEAKING UP ON ME, EH?
I WOULD THROW YOU OVERBOARD, EXCEPT YOU GAVE ME A GOOD IDEA.
TO CATCH A SPIDER, I'LL NEED A FLY.
AAAAAAAAAH!

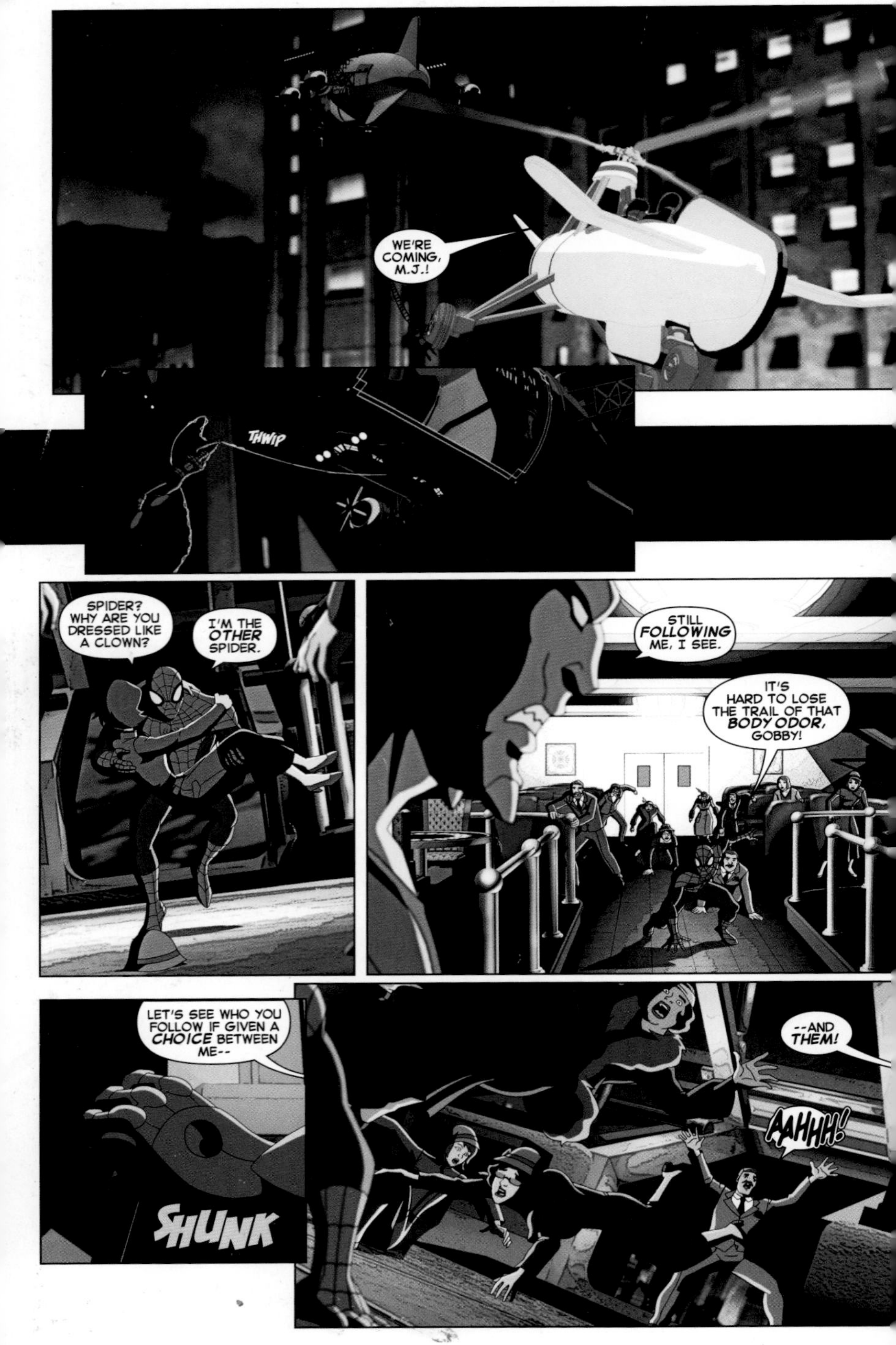
WE'RE COMING, M.J.!
THWIP
SPIDER? WHY ARE YOU DRESSED LIKE A CLOWN?
I'M THE OTHER SPIDER.
STILL FOLLOWING ME, I SEE.
IT'S HARD TO LOSE THE TRAIL OF THAT BODY ODOR, GOBBY!
LET'S SEE WHO YOU FOLLOW IF GIVEN A CHOICE BETWEEN ME--
SHUNK
--AND THEM!
AAHHH!

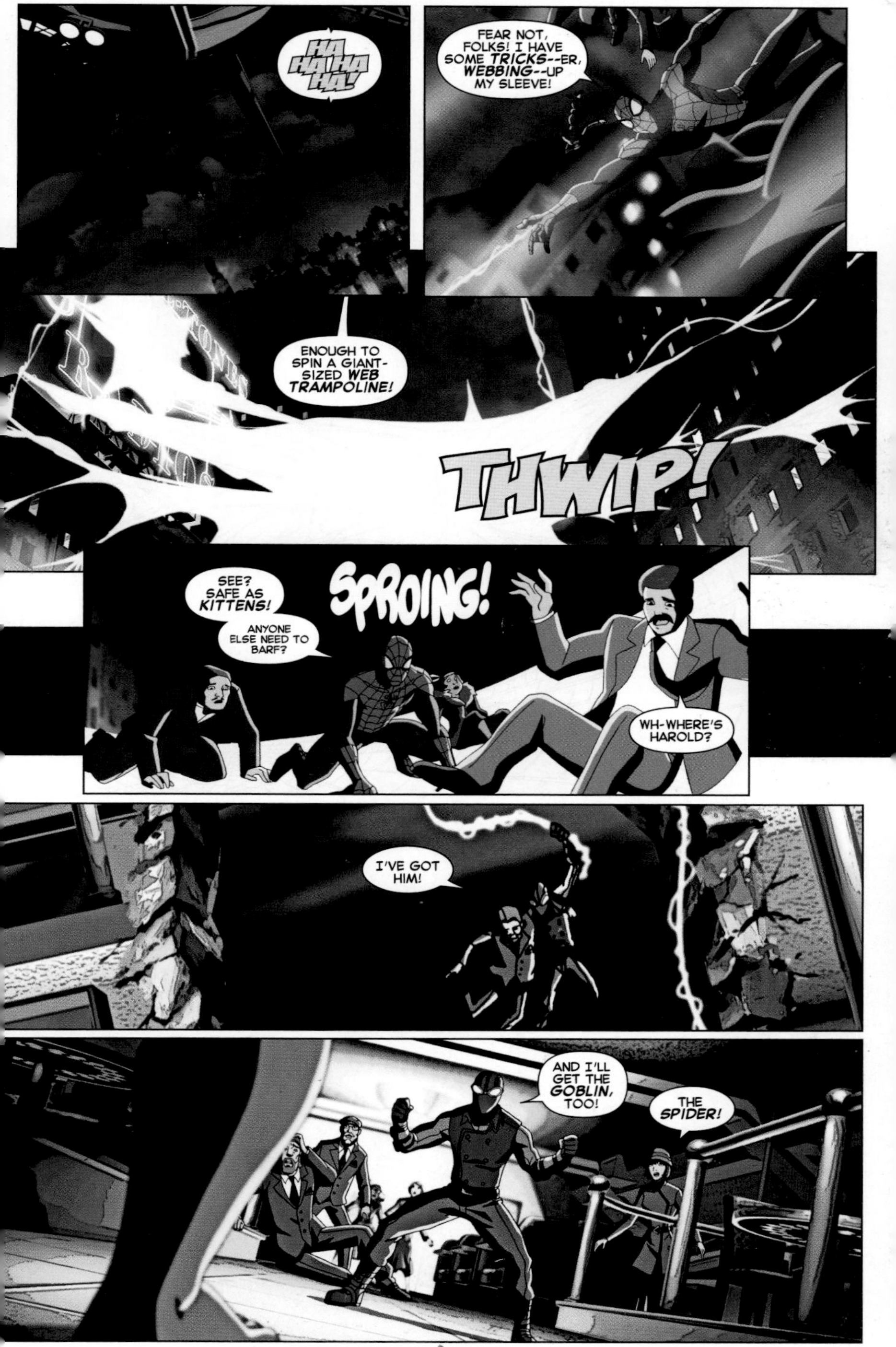
HA HA HA HA!
FEAR NOT, FOLKS! I HAVE SOME TRICKS--ER, WEBBING--UP MY SLEEVE!
ENOUGH TO SPIN A GIANT-SIZED WEB TRAMPOLINE!
THWIP!
SEE? SAFE AS KITTENS!
SPROING!
ANYONE ELSE NEED TO BARF?
WH-WHERE'S HAROLD?
I'VE GOT HIM!
AND I'LL GET THE GOBLIN, TOO!
THE SPIDER!

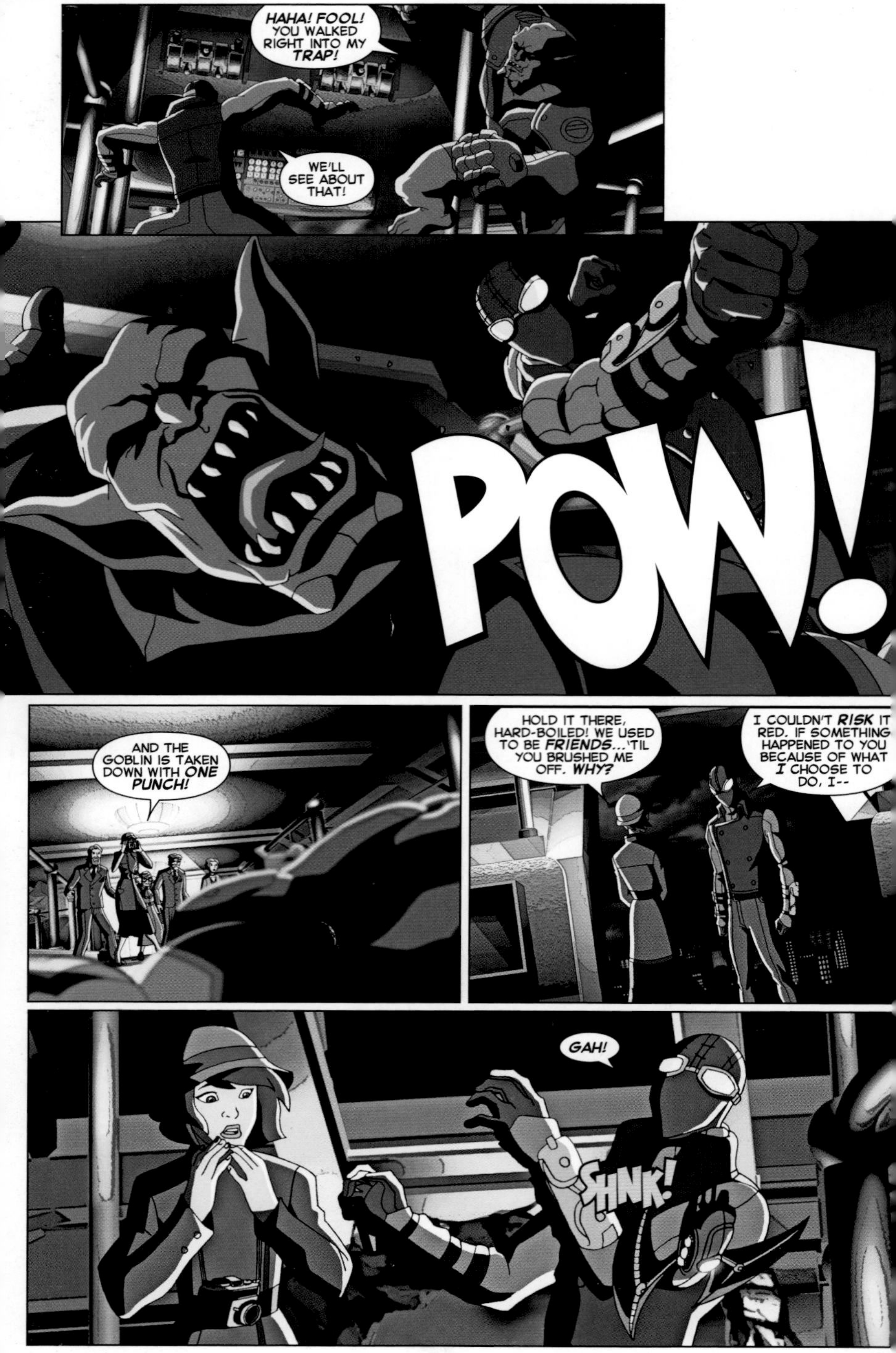
HAHA! FOOL! YOU WALKED RIGHT INTO MY TRAP!
WE'LL SEE ABOUT THAT!
POW!
AND THE GOBLIN IS TAKEN DOWN WITH ONE PUNCH!
HOLD IT THERE, HARD-BOILED! WE USED TO BE FRIENDS...'TIL YOU BRUSHED ME OFF. WHY?
I COULDN'T RISK IT, RED. IF SOMETHING HAPPENED TO YOU BECAUSE OF WHAT I CHOOSE TO DO, I--
GAH!
SHNK!

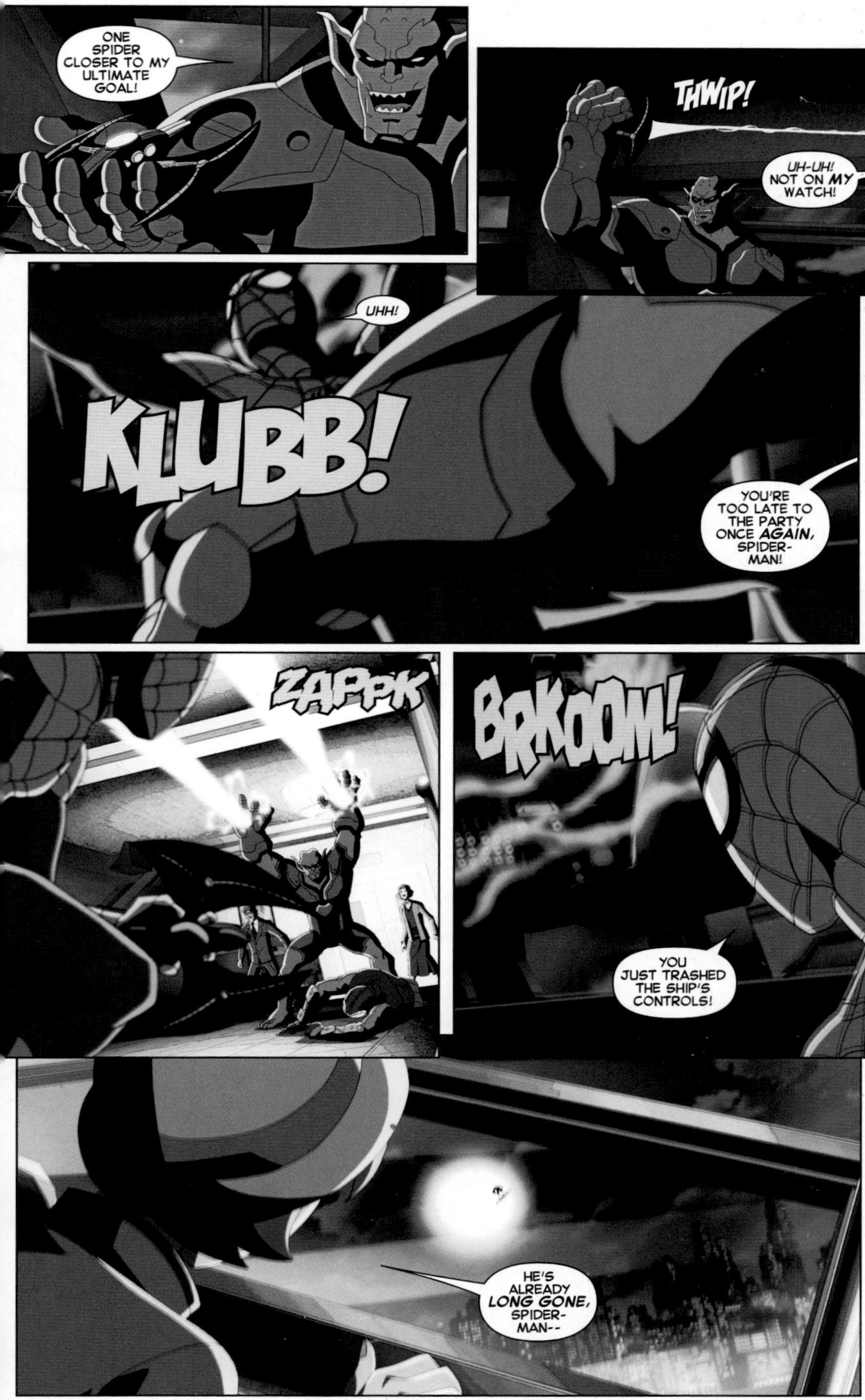
ONE SPIDER CLOSER TO MY ULTIMATE GOAL!
THWIP!
UH-UH! NOT ON MY WATCH!
UHH!
KLUBB!
YOU'RE TOO LATE TO THE PARTY ONCE AGAIN, SPIDER-MAN!
ZAPPK
BRKOOM!
YOU JUST TRASHED THE SHIP'S CONTROLS!
HE'S ALREADY LONG GONE, SPIDER-MAN--

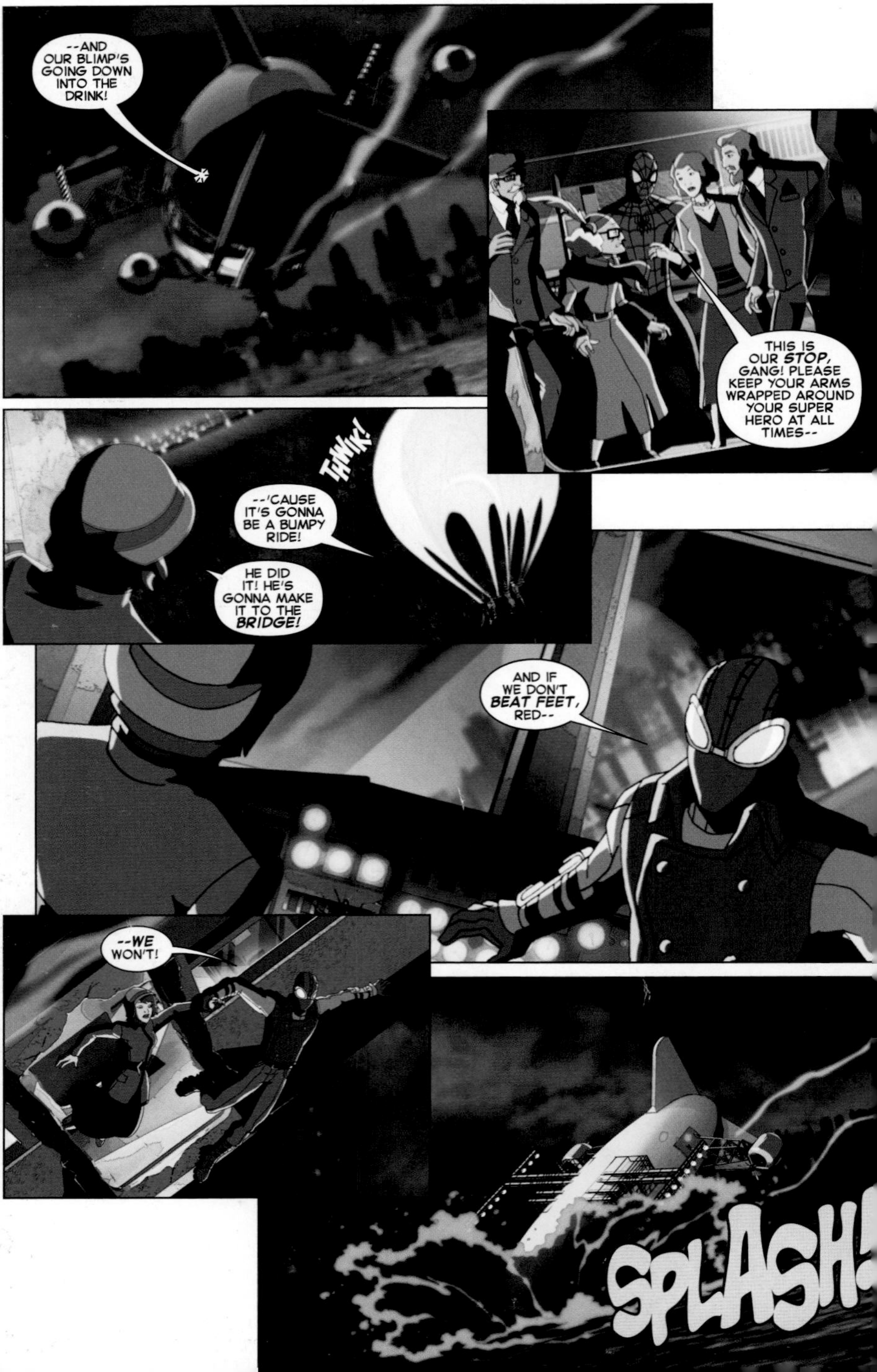
--AND OUR BLIMP'S GOING DOWN INTO THE DRINK!
THIS IS OUR STOP, GANG! PLEASE KEEP YOUR ARMS WRAPPED AROUND YOUR SUPER HERO AT ALL TIMES--
THWIK!
--'CAUSE IT'S GONNA BE A BUMPY RIDE!
HE DID IT! HE'S GONNA MAKE IT TO THE BRIDGE!
AND IF WE DON'T BEAT FEET, RED--
--WE WON'T!
SPLASH!

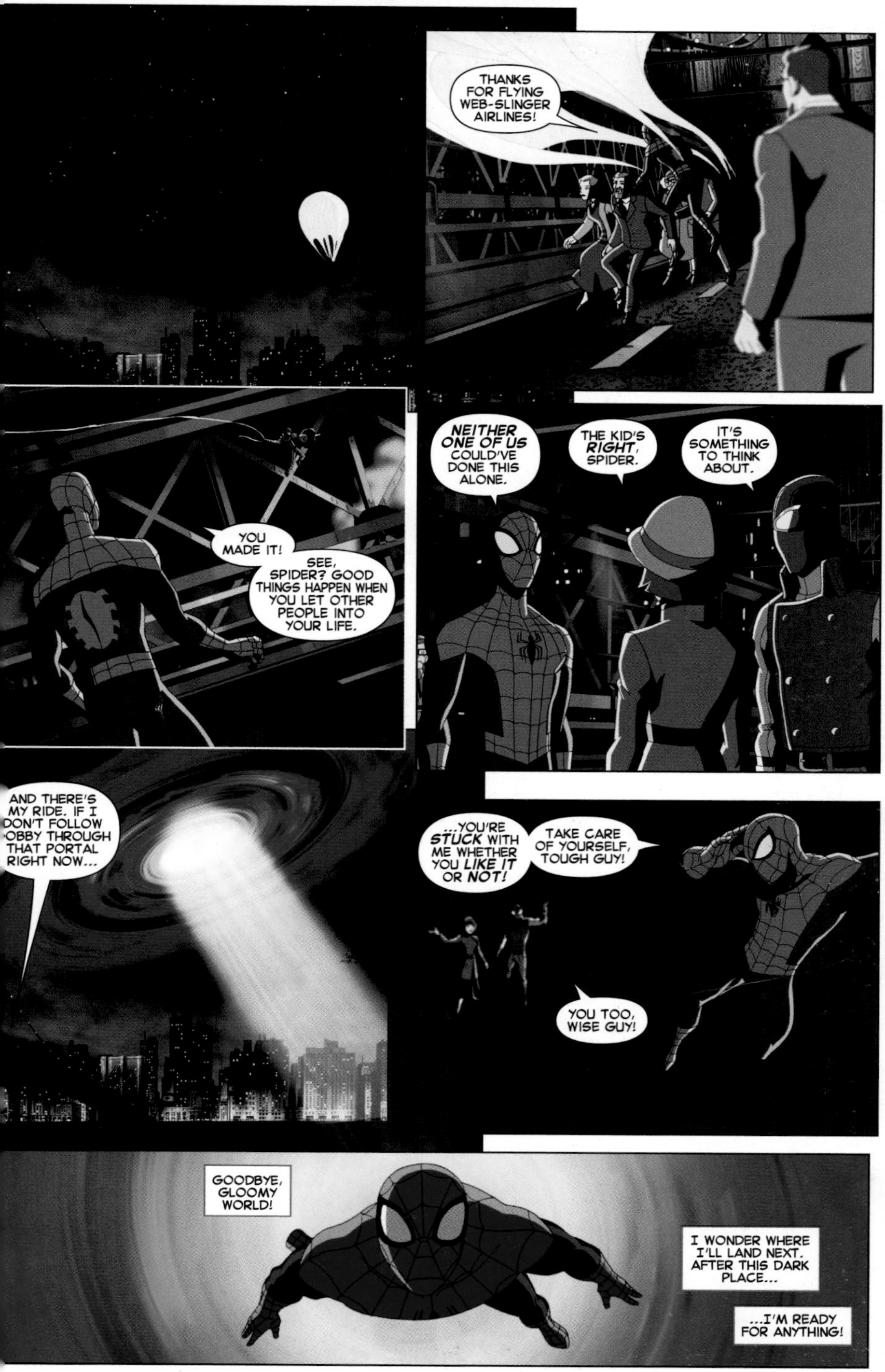
THANKS FOR FLYING WEB-SLINGER AIRLINES!
YOU MADE IT!
SEE, SPIDER? GOOD THINGS HAPPEN WHEN YOU LET OTHER PEOPLE INTO YOUR LIFE.
NEITHER ONE OF US COULD'VE DONE THIS ALONE.
THE KID'S RIGHT, SPIDER.
IT'S SOMETHING TO THINK ABOUT.
AND THERE'S MY RIDE. IF I DON'T FOLLOW OBBY THROUGH THAT PORTAL RIGHT NOW...
...YOU'RE STUCK WITH ME WHETHER YOU LIKE IT OR NOT!
TAKE CARE OF YOURSELF, TOUGH GUY!
YOU TOO, WISE GUY!
GOODBYE, GLOOMY WORLD!
I WONDER WHERE I'LL LAND NEXT. AFTER THIS DARK PLACE...
...I'M READY FOR ANYTHING!

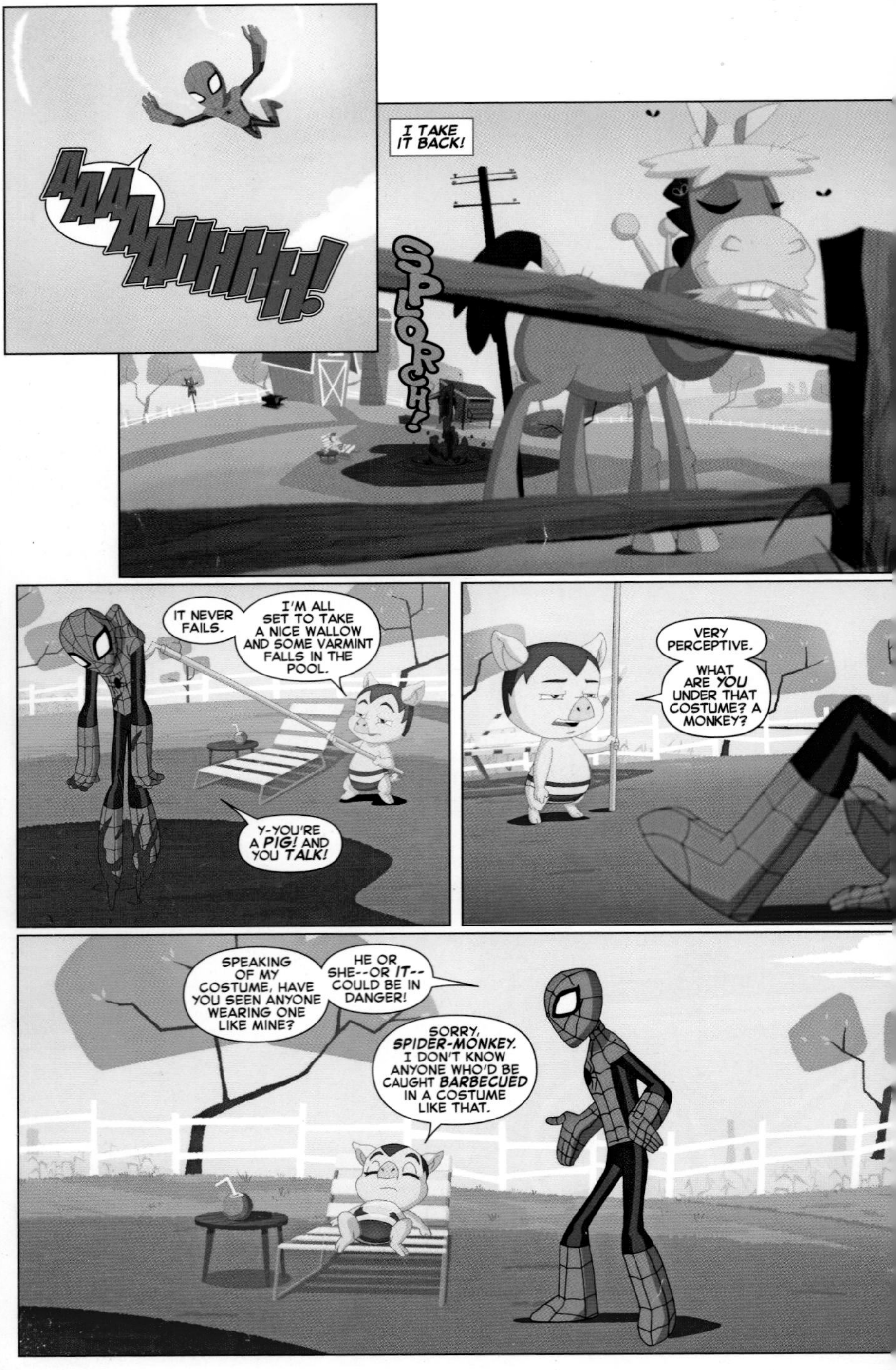
AAAAAAHHHHH!
I TAKE IT BACK!
SPLORCH!
IT NEVER FAILS.
I'M ALL SET TO TAKE A NICE WALLOW AND SOME VARMINT FALLS IN THE POOL.
Y-YOU'RE A PIG! AND YOU TALK!
VERY PERCEPTIVE.
WHAT ARE YOU UNDER THAT COSTUME? A MONKEY?
SPEAKING OF MY COSTUME, HAVE YOU SEEN ANYONE WEARING ONE LIKE MINE?
HE OR SHE--OR IT--COULD BE IN DANGER!
SORRY, SPIDER-MONKEY. I DON'T KNOW ANYONE WHO'D BE CAUGHT BARBECUED IN A COSTUME LIKE THAT.

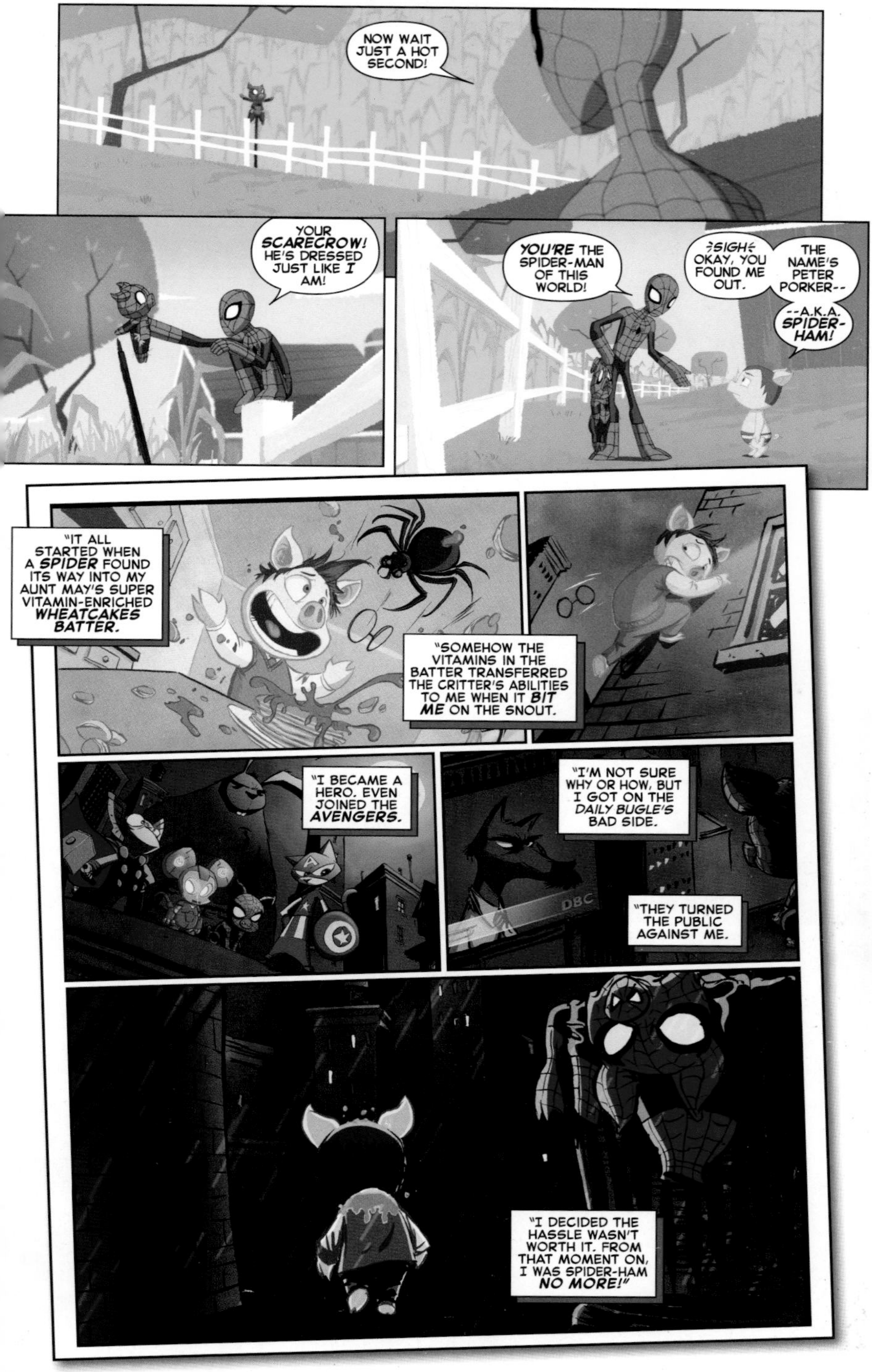
NOW WAIT JUST A HOT SECOND!
YOUR *SCARECROW!* HE'S DRESSED JUST LIKE *I* AM!
YOU'RE THE SPIDER-MAN OF THIS WORLD!
⇒SIGH⇐ OKAY, YOU FOUND ME OUT.
THE NAME'S PETER PORKER--
--A.K.A. *SPIDER-HAM!*
"IT ALL STARTED WHEN A *SPIDER* FOUND ITS WAY INTO MY AUNT MAY'S SUPER VITAMIN-ENRICHED *WHEATCAKES BATTER.*
"SOMEHOW THE VITAMINS IN THE BATTER TRANSFERRED THE CRITTER'S ABILITIES TO ME WHEN IT *BIT ME* ON THE SNOUT.
"I BECAME A HERO. EVEN JOINED THE *AVENGERS.*
"I'M NOT SURE WHY OR HOW, BUT I GOT ON THE *DAILY BUGLE'S* BAD SIDE.
DBC
"THEY TURNED THE PUBLIC AGAINST ME.
"I DECIDED THE HASSLE WASN'T WORTH IT. FROM THAT MOMENT ON, I WAS SPIDER-HAM *NO MORE!"*

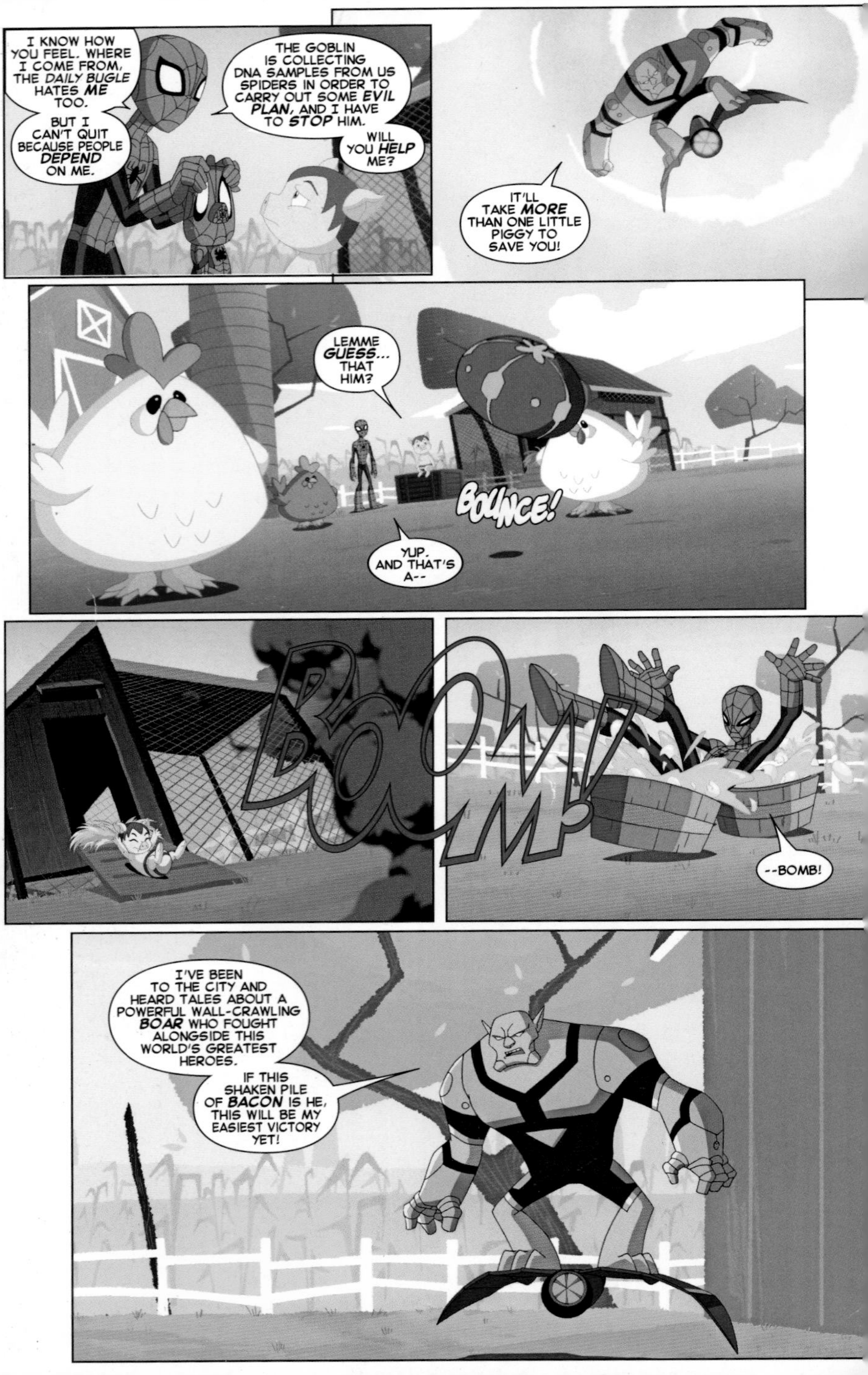
I KNOW HOW YOU FEEL. WHERE I COME FROM, THE *DAILY BUGLE* HATES **ME** TOO.
BUT I CAN'T QUIT BECAUSE PEOPLE **DEPEND** ON ME.
THE GOBLIN IS COLLECTING DNA SAMPLES FROM US SPIDERS IN ORDER TO CARRY OUT SOME **EVIL PLAN,** AND I HAVE TO **STOP** HIM.
WILL YOU **HELP** ME?
IT'LL TAKE **MORE** THAN ONE LITTLE PIGGY TO SAVE YOU!
LEMME **GUESS...** THAT HIM?
BOUNCE!
YUP. AND THAT'S A--
BOOM!
--BOMB!
I'VE BEEN TO THE CITY AND HEARD TALES ABOUT A POWERFUL WALL-CRAWLING **BOAR** WHO FOUGHT ALONGSIDE THIS WORLD'S GREATEST HEROES.
IF THIS SHAKEN PILE OF **BACON** IS HE, THIS WILL BE MY EASIEST VICTORY YET!

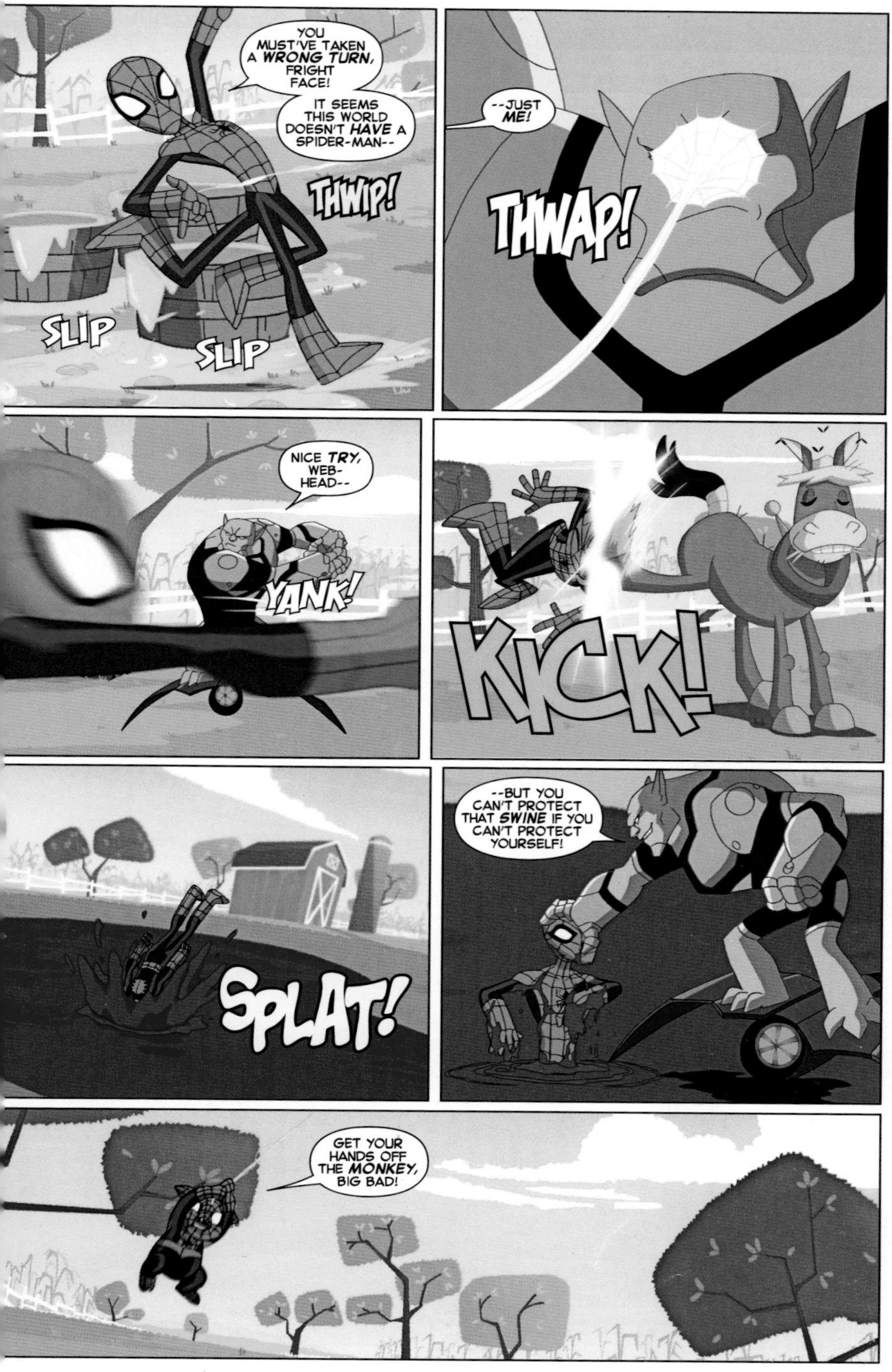
YOU MUST'VE TAKEN A WRONG TURN, FRIGHT FACE!
IT SEEMS THIS WORLD DOESN'T HAVE A SPIDER-MAN--
THWIP!
SLIP
SLIP
--JUST ME!
THWAP!
NICE TRY, WEB-HEAD--
YANK!
KICK!
SPLAT!
--BUT YOU CAN'T PROTECT THAT SWINE IF YOU CAN'T PROTECT YOURSELF!
GET YOUR HANDS OFF THE MONKEY, BIG BAD!

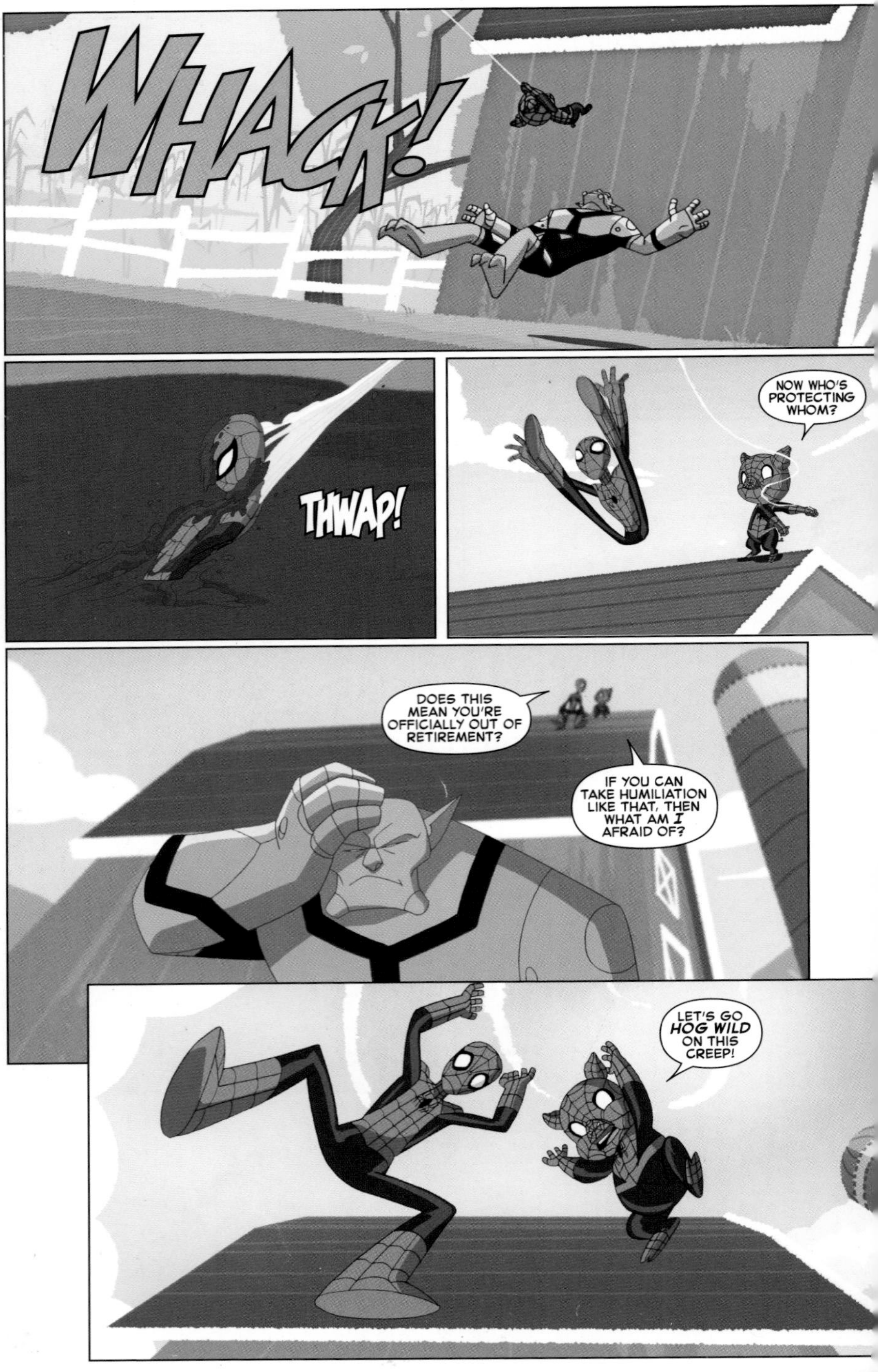
WHACK!
THWAP!
NOW WHO'S PROTECTING WHOM?
DOES THIS MEAN YOU'RE OFFICIALLY OUT OF RETIREMENT?
IF YOU CAN TAKE HUMILIATION LIKE THAT, THEN WHAT AM *I* AFRAID OF?
LET'S GO ***HOG WILD*** ON THIS CREEP!

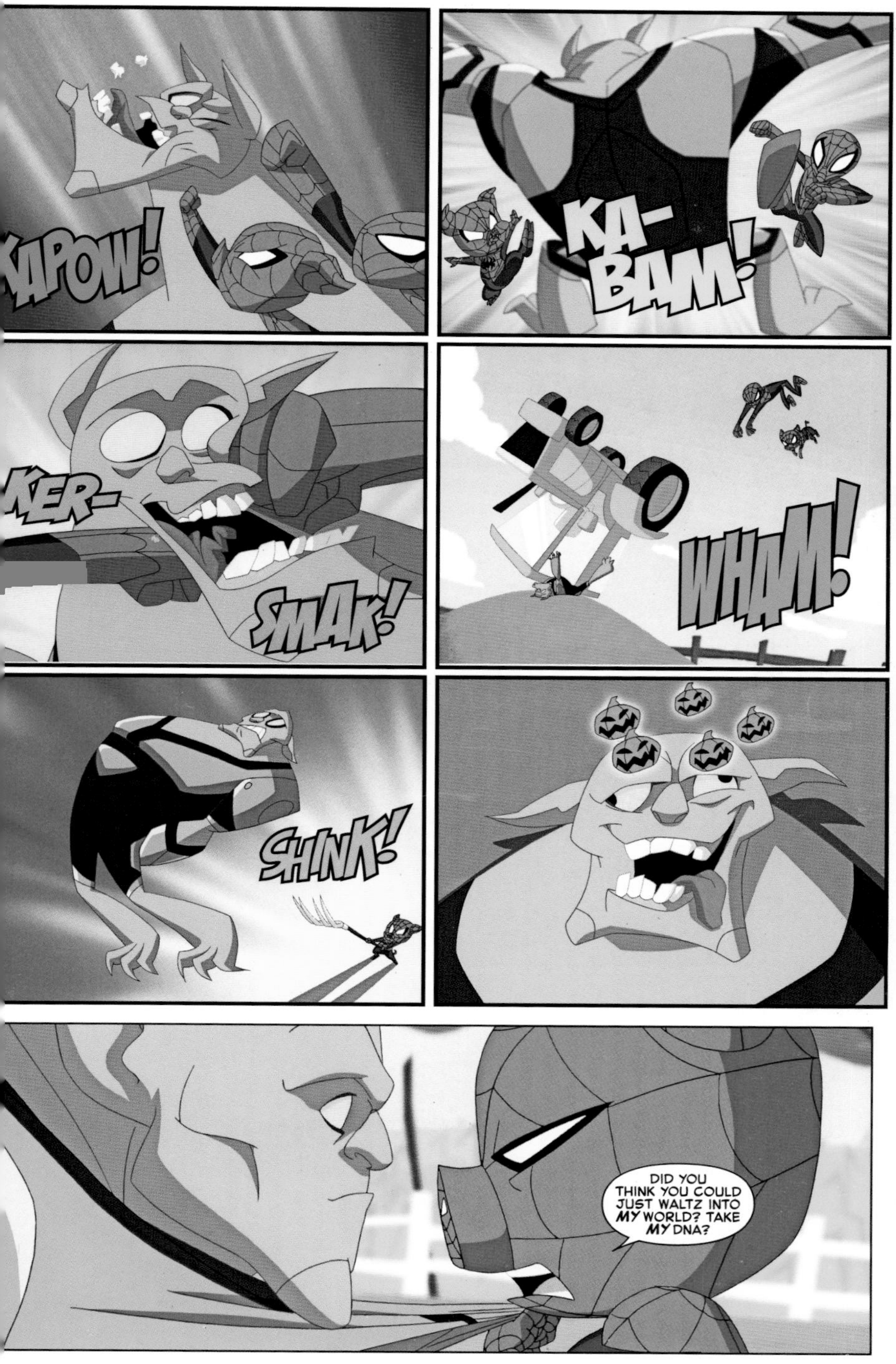
KAPOW!
KA-BAM!
KER-
SMAK!
WHAM!
SHINK!
DID YOU THINK YOU COULD JUST WALTZ INTO MY WORLD? TAKE MY DNA?

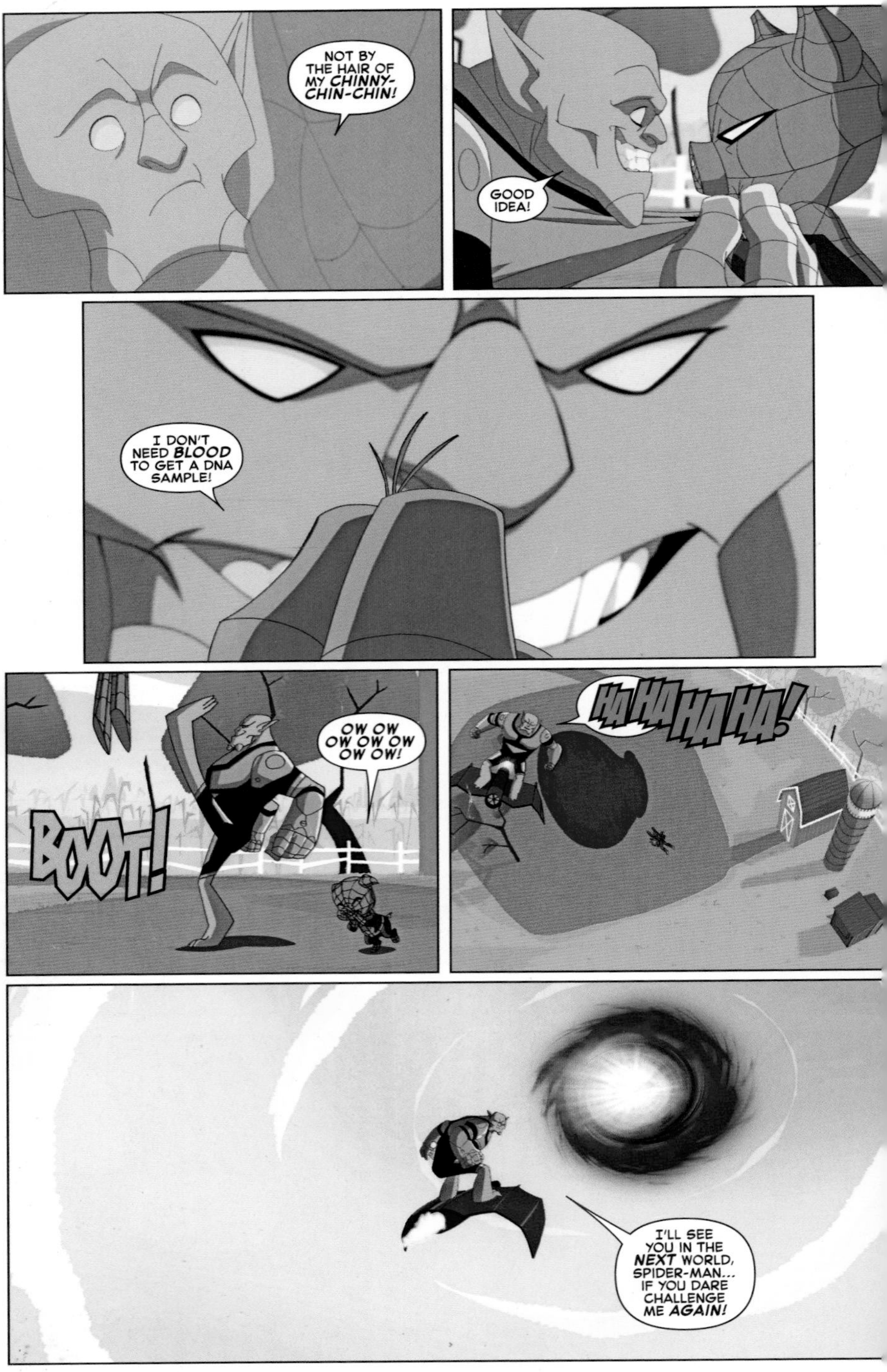
NOT BY THE HAIR OF MY CHINNY-CHIN-CHIN!
GOOD IDEA!
I DON'T NEED BLOOD TO GET A DNA SAMPLE!
BOOT!
OW OW OW OW OW OW OW!
HA HA HA HA!
I'LL SEE YOU IN THE NEXT WORLD, SPIDER-MAN... IF YOU DARE CHALLENGE ME AGAIN!

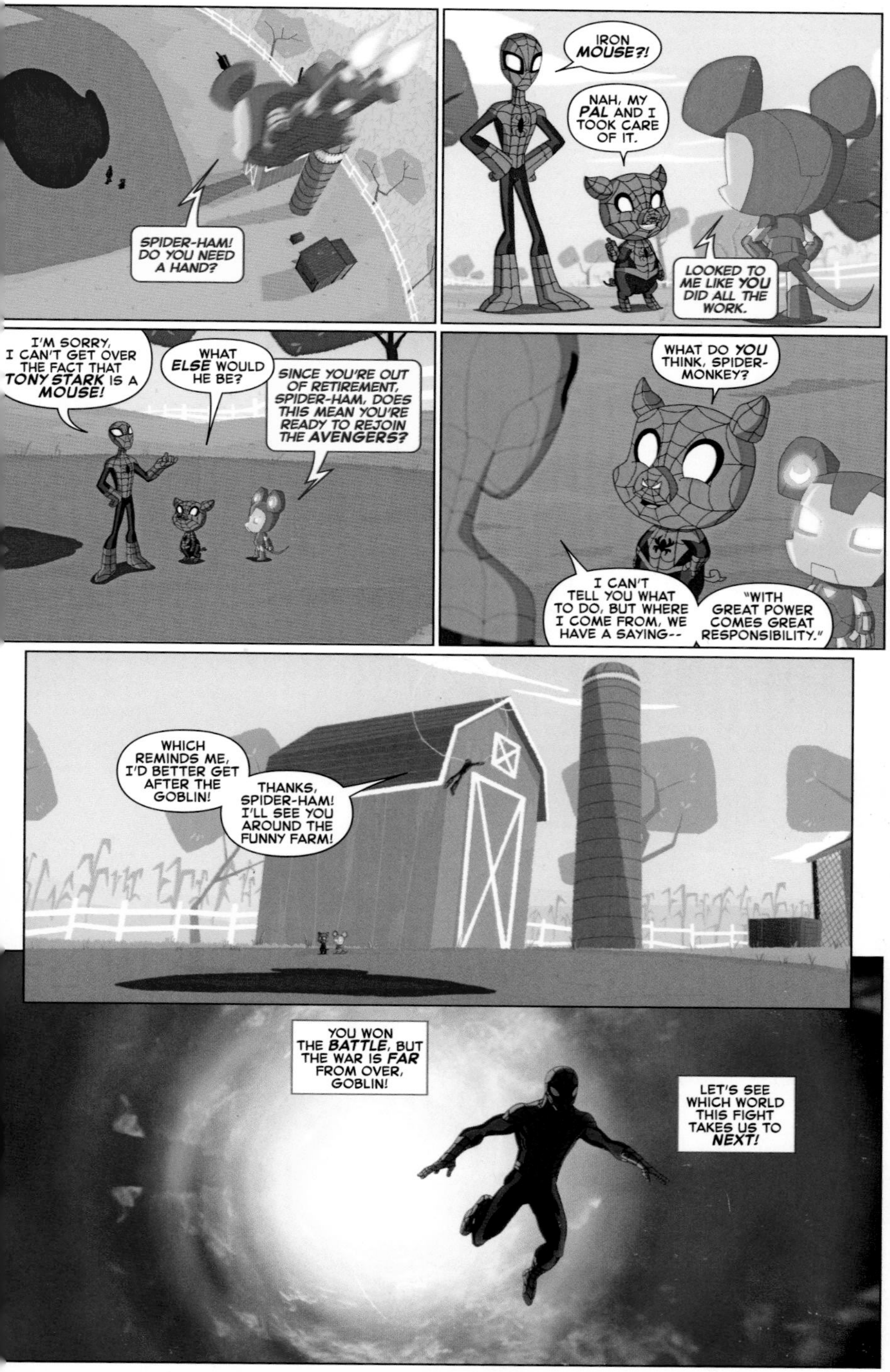
SPIDER-HAM! DO YOU NEED A HAND?
IRON MOUSE?!
NAH, MY PAL AND I TOOK CARE OF IT.
LOOKED TO ME LIKE YOU DID ALL THE WORK.
I'M SORRY, I CAN'T GET OVER THE FACT THAT TONY STARK IS A MOUSE!
WHAT ELSE WOULD HE BE?
SINCE YOU'RE OUT OF RETIREMENT, SPIDER-HAM, DOES THIS MEAN YOU'RE READY TO REJOIN THE AVENGERS?
WHAT DO YOU THINK, SPIDER-MONKEY?
I CAN'T TELL YOU WHAT TO DO, BUT WHERE I COME FROM, WE HAVE A SAYING--
"WITH GREAT POWER COMES GREAT RESPONSIBILITY."
WHICH REMINDS ME, I'D BETTER GET AFTER THE GOBLIN!
THANKS, SPIDER-HAM! I'LL SEE YOU AROUND THE FUNNY FARM!
YOU WON THE BATTLE, BUT THE WAR IS FAR FROM OVER, GOBLIN!
LET'S SEE WHICH WORLD THIS FIGHT TAKES US TO NEXT!

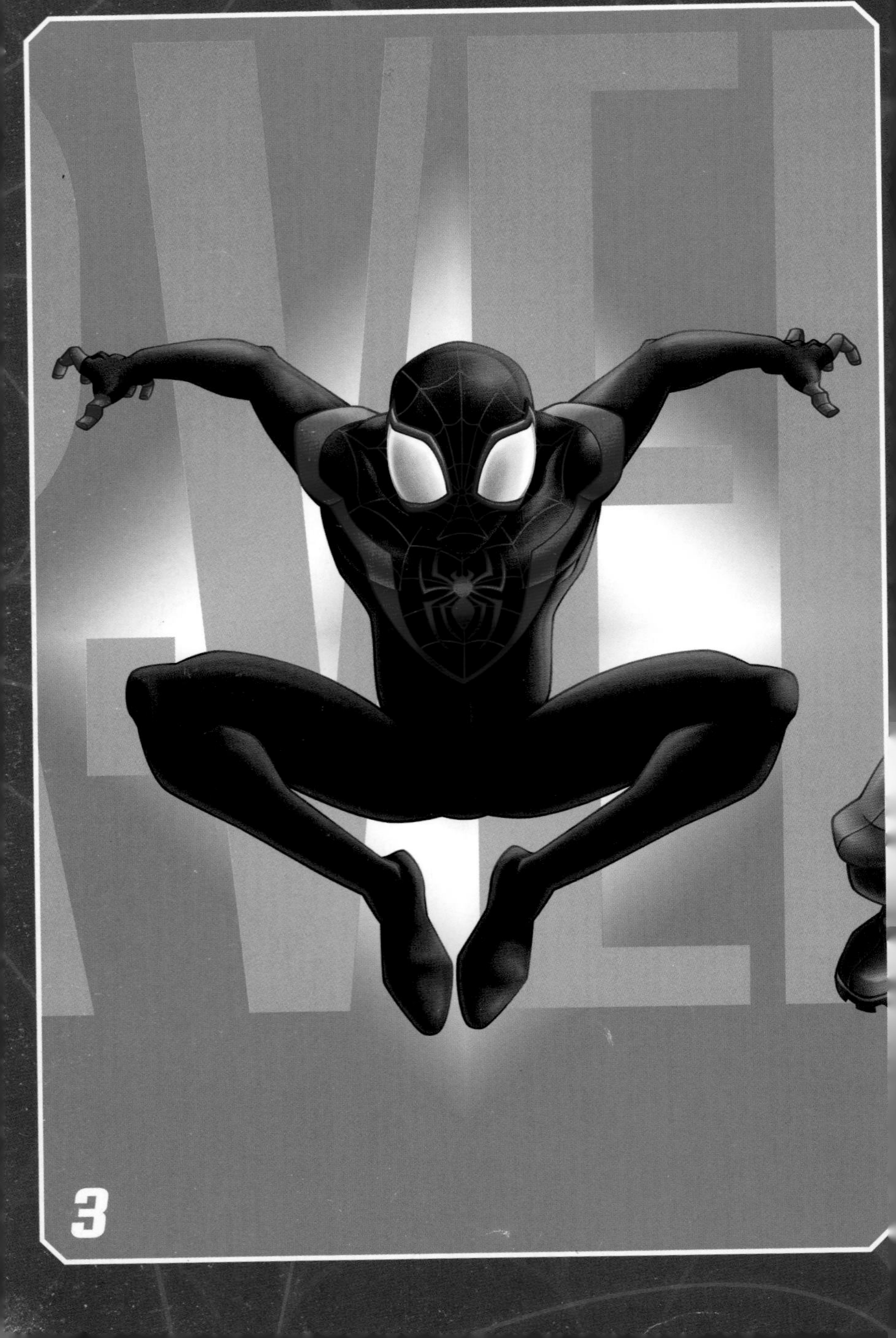

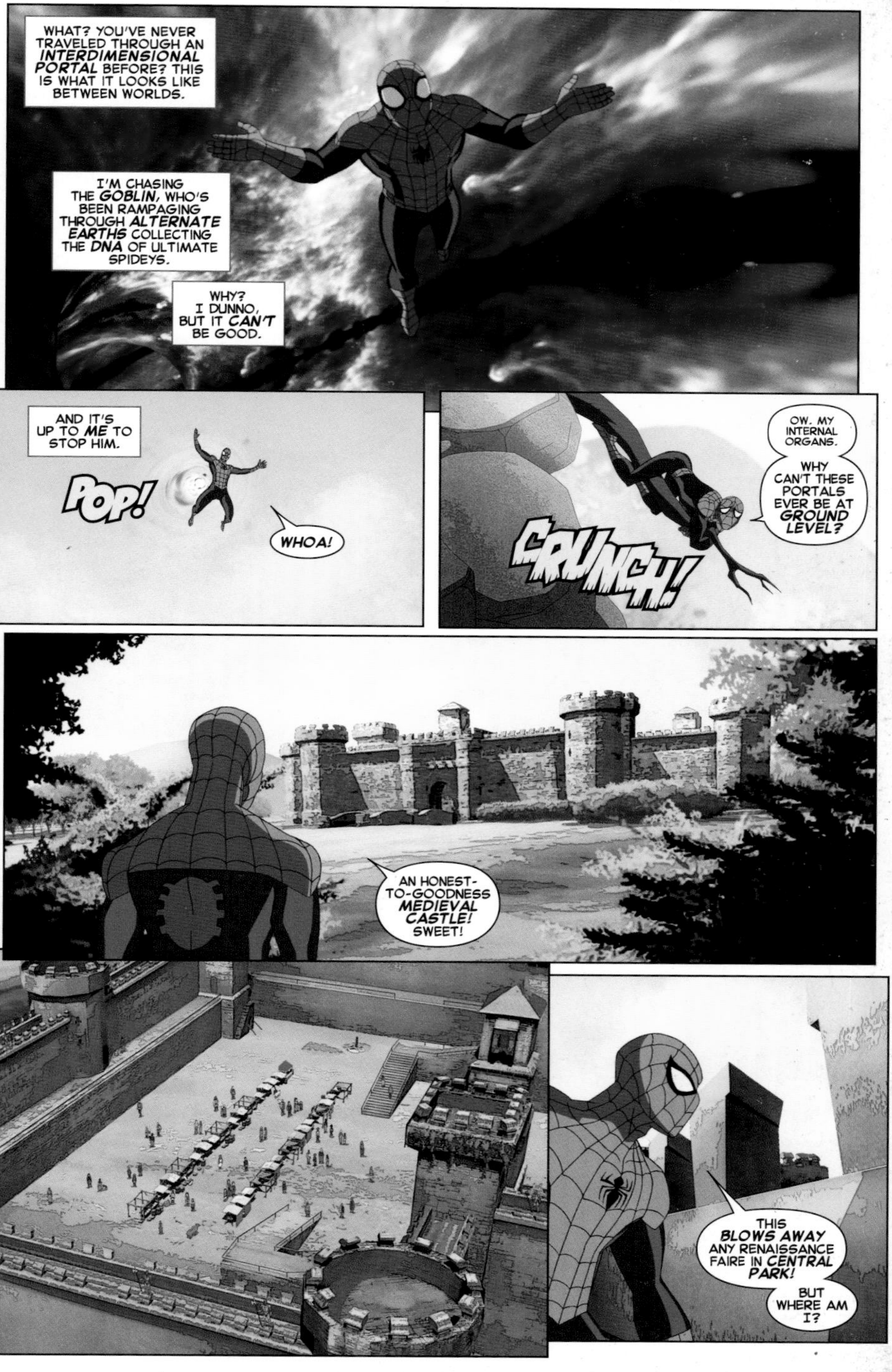
WHAT? YOU'VE NEVER TRAVELED THROUGH AN INTERDIMENSIONAL PORTAL BEFORE? THIS IS WHAT IT LOOKS LIKE BETWEEN WORLDS.
I'M CHASING THE GOBLIN, WHO'S BEEN RAMPAGING THROUGH ALTERNATE EARTHS COLLECTING THE DNA OF ULTIMATE SPIDEYS.
WHY? I DUNNO, BUT IT CAN'T BE GOOD.
AND IT'S UP TO ME TO STOP HIM.
POP!
WHOA!
CRUNCH!
OW. MY INTERNAL ORGANS.
WHY CAN'T THESE PORTALS EVER BE AT GROUND LEVEL?
AN HONEST-TO-GOODNESS MEDIEVAL CASTLE! SWEET!
THIS BLOWS AWAY ANY RENAISSANCE FAIRE IN CENTRAL PARK!
BUT WHERE AM I?

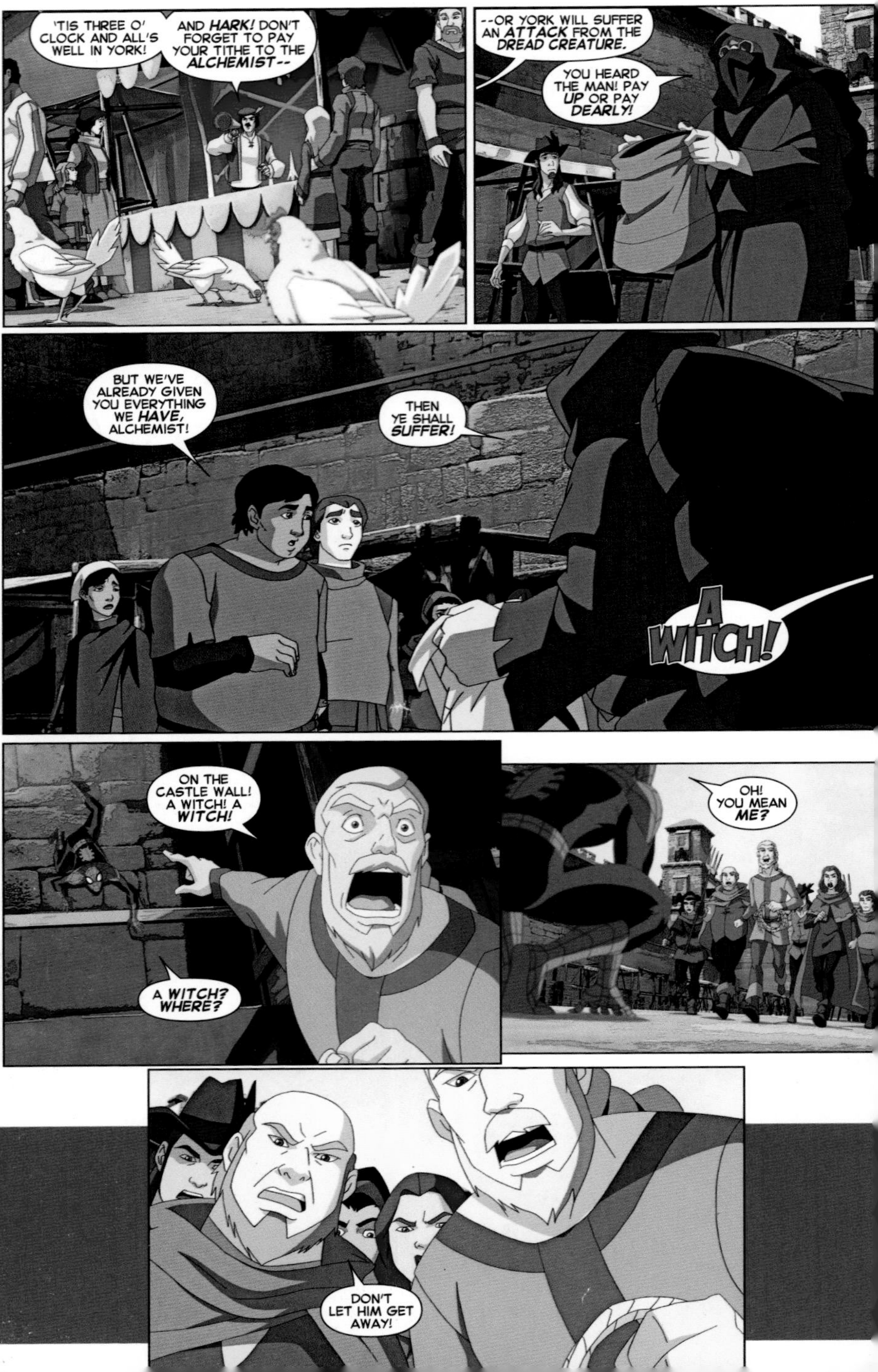
'TIS THREE O' CLOCK AND ALL'S WELL IN YORK!
AND HARK! DON'T FORGET TO PAY YOUR TITHE TO THE ALCHEMIST--
--OR YORK WILL SUFFER AN ATTACK FROM THE DREAD CREATURE.
YOU HEARD THE MAN! PAY UP OR PAY DEARLY!
BUT WE'VE ALREADY GIVEN YOU EVERYTHING WE HAVE, ALCHEMIST!
THEN YE SHALL SUFFER!
A WITCH!
ON THE CASTLE WALL! A WITCH! A WITCH!
A WITCH? WHERE?
OH! YOU MEAN ME?
DON'T LET HIM GET AWAY!

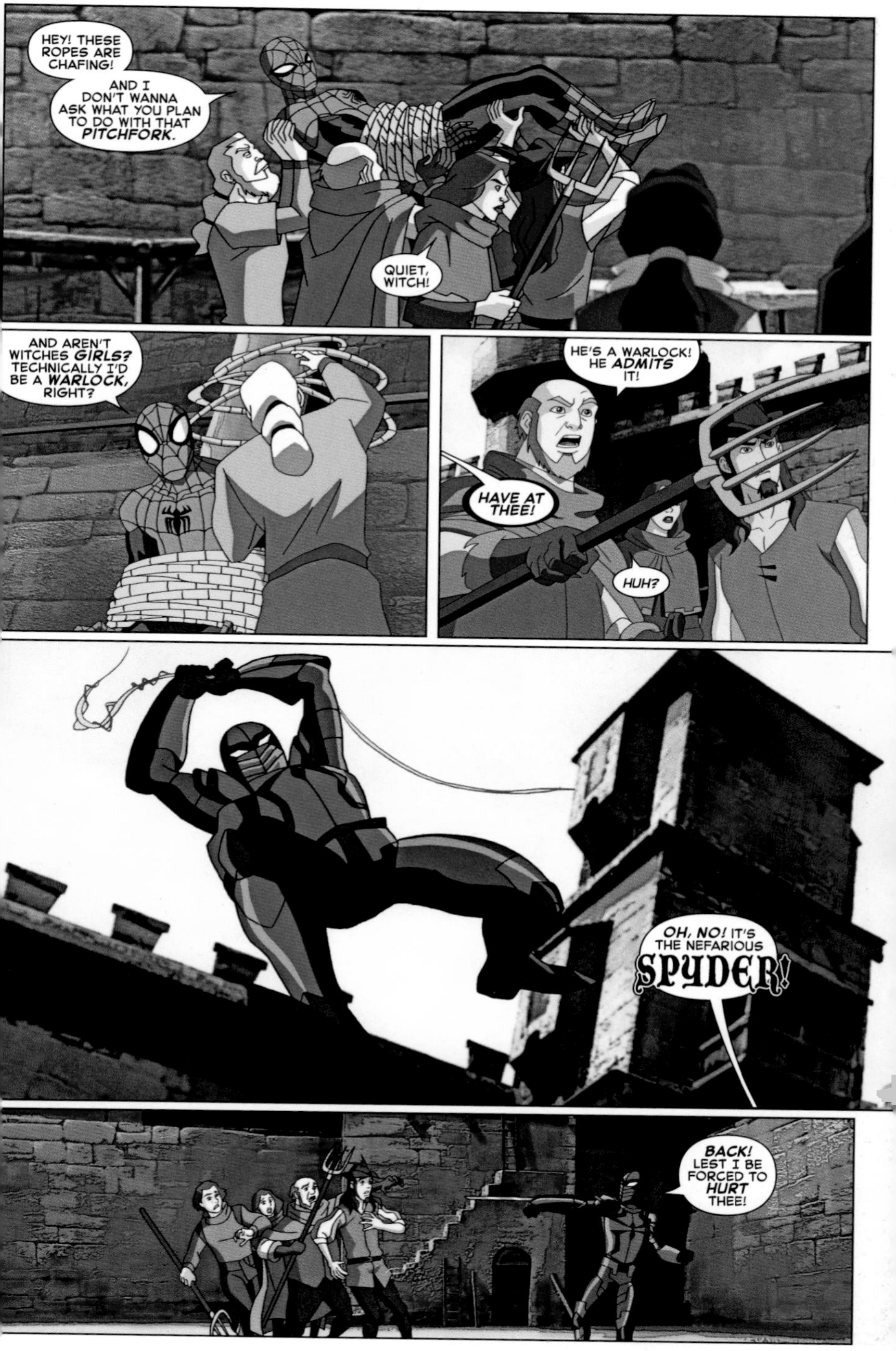
HEY! THESE ROPES ARE CHAFING!
AND I DON'T WANNA ASK WHAT YOU PLAN TO DO WITH THAT PITCHFORK.
QUIET, WITCH!
AND AREN'T WITCHES GIRLS? TECHNICALLY I'D BE A WARLOCK, RIGHT?
HE'S A WARLOCK! HE ADMITS IT!
HAVE AT THEE!
HUH?
OH, NO! IT'S THE NEFARIOUS SPYDER!
BACK! LEST I BE FORCED TO HURT THEE!

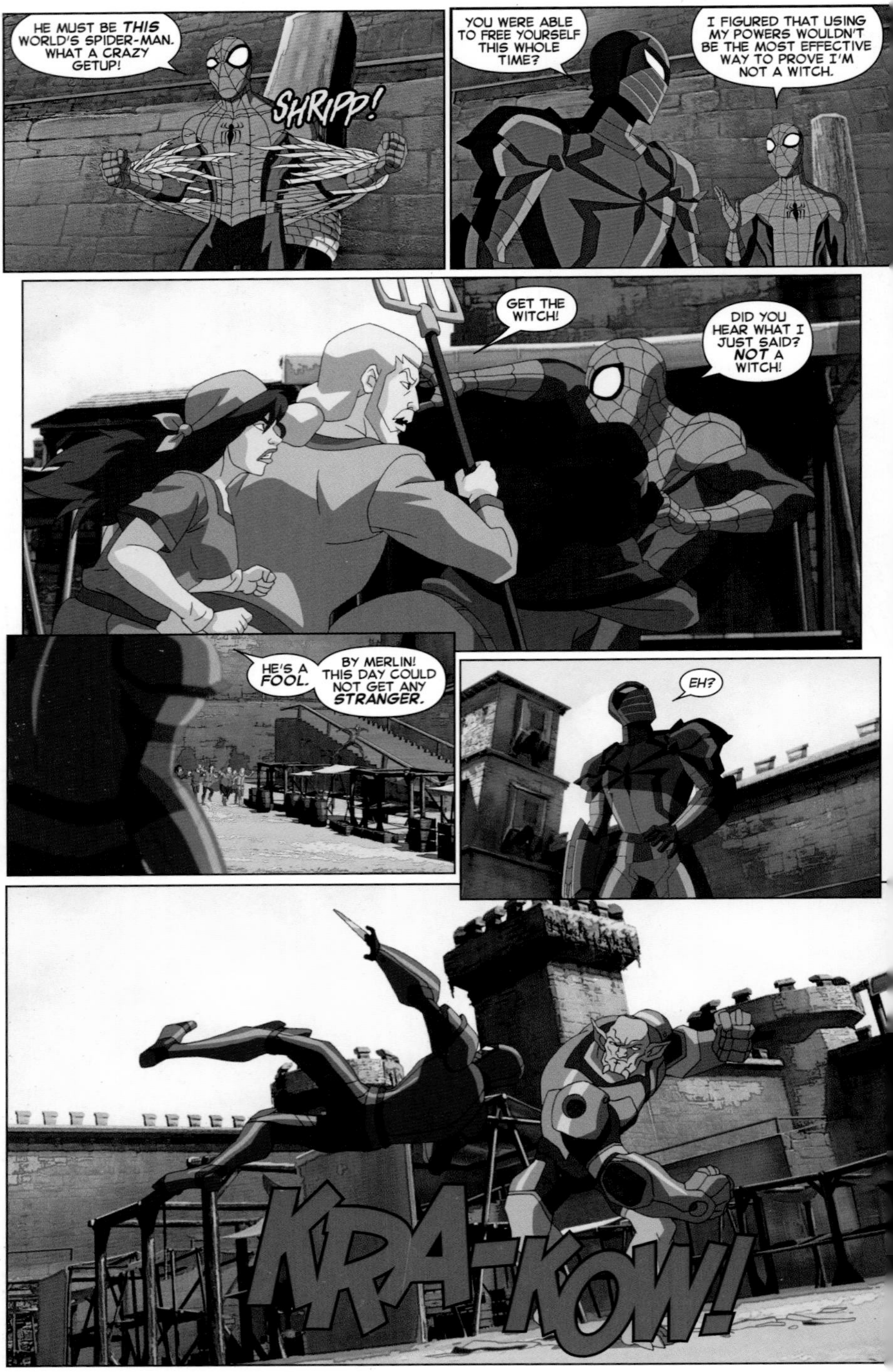
HE MUST BE THIS WORLD'S SPIDER-MAN. WHAT A CRAZY GETUP!
SHRIPP!
YOU WERE ABLE TO FREE YOURSELF THIS WHOLE TIME?
I FIGURED THAT USING MY POWERS WOULDN'T BE THE MOST EFFECTIVE WAY TO PROVE I'M NOT A WITCH.
GET THE WITCH!
DID YOU HEAR WHAT I JUST SAID? NOT A WITCH!
HE'S A FOOL.
BY MERLIN! THIS DAY COULD NOT GET ANY STRANGER.
EH?
KRA-KOW!

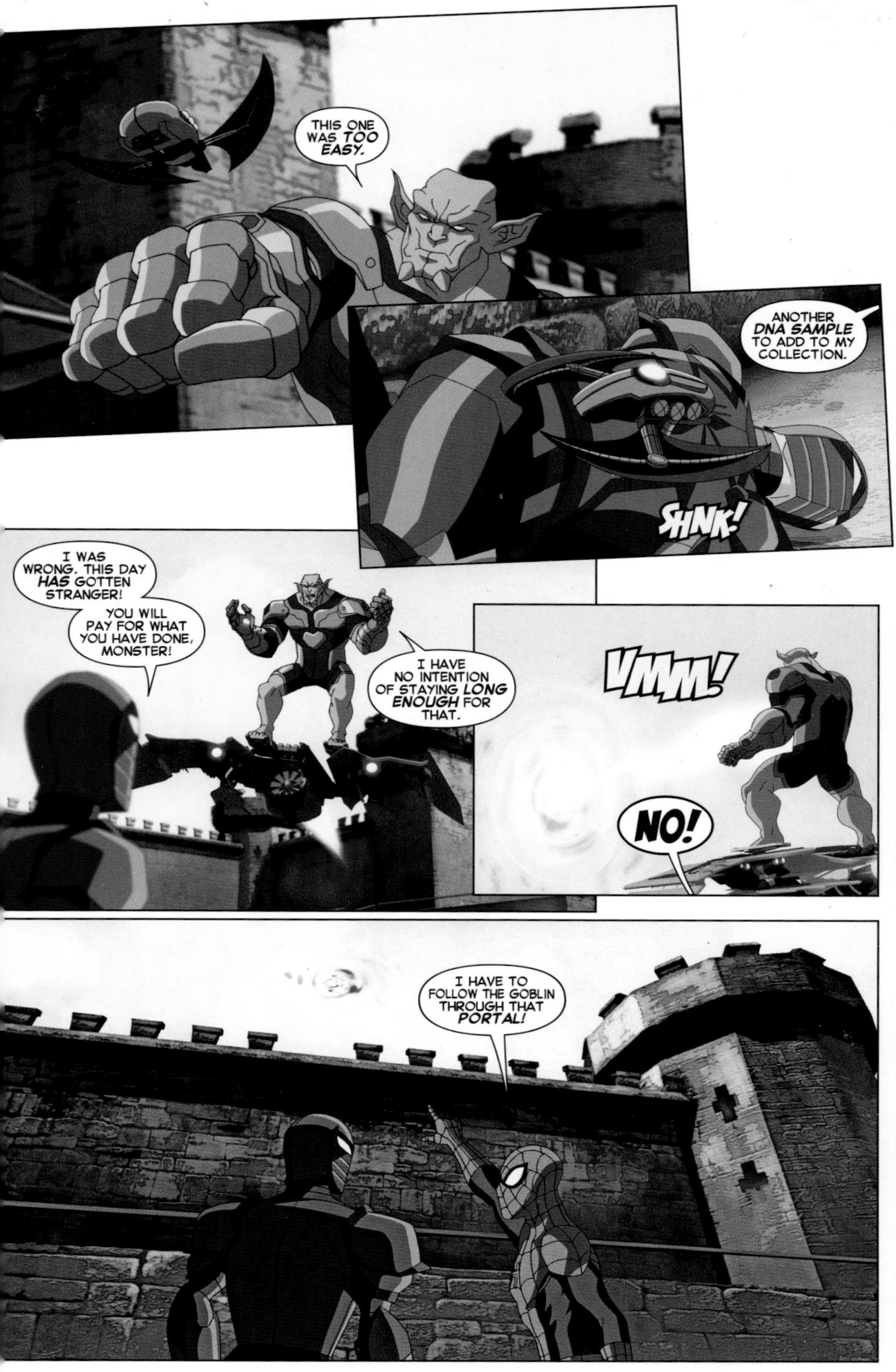
THIS ONE WAS TOO EASY.
ANOTHER DNA SAMPLE TO ADD TO MY COLLECTION.
SHNK!
I WAS WRONG. THIS DAY HAS GOTTEN STRANGER!
YOU WILL PAY FOR WHAT YOU HAVE DONE, MONSTER!
I HAVE NO INTENTION OF STAYING LONG ENOUGH FOR THAT.
VMM!
NO!
I HAVE TO FOLLOW THE GOBLIN THROUGH THAT PORTAL!

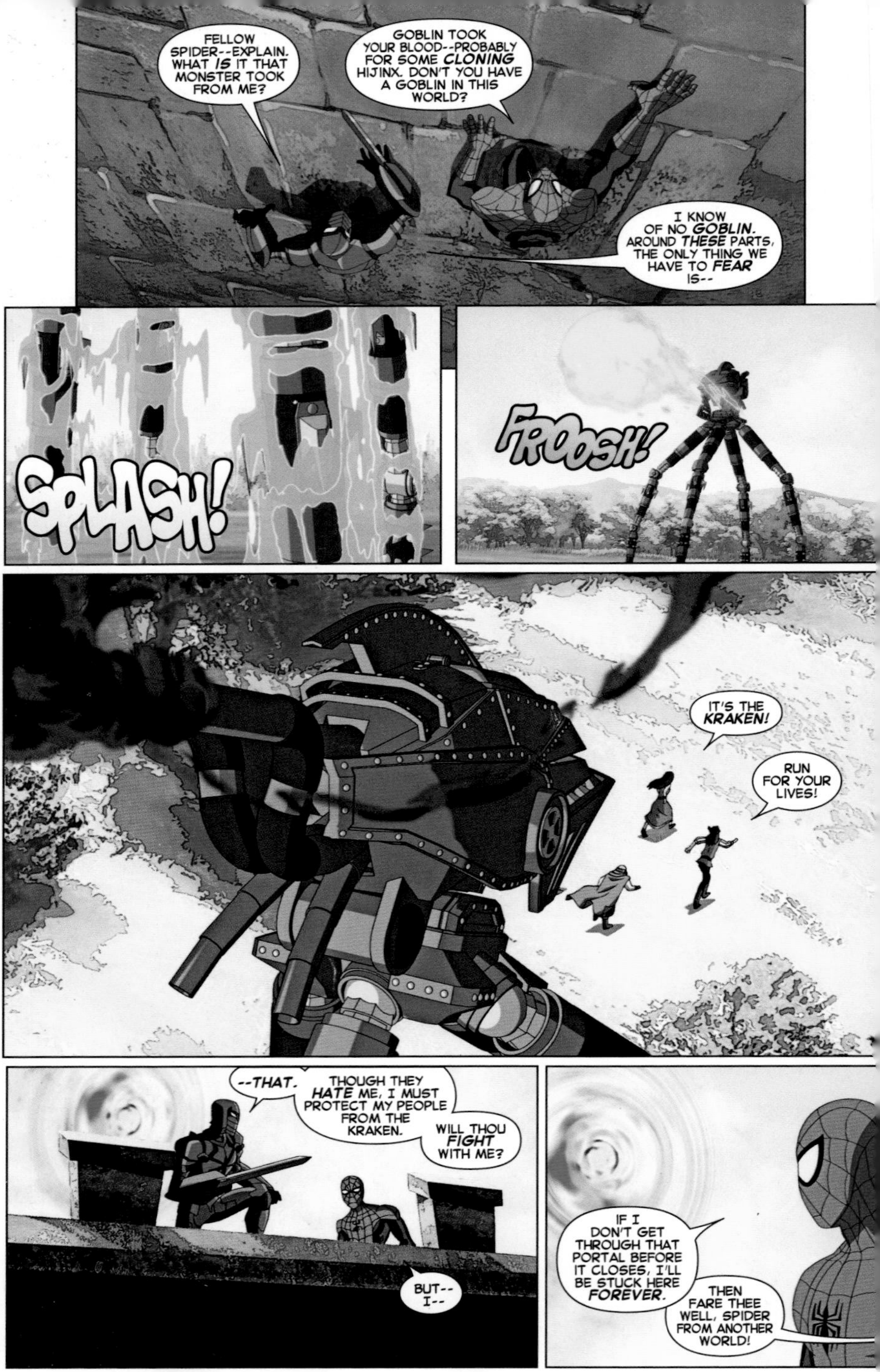

FELLOW SPIDER--EXPLAIN. WHAT IS IT THAT MONSTER TOOK FROM ME?
GOBLIN TOOK YOUR BLOOD--PROBABLY FOR SOME CLONING HIJINX. DON'T YOU HAVE A GOBLIN IN THIS WORLD?
I KNOW OF NO GOBLIN. AROUND THESE PARTS, THE ONLY THING WE HAVE TO FEAR IS--
SPLASH!
FROOSH!
IT'S THE KRAKEN!
RUN FOR YOUR LIVES!
--THAT.
THOUGH THEY HATE ME, I MUST PROTECT MY PEOPLE FROM THE KRAKEN.
WILL THOU FIGHT WITH ME?
BUT-- I--
IF I DON'T GET THROUGH THAT PORTAL BEFORE IT CLOSES, I'LL BE STUCK HERE FOREVER.
THEN FARE THEE WELL, SPIDER FROM ANOTHER WORLD!

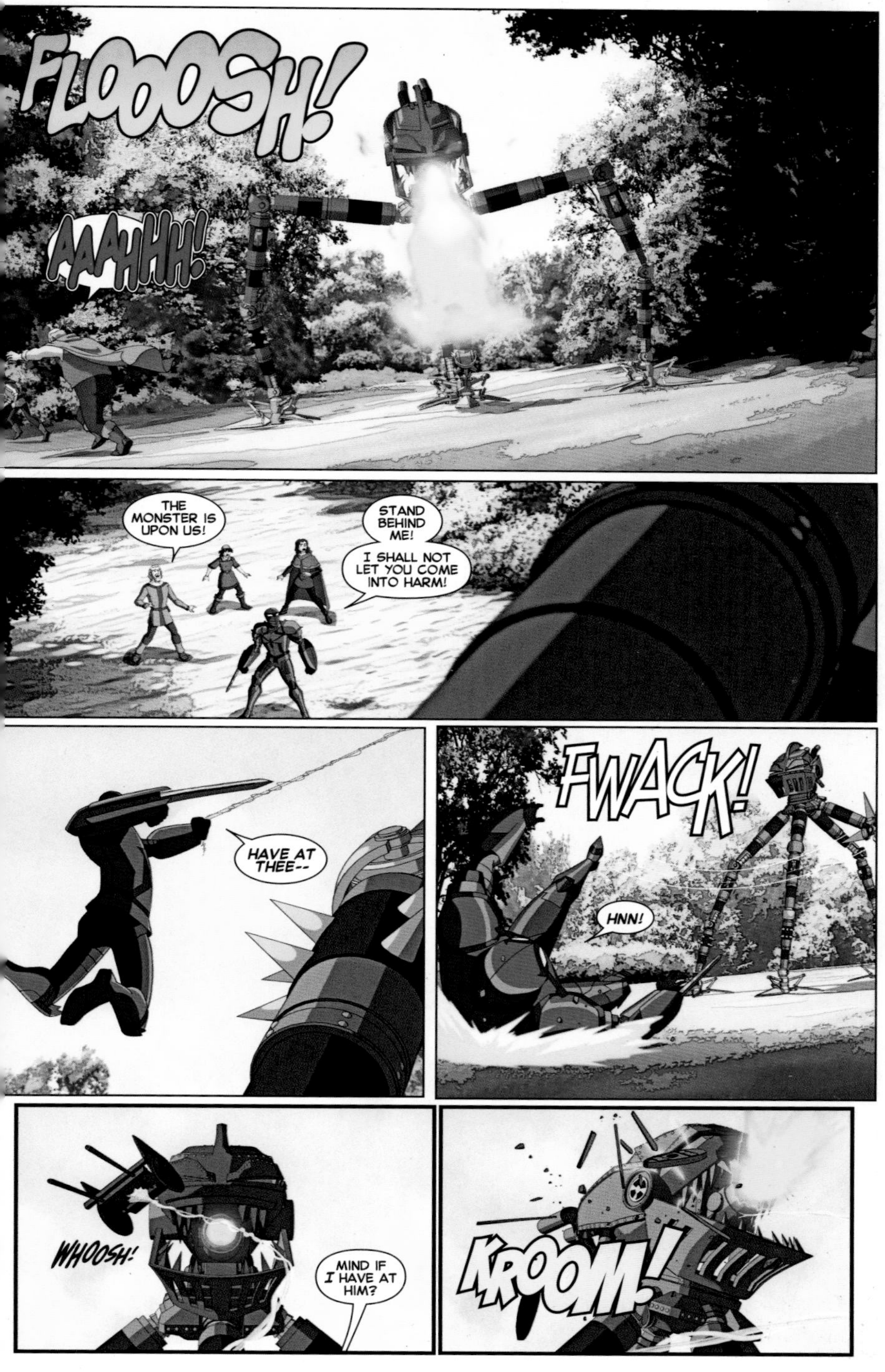
FLOOOSH!
AAAHHH!
THE MONSTER IS UPON US!
STAND BEHIND ME!
I SHALL NOT LET YOU COME INTO HARM!
HAVE AT THEE--
FWACK!
HNN!
WHOOSH!
MIND IF I HAVE AT HIM?
KROOM!

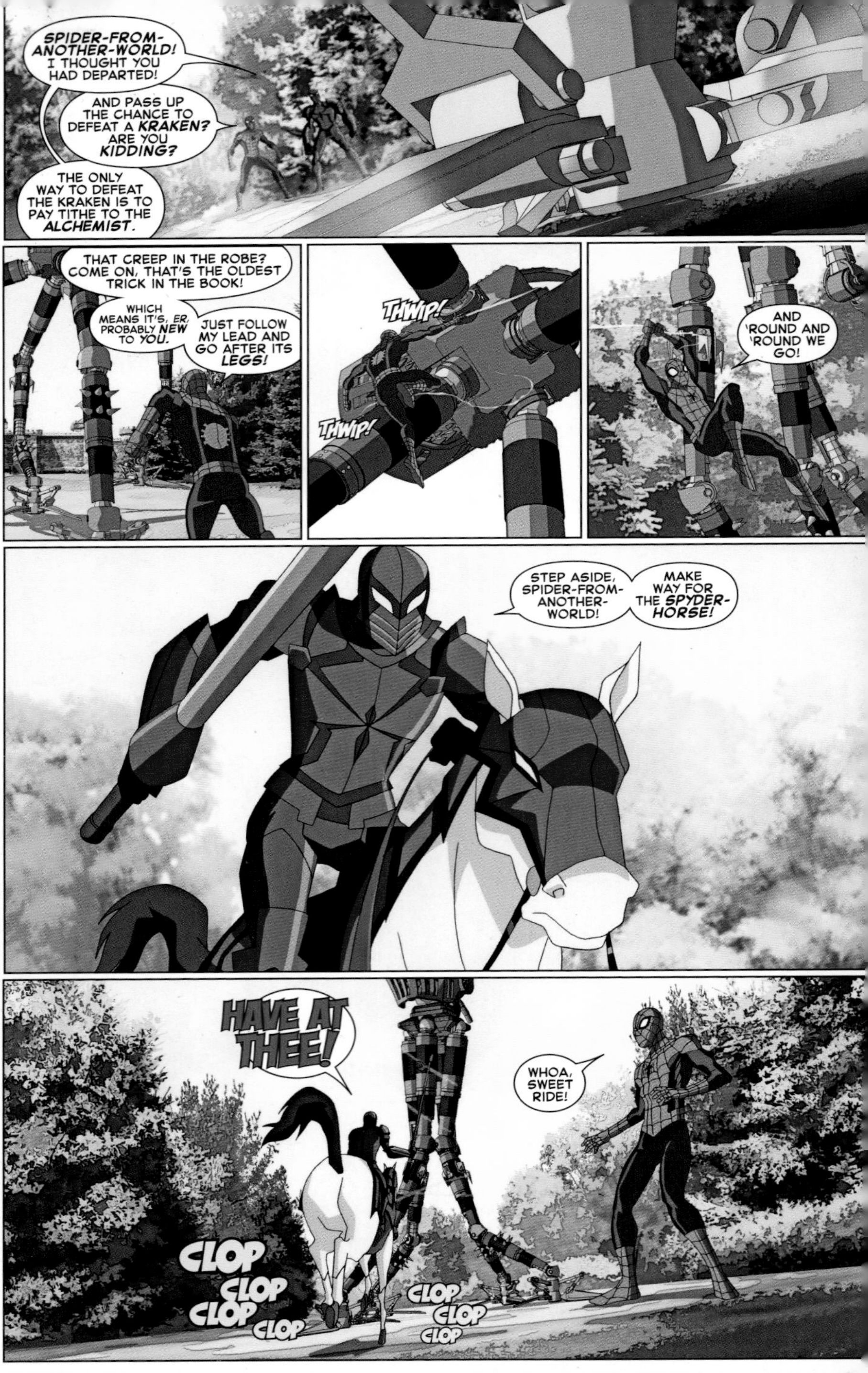
SPIDER-FROM-ANOTHER-WORLD! I THOUGHT YOU HAD DEPARTED!
AND PASS UP THE CHANCE TO DEFEAT A KRAKEN? ARE YOU KIDDING?
THE ONLY WAY TO DEFEAT THE KRAKEN IS TO PAY TITHE TO THE ALCHEMIST.
THAT CREEP IN THE ROBE? COME ON, THAT'S THE OLDEST TRICK IN THE BOOK!
WHICH MEANS IT'S, ER, PROBABLY NEW TO YOU.
JUST FOLLOW MY LEAD AND GO AFTER ITS LEGS!
THWIP!
THWIP!
AND 'ROUND AND 'ROUND WE GO!
STEP ASIDE, SPIDER-FROM-ANOTHER-WORLD!
MAKE WAY FOR THE SPYDER-HORSE!
HAVE AT THEE!
WHOA, SWEET RIDE!
CLOP
CLOP
CLOP
CLOP
CLOP
CLOP
CLOP

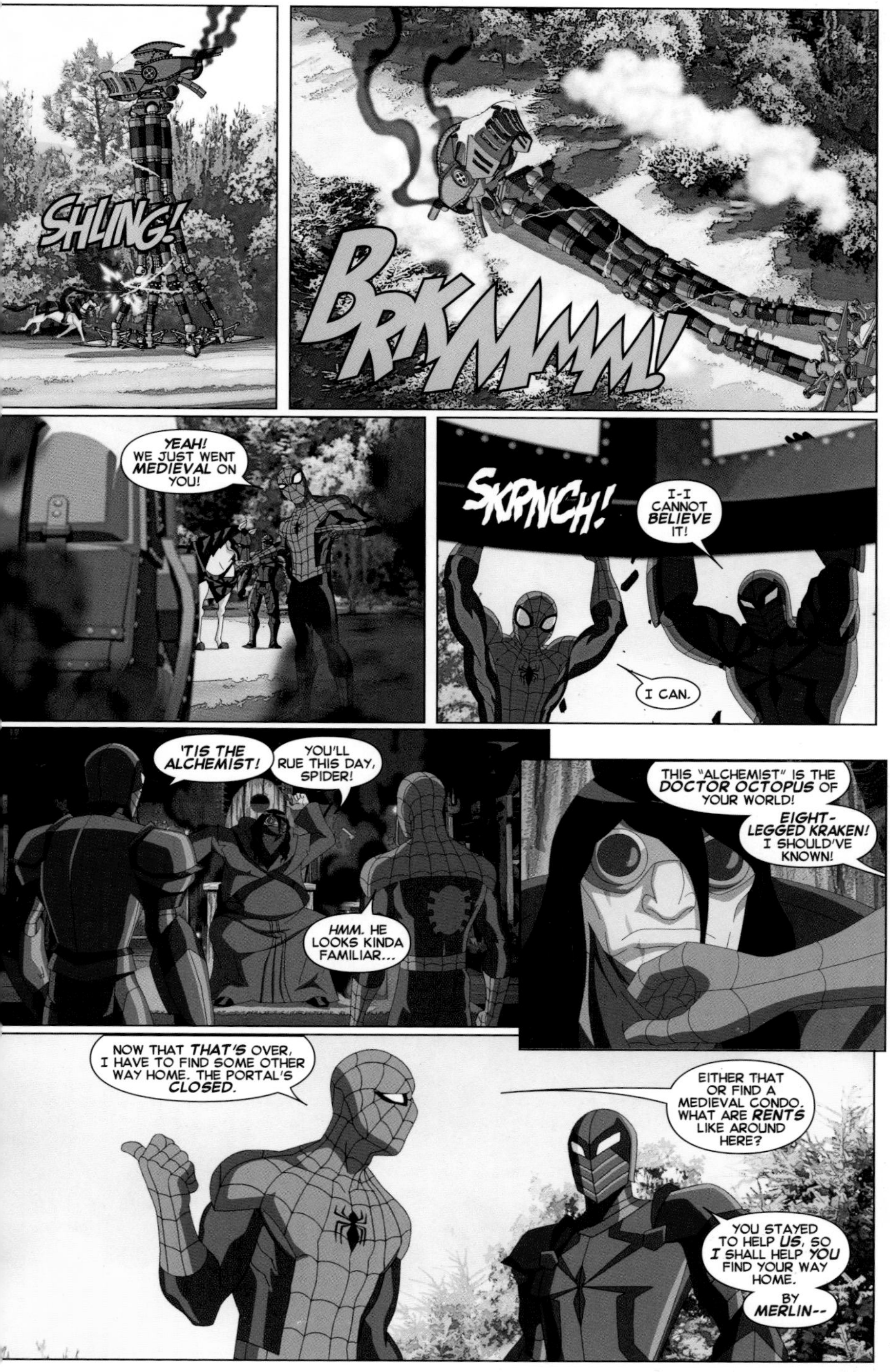
SHLING!
BRKMMM!
YEAH! WE JUST WENT MEDIEVAL ON YOU!
SKRNCH!
I-I CANNOT BELIEVE IT!
I CAN.
'TIS THE ALCHEMIST!
YOU'LL RUE THIS DAY, SPIDER!
HMM. HE LOOKS KINDA FAMILIAR...
THIS "ALCHEMIST" IS THE DOCTOR OCTOPUS OF YOUR WORLD!
EIGHT-LEGGED KRAKEN! I SHOULD'VE KNOWN!
NOW THAT THAT'S OVER, I HAVE TO FIND SOME OTHER WAY HOME. THE PORTAL'S CLOSED.
EITHER THAT OR FIND A MEDIEVAL CONDO. WHAT ARE RENTS LIKE AROUND HERE?
YOU STAYED TO HELP US, SO I SHALL HELP YOU FIND YOUR WAY HOME.
BY MERLIN--

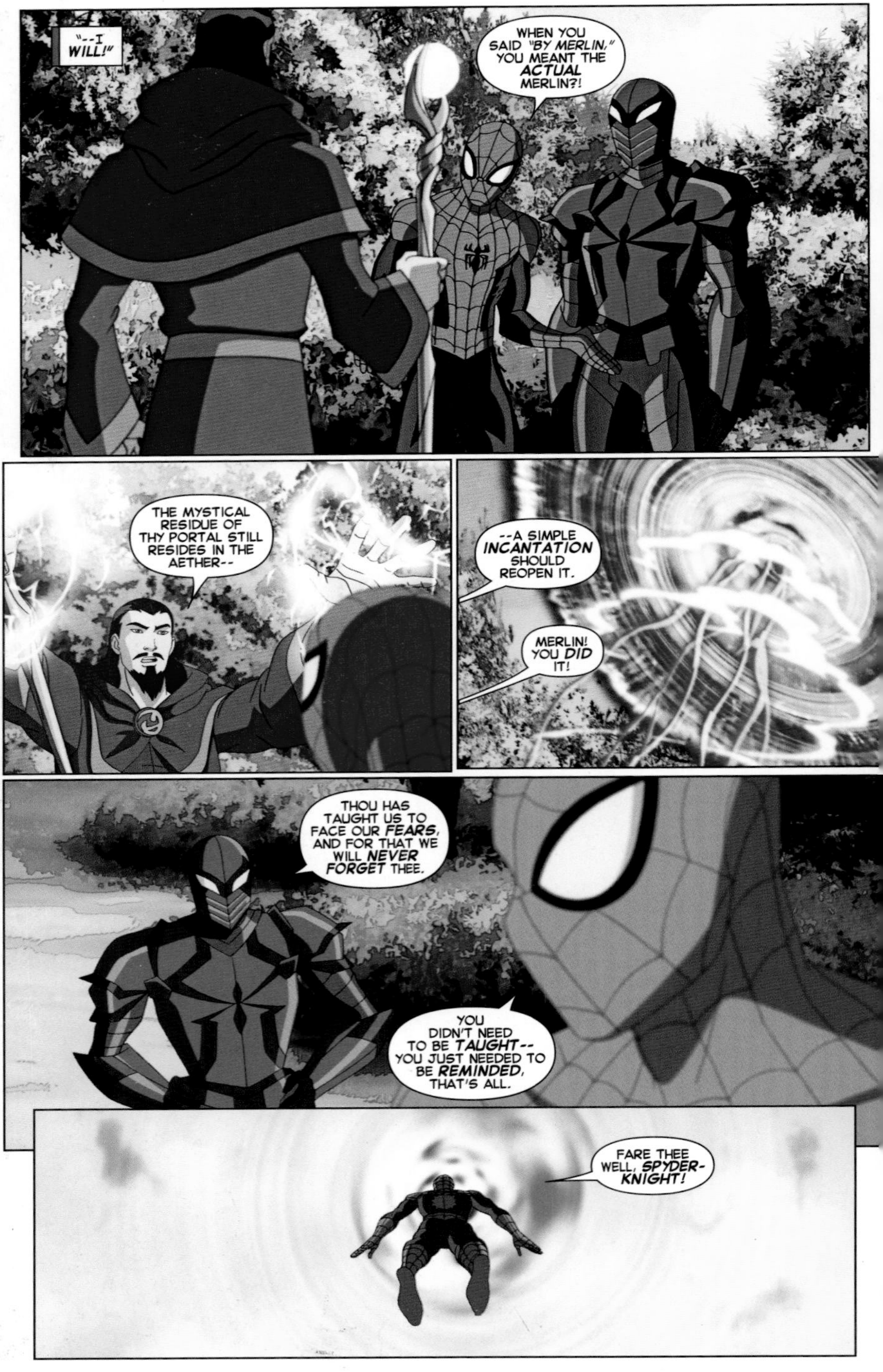
"--I WILL!"
WHEN YOU SAID "BY MERLIN," YOU MEANT THE ACTUAL MERLIN?!
THE MYSTICAL RESIDUE OF THY PORTAL STILL RESIDES IN THE AETHER--
--A SIMPLE INCANTATION SHOULD REOPEN IT.
MERLIN! YOU DID IT!
THOU HAS TAUGHT US TO FACE OUR FEARS, AND FOR THAT WE WILL NEVER FORGET THEE.
YOU DIDN'T NEED TO BE TAUGHT-- YOU JUST NEEDED TO BE REMINDED, THAT'S ALL.
FARE THEE WELL, SPYDER-KNIGHT!

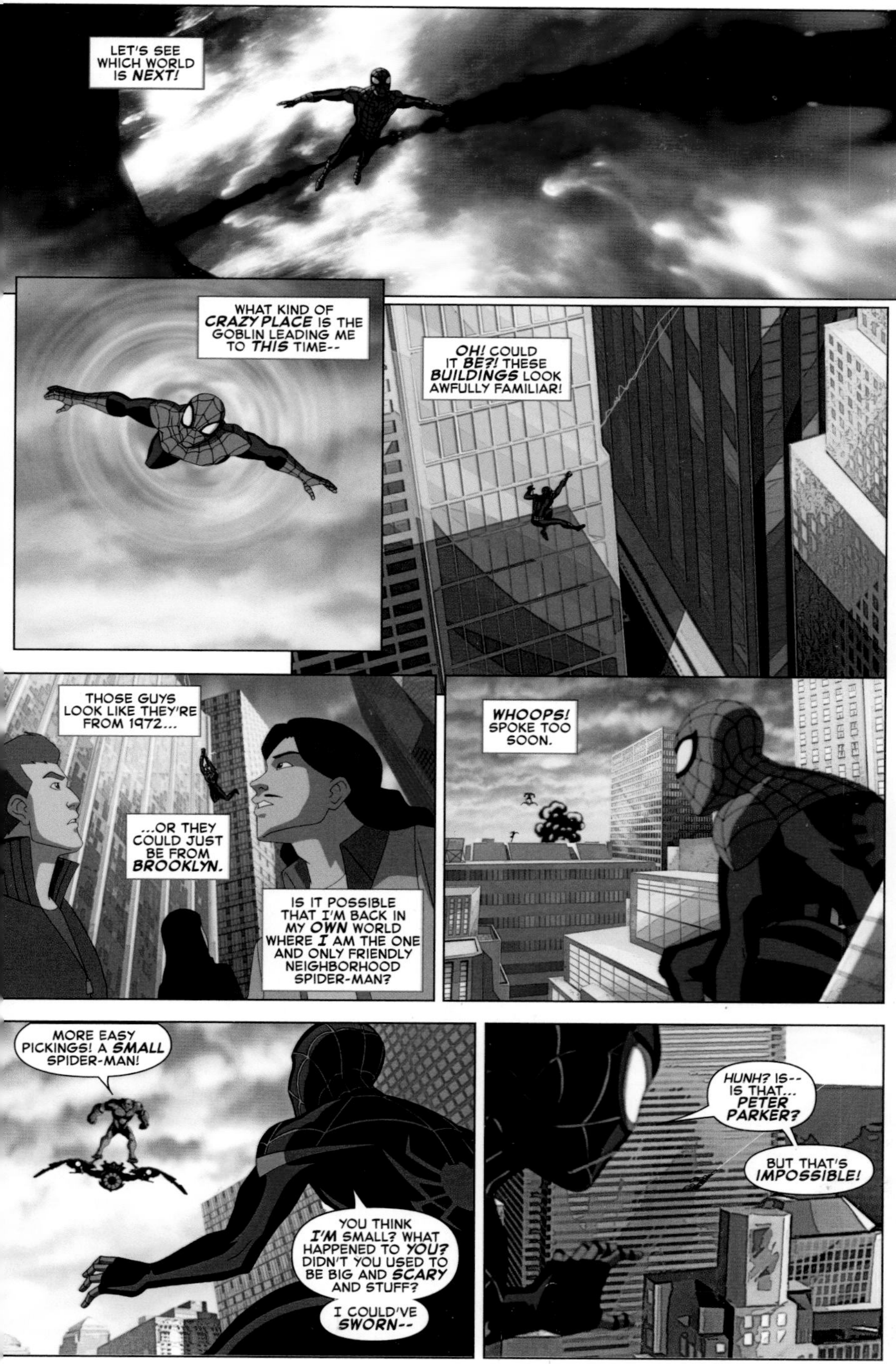

LET'S SEE WHICH WORLD IS NEXT!
WHAT KIND OF CRAZY PLACE IS THE GOBLIN LEADING ME TO THIS TIME--
OH! COULD IT BE?! THESE BUILDINGS LOOK AWFULLY FAMILIAR!
THOSE GUYS LOOK LIKE THEY'RE FROM 1972...
...OR THEY COULD JUST BE FROM BROOKLYN.
IS IT POSSIBLE THAT I'M BACK IN MY OWN WORLD WHERE I AM THE ONE AND ONLY FRIENDLY NEIGHBORHOOD SPIDER-MAN?
WHOOPS! SPOKE TOO SOON.
MORE EASY PICKINGS! A SMALL SPIDER-MAN!
YOU THINK I'M SMALL? WHAT HAPPENED TO YOU? DIDN'T YOU USED TO BE BIG AND SCARY AND STUFF?
I COULD'VE SWORN--
HUNH? IS-- IS THAT... PETER PARKER?
BUT THAT'S IMPOSSIBLE!

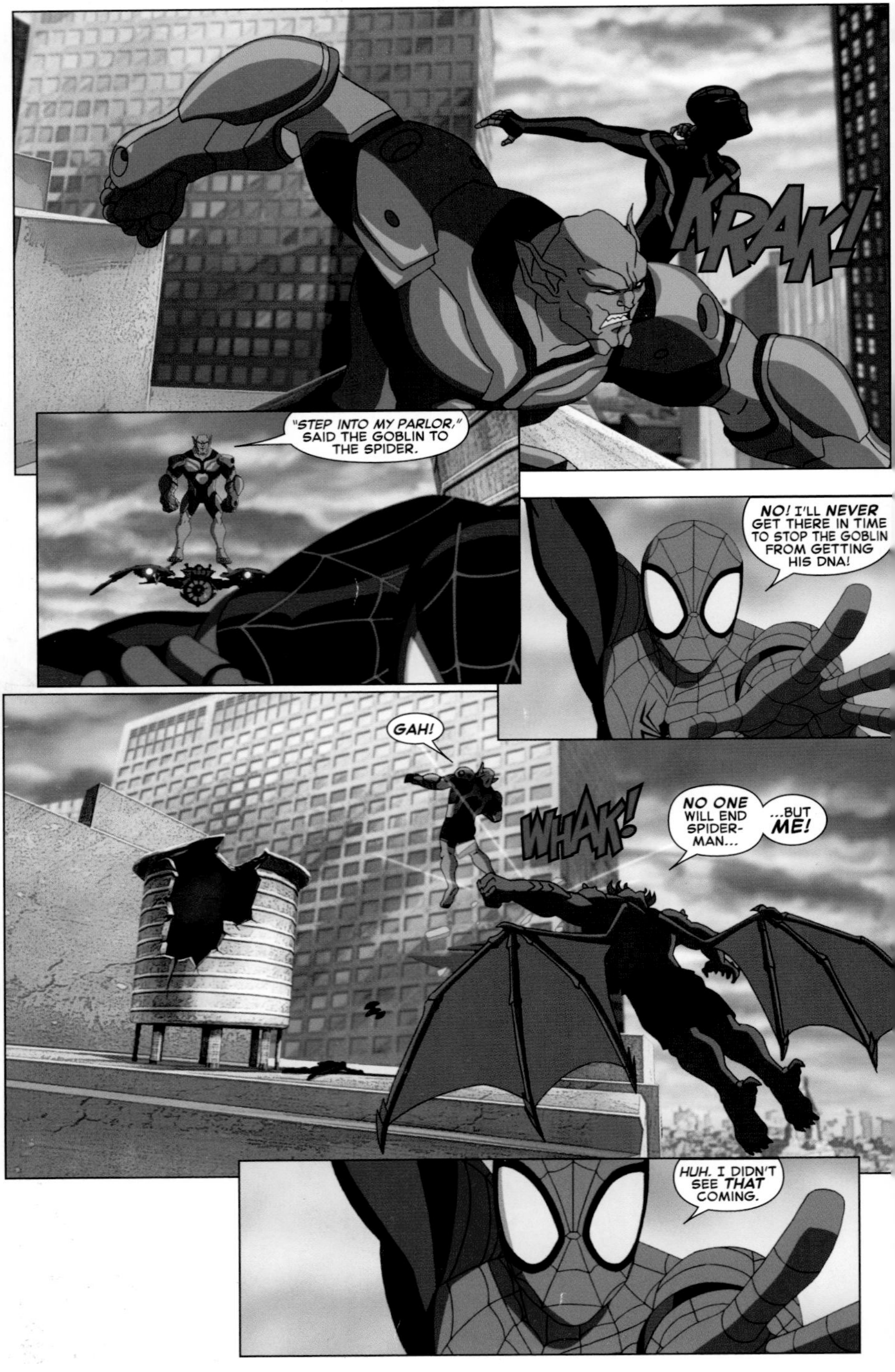
KRAK!
"STEP INTO MY PARLOR," SAID THE GOBLIN TO THE SPIDER.
NO! I'LL NEVER GET THERE IN TIME TO STOP THE GOBLIN FROM GETTING HIS DNA!
GAH!
WHAK!
NO ONE WILL END SPIDER-MAN...
...BUT ME!
HUH. I DIDN'T SEE THAT COMING.

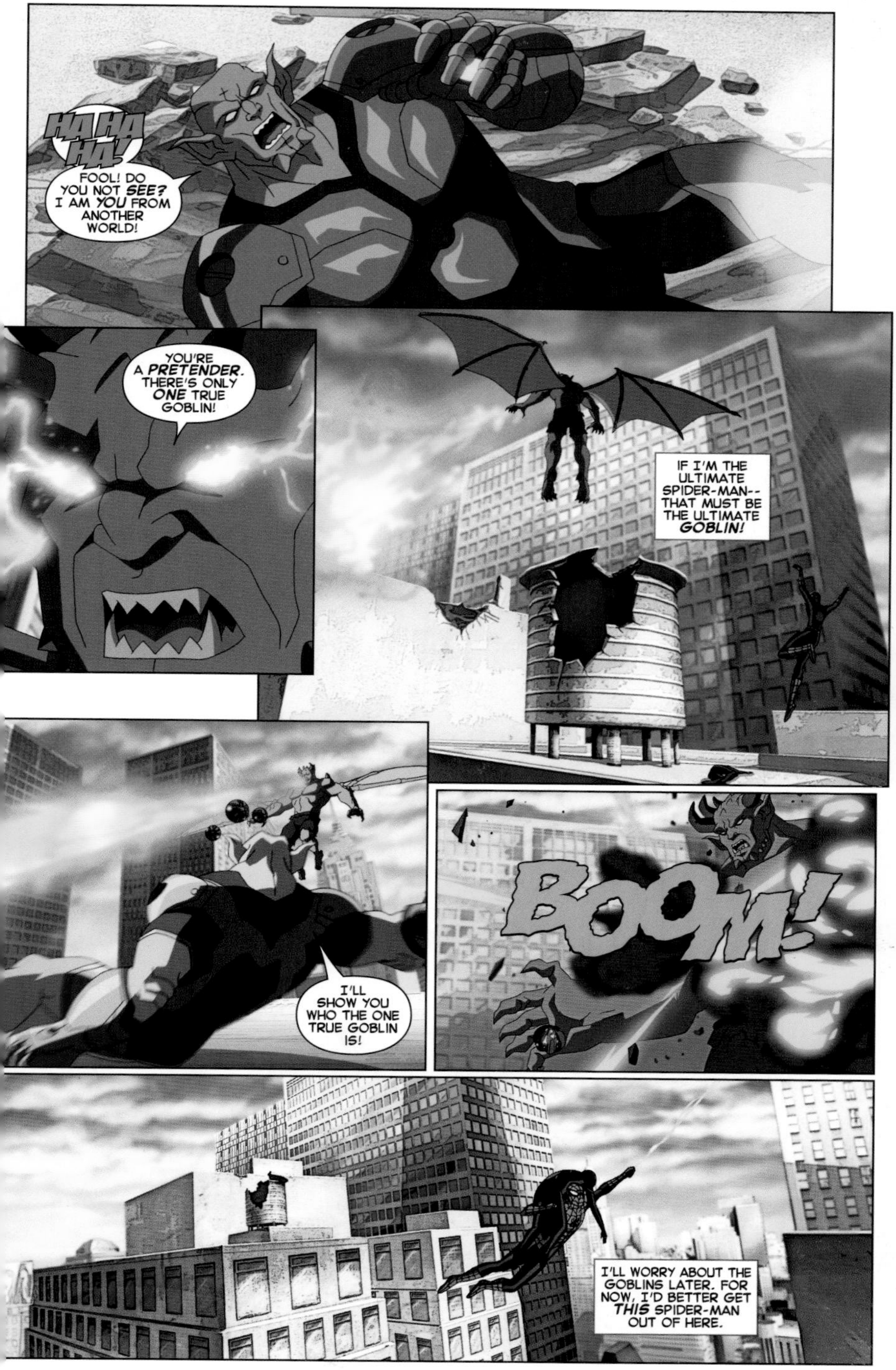
HA HA HA!
FOOL! DO YOU NOT SEE? I AM YOU FROM ANOTHER WORLD!
YOU'RE A PRETENDER. THERE'S ONLY ONE TRUE GOBLIN!
IF I'M THE ULTIMATE SPIDER-MAN-- THAT MUST BE THE ULTIMATE GOBLIN!
I'LL SHOW YOU WHO THE ONE TRUE GOBLIN IS!
BOOM!
I'LL WORRY ABOUT THE GOBLINS LATER. FOR NOW, I'D BETTER GET THIS SPIDER-MAN OUT OF HERE.

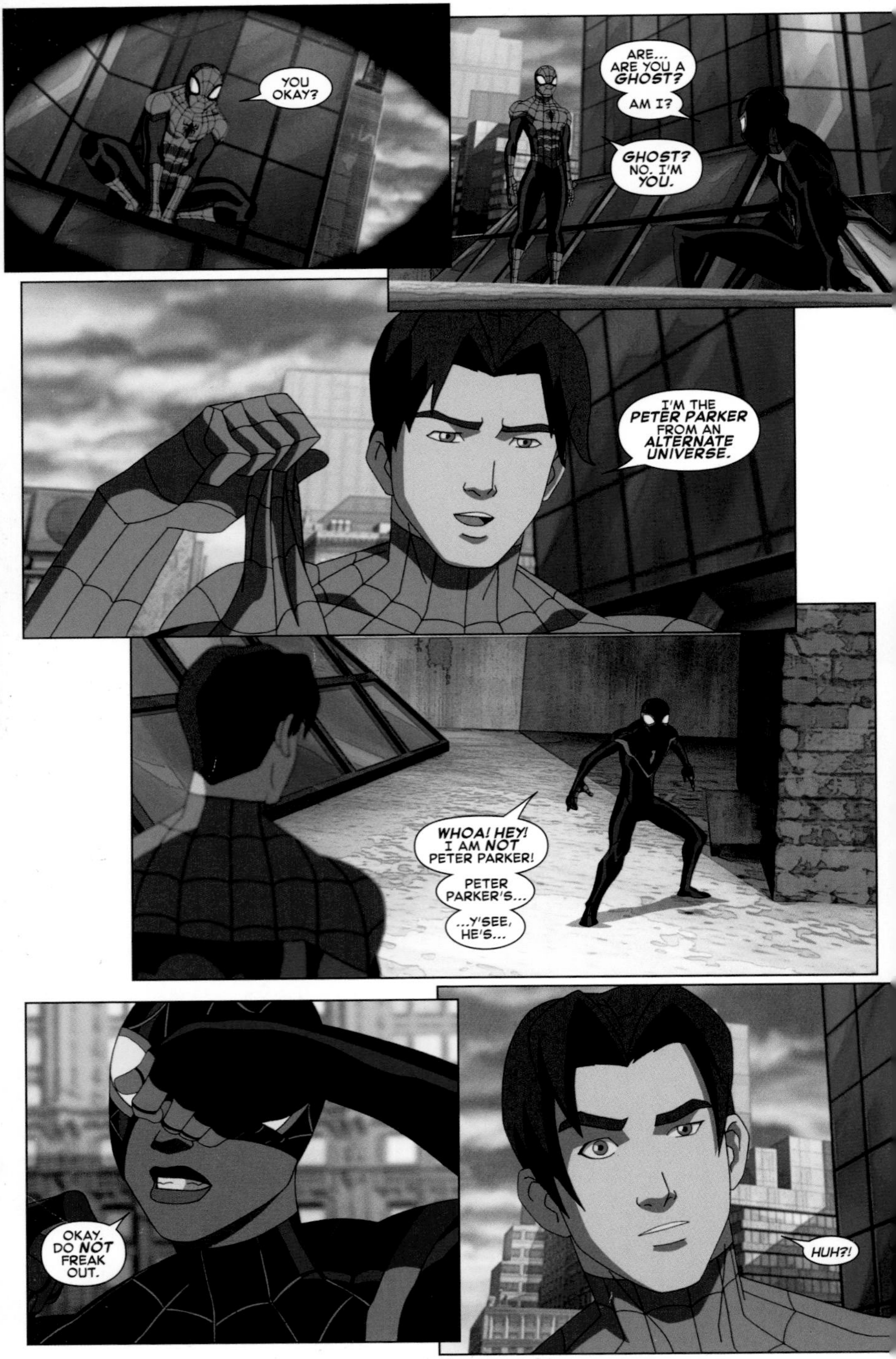
YOU OKAY?
ARE... ARE YOU A GHOST?
AM I?
GHOST? NO. I'M YOU.
I'M THE PETER PARKER FROM AN ALTERNATE UNIVERSE.
WHOA! HEY! I AM NOT PETER PARKER!
PETER PARKER'S...
...Y'SEE, HE'S...
OKAY. DO NOT FREAK OUT.
HUH?!

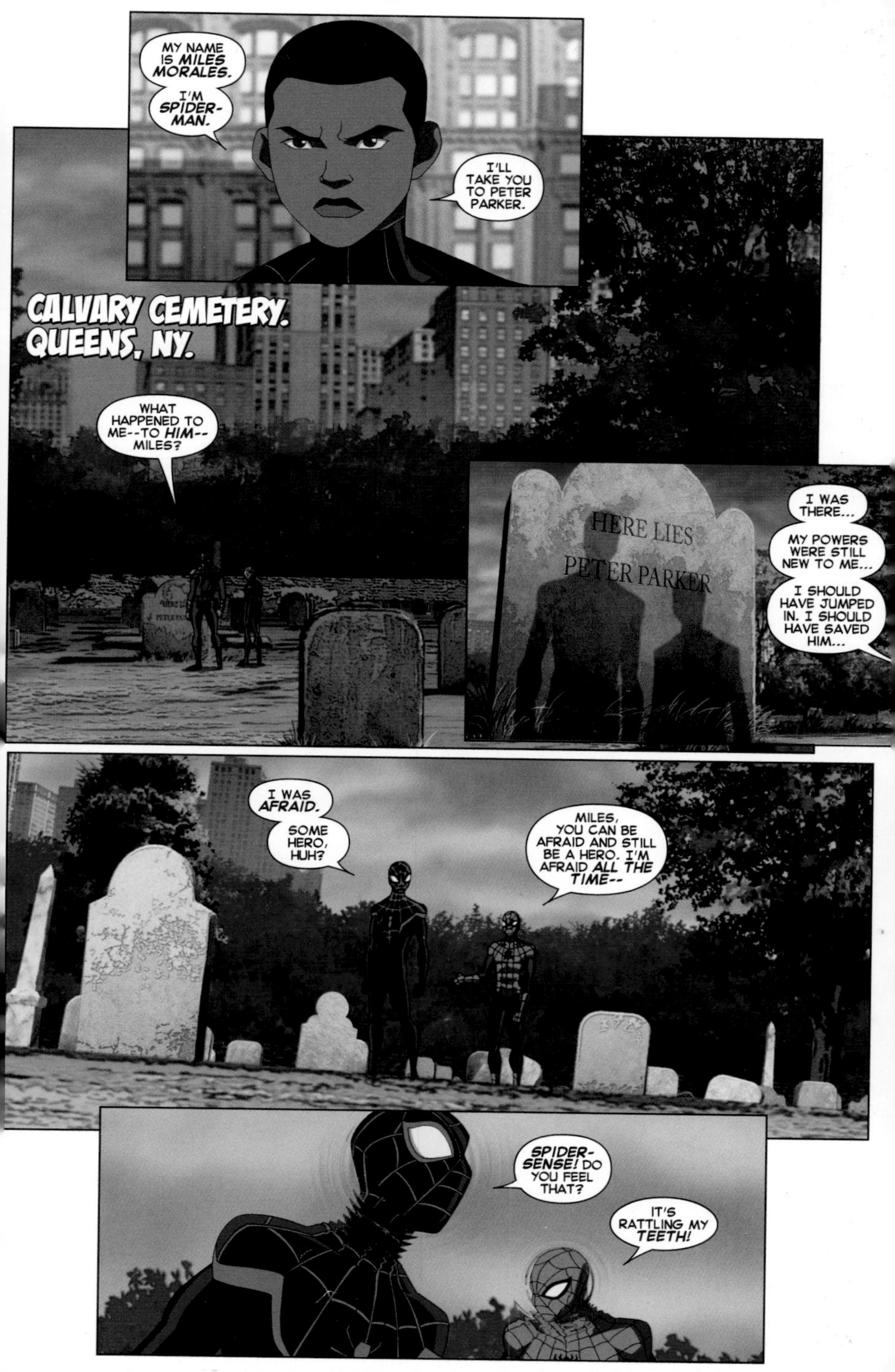
MY NAME IS MILES MORALES.
I'M SPIDER-MAN.
I'LL TAKE YOU TO PETER PARKER.
CALVARY CEMETERY. QUEENS, NY.
WHAT HAPPENED TO ME--TO HIM-- MILES?
HERE LIES PETER PARKER
I WAS THERE...
MY POWERS WERE STILL NEW TO ME...
I SHOULD HAVE JUMPED IN. I SHOULD HAVE SAVED HIM...
I WAS AFRAID.
SOME HERO, HUH?
MILES, YOU CAN BE AFRAID AND STILL BE A HERO. I'M AFRAID ALL THE TIME--
SPIDER-SENSE! DO YOU FEEL THAT?
IT'S RATTLING MY TEETH!

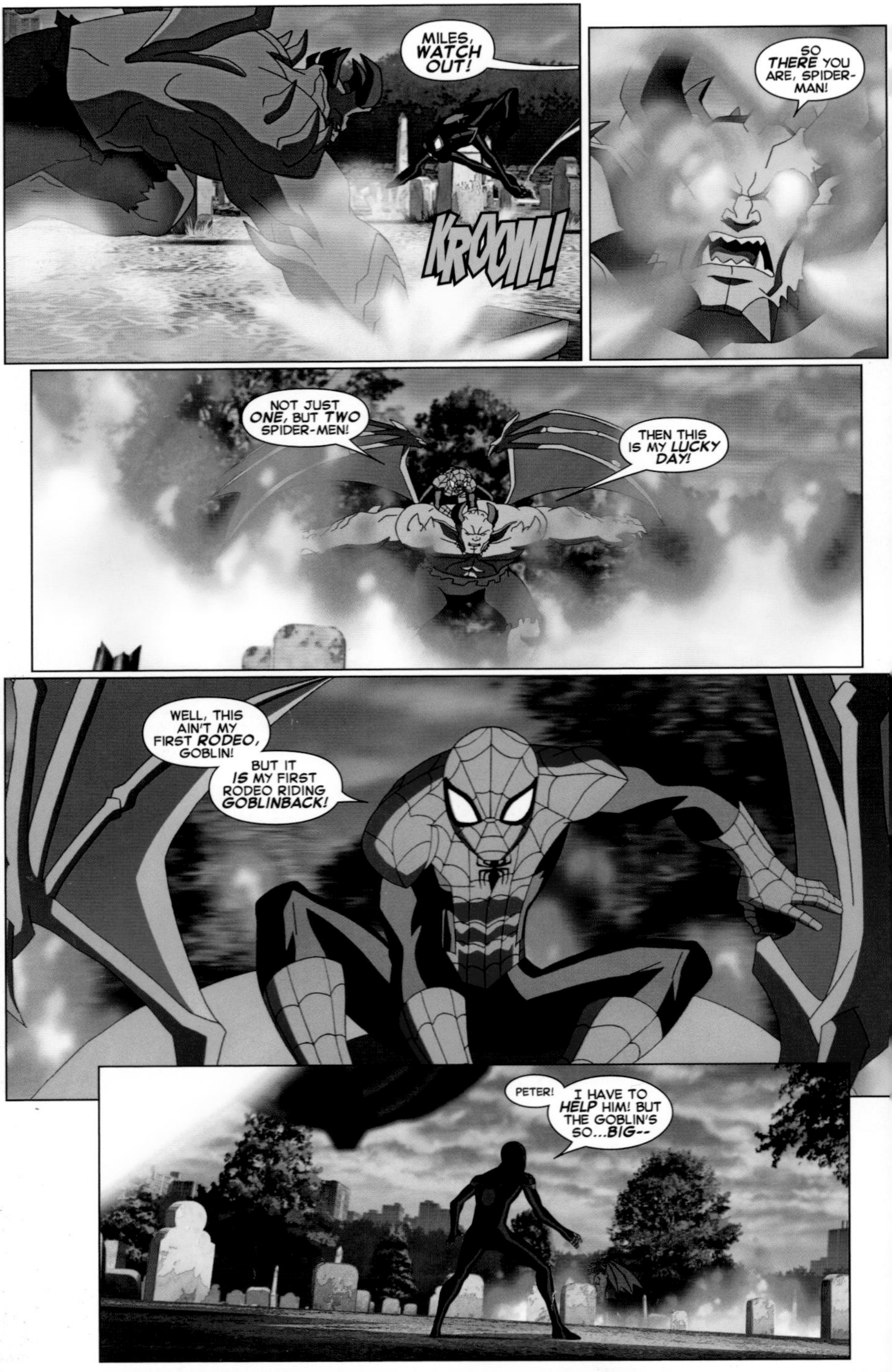
MILES, WATCH OUT!
KROOOM!
SO THERE YOU ARE, SPIDER-MAN!
NOT JUST ONE, BUT TWO SPIDER-MEN!
THEN THIS IS MY LUCKY DAY!
WELL, THIS AIN'T MY FIRST RODEO, GOBLIN!
BUT IT IS MY FIRST RODEO RIDING GOBLINBACK!
PETER!
I HAVE TO HELP HIM! BUT THE GOBLIN'S SO...BIG--

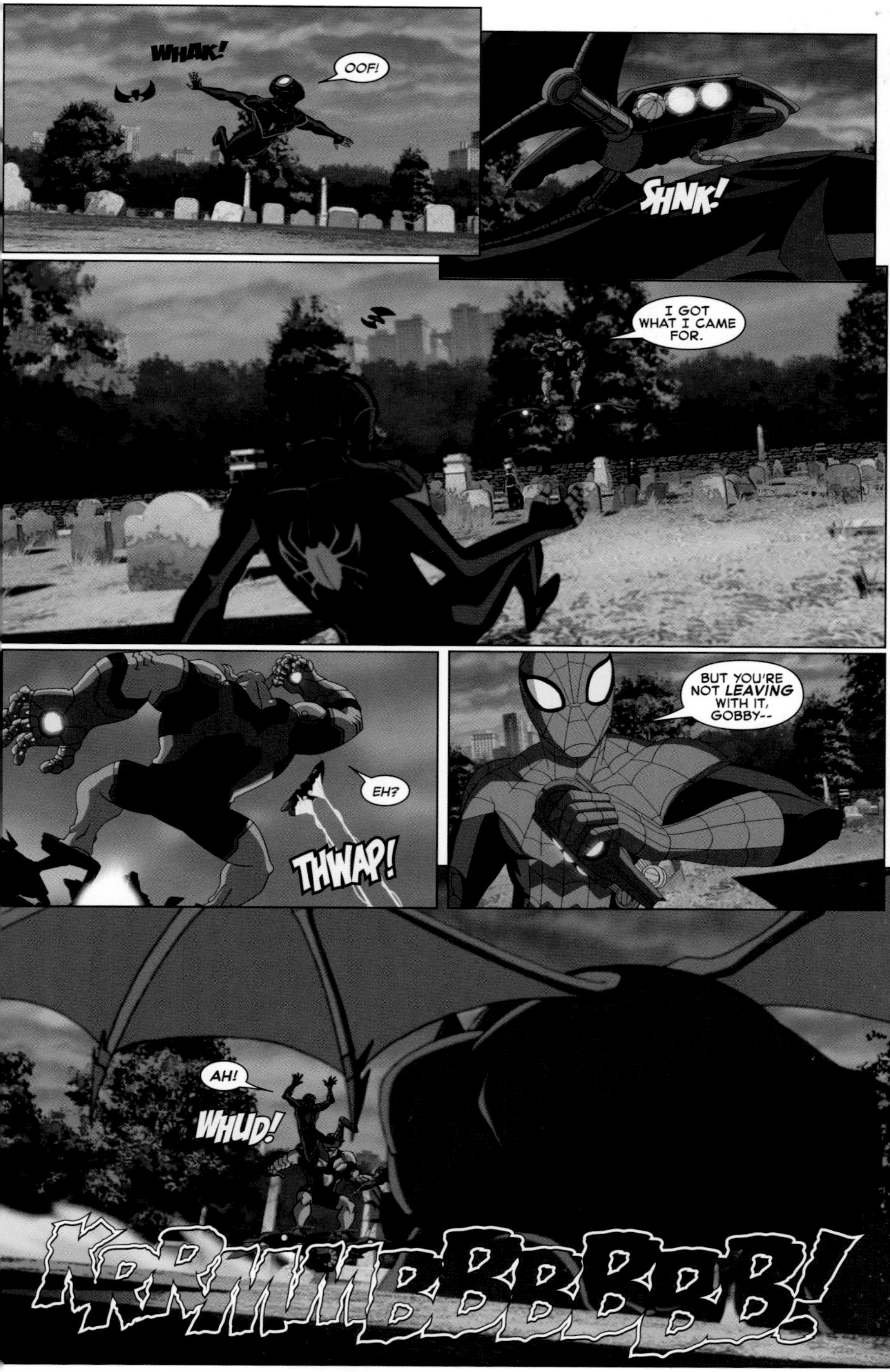

WHAK!
OOF!
SHNK!
I GOT WHAT I CAME FOR.
EH?
THWAP!
BUT YOU'RE NOT *LEAVING* WITH IT, GOBBY--
AH!
WHUD!
KRRMMMBBBBBB!

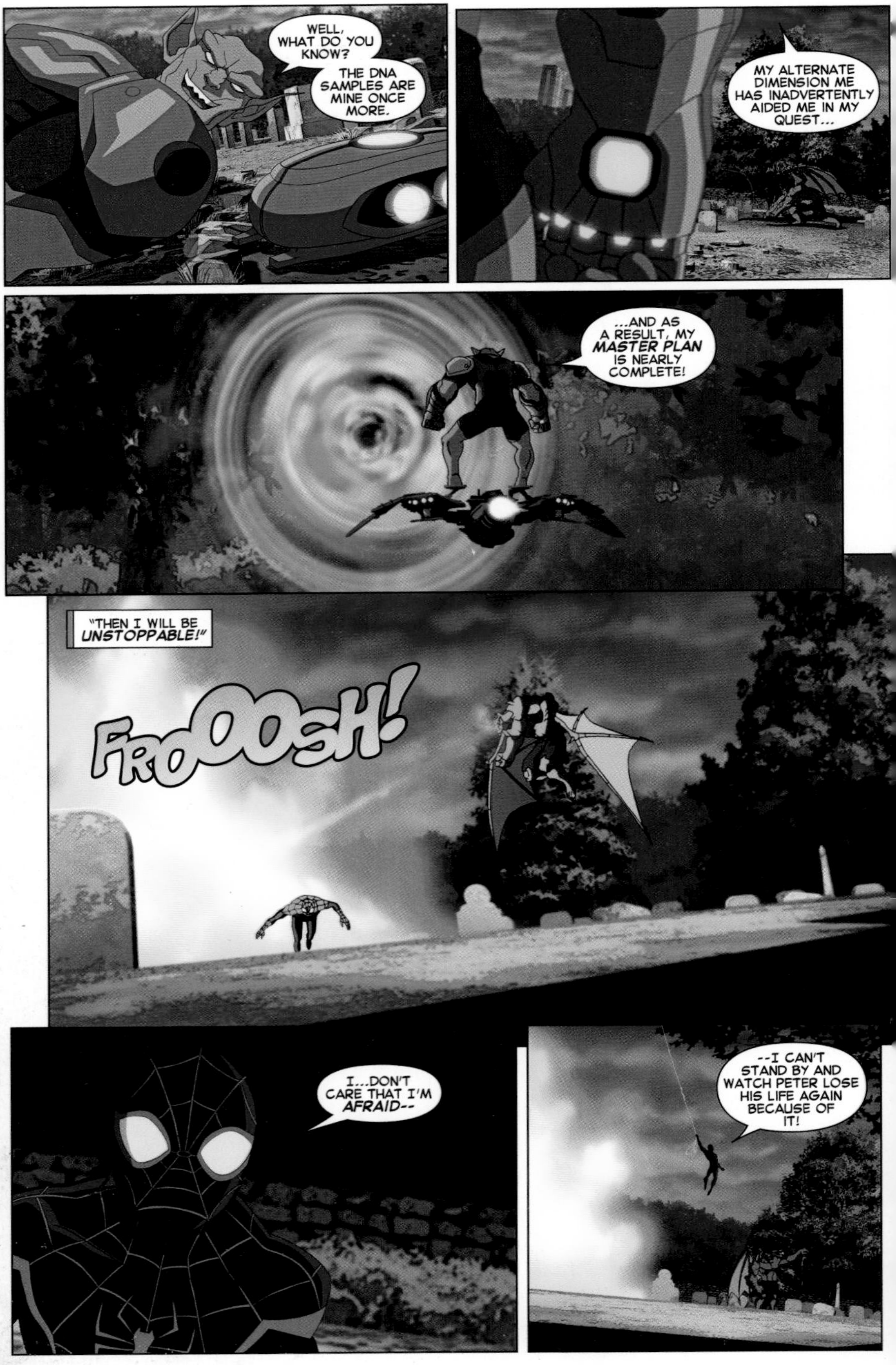
WELL, WHAT DO YOU KNOW?
THE DNA SAMPLES ARE MINE ONCE MORE.
MY ALTERNATE DIMENSION ME HAS INADVERTENTLY AIDED ME IN MY QUEST...
...AND AS A RESULT, MY MASTER PLAN IS NEARLY COMPLETE!
"THEN I WILL BE UNSTOPPABLE!"
FROOOOSH!
I...DON'T CARE THAT I'M AFRAID--
--I CAN'T STAND BY AND WATCH PETER LOSE HIS LIFE AGAIN BECAUSE OF IT!

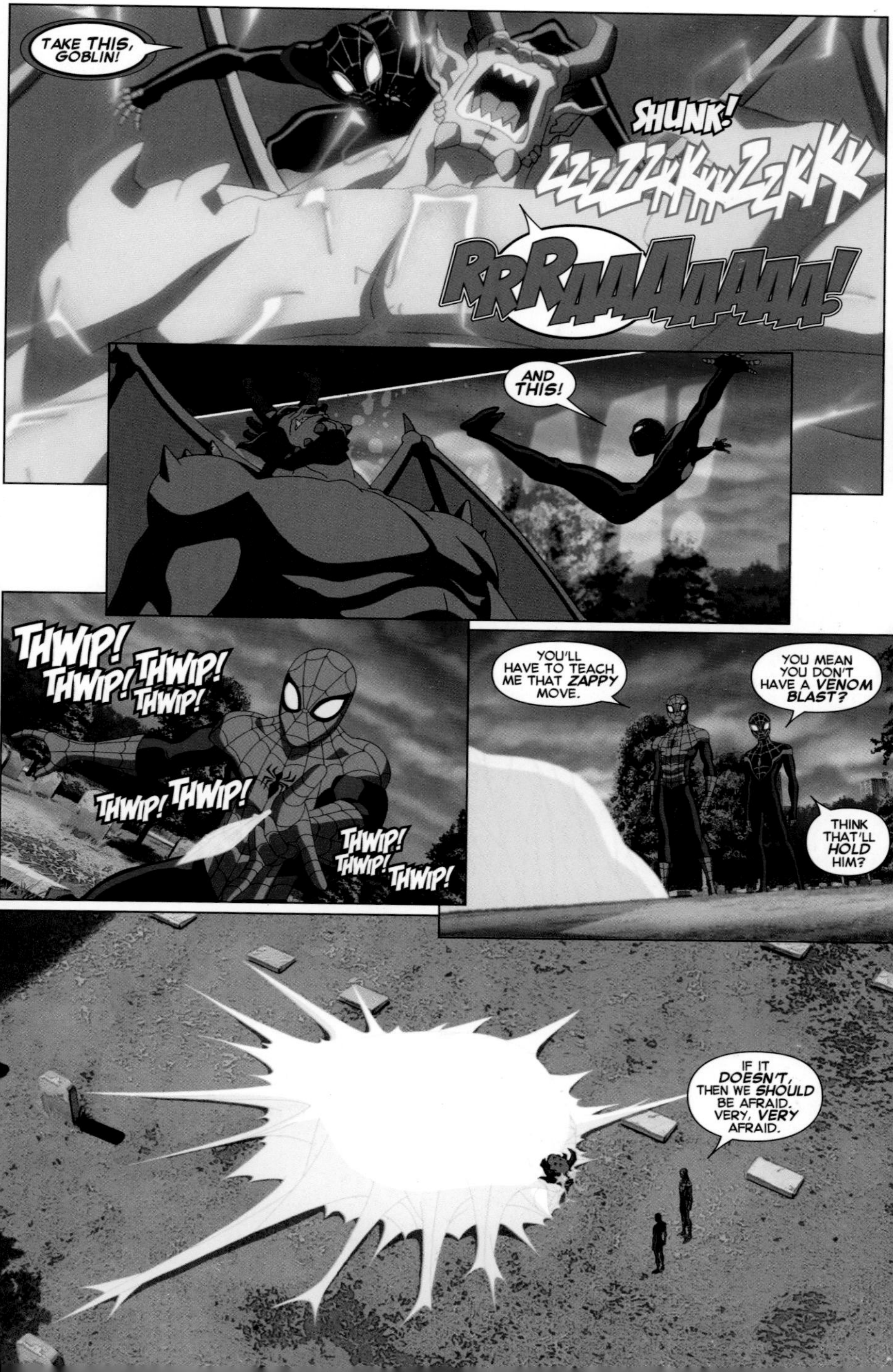
TAKE THIS, GOBLIN!
SHUNK!
ZZZZZKKKZZKKK
RRRAAAAAAA!
AND THIS!
THWIP! THWIP! THWIP! THWIP!
THWIP! THWIP!
THWIP! THWIP! THWIP!
YOU'LL HAVE TO TEACH ME THAT ZAPPY MOVE.
YOU MEAN YOU DON'T HAVE A VENOM BLAST?
THINK THAT'LL HOLD HIM?
IF IT DOESN'T, THEN WE SHOULD BE AFRAID. VERY, VERY AFRAID.

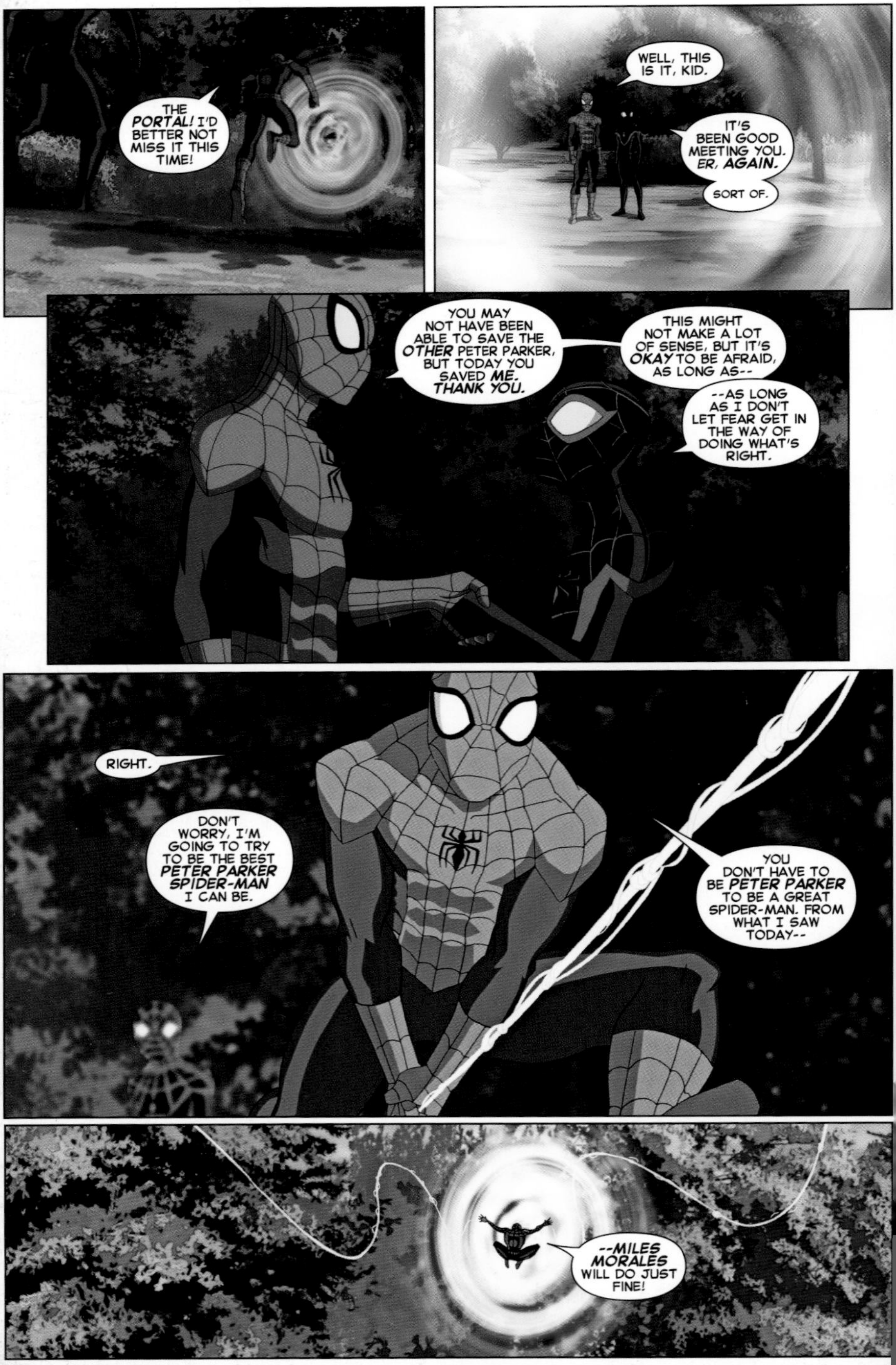
THE PORTAL! I'D BETTER NOT MISS IT THIS TIME!
WELL, THIS IS IT, KID.
IT'S BEEN GOOD MEETING YOU. ER, AGAIN.
SORT OF.
YOU MAY NOT HAVE BEEN ABLE TO SAVE THE OTHER PETER PARKER, BUT TODAY YOU SAVED ME. THANK YOU.
THIS MIGHT NOT MAKE A LOT OF SENSE, BUT IT'S OKAY TO BE AFRAID, AS LONG AS--
--AS LONG AS I DON'T LET FEAR GET IN THE WAY OF DOING WHAT'S RIGHT.
RIGHT.
DON'T WORRY, I'M GOING TO TRY TO BE THE BEST PETER PARKER SPIDER-MAN I CAN BE.
YOU DON'T HAVE TO BE PETER PARKER TO BE A GREAT SPIDER-MAN. FROM WHAT I SAW TODAY--
--MILES MORALES WILL DO JUST FINE!

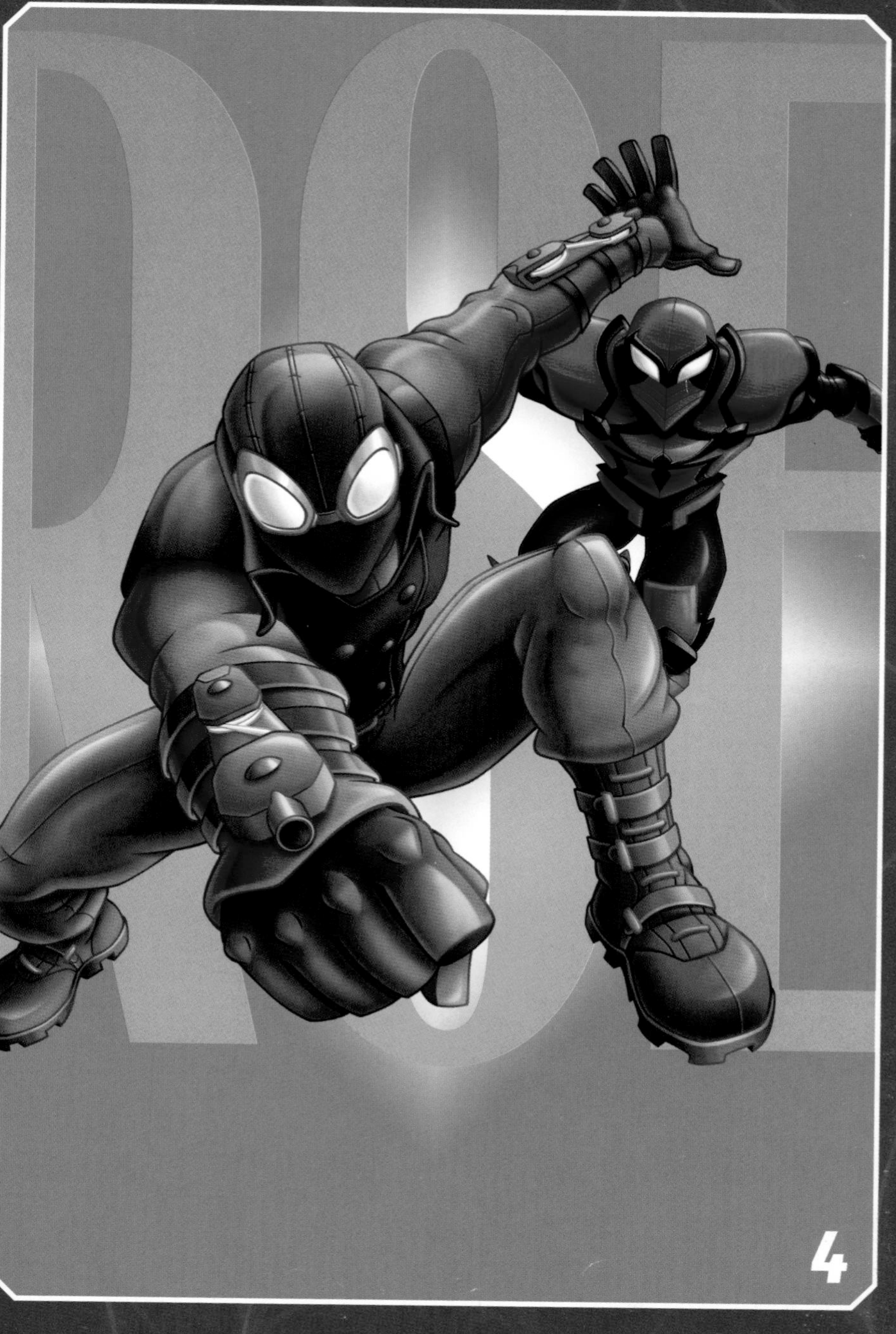
4

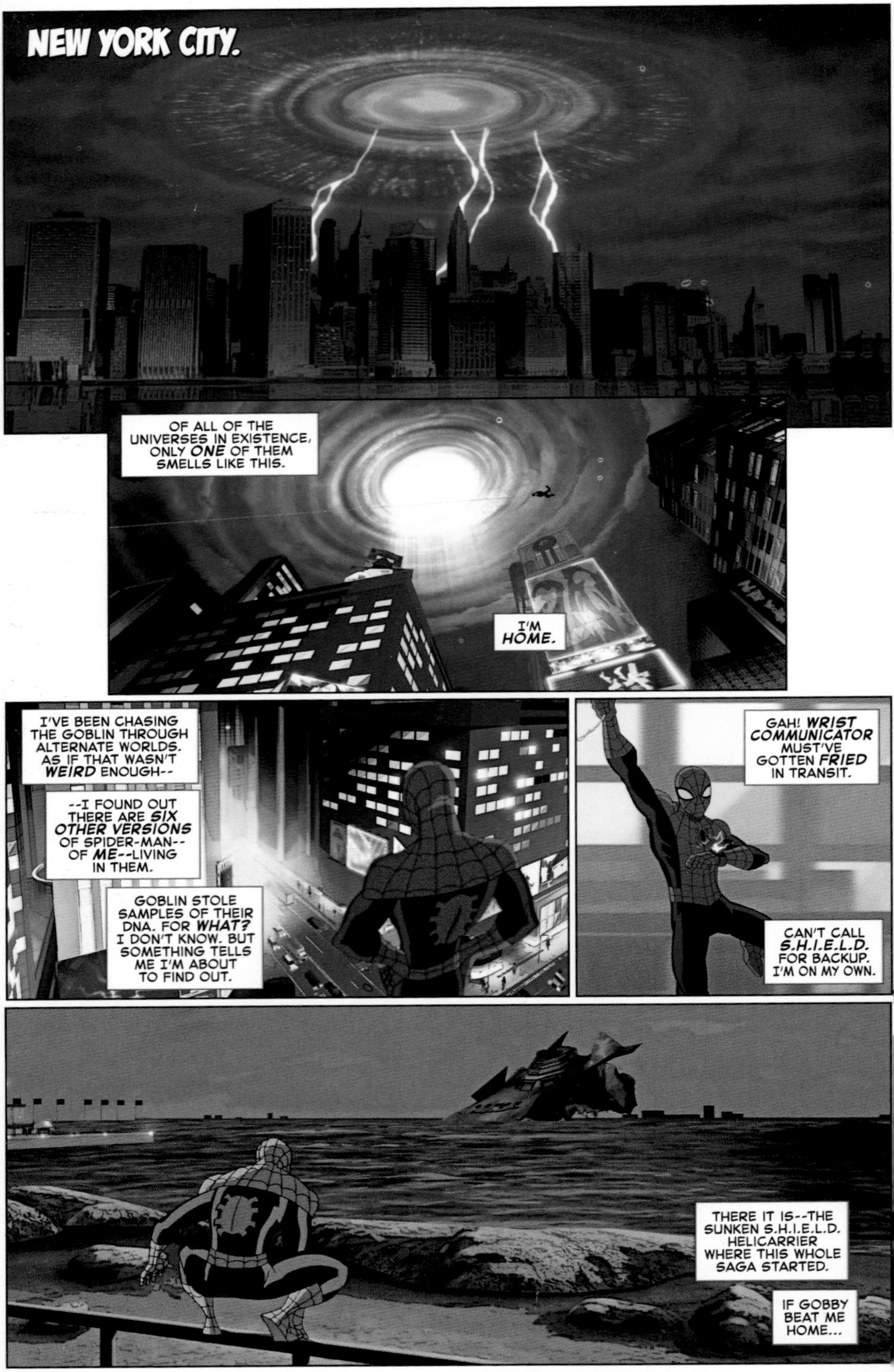
NEW YORK CITY.
OF ALL OF THE UNIVERSES IN EXISTENCE, ONLY ONE OF THEM SMELLS LIKE THIS.
I'M HOME.
I'VE BEEN CHASING THE GOBLIN THROUGH ALTERNATE WORLDS. AS IF THAT WASN'T WEIRD ENOUGH--
--I FOUND OUT THERE ARE SIX OTHER VERSIONS OF SPIDER-MAN--OF ME--LIVING IN THEM.
GOBLIN STOLE SAMPLES OF THEIR DNA. FOR WHAT? I DON'T KNOW. BUT SOMETHING TELLS ME I'M ABOUT TO FIND OUT.
GAH! WRIST COMMUNICATOR MUST'VE GOTTEN FRIED IN TRANSIT.
CAN'T CALL S.H.I.E.L.D. FOR BACKUP. I'M ON MY OWN.
THERE IT IS--THE SUNKEN S.H.I.E.L.D. HELICARRIER WHERE THIS WHOLE SAGA STARTED.
IF GOBBY BEAT ME HOME...

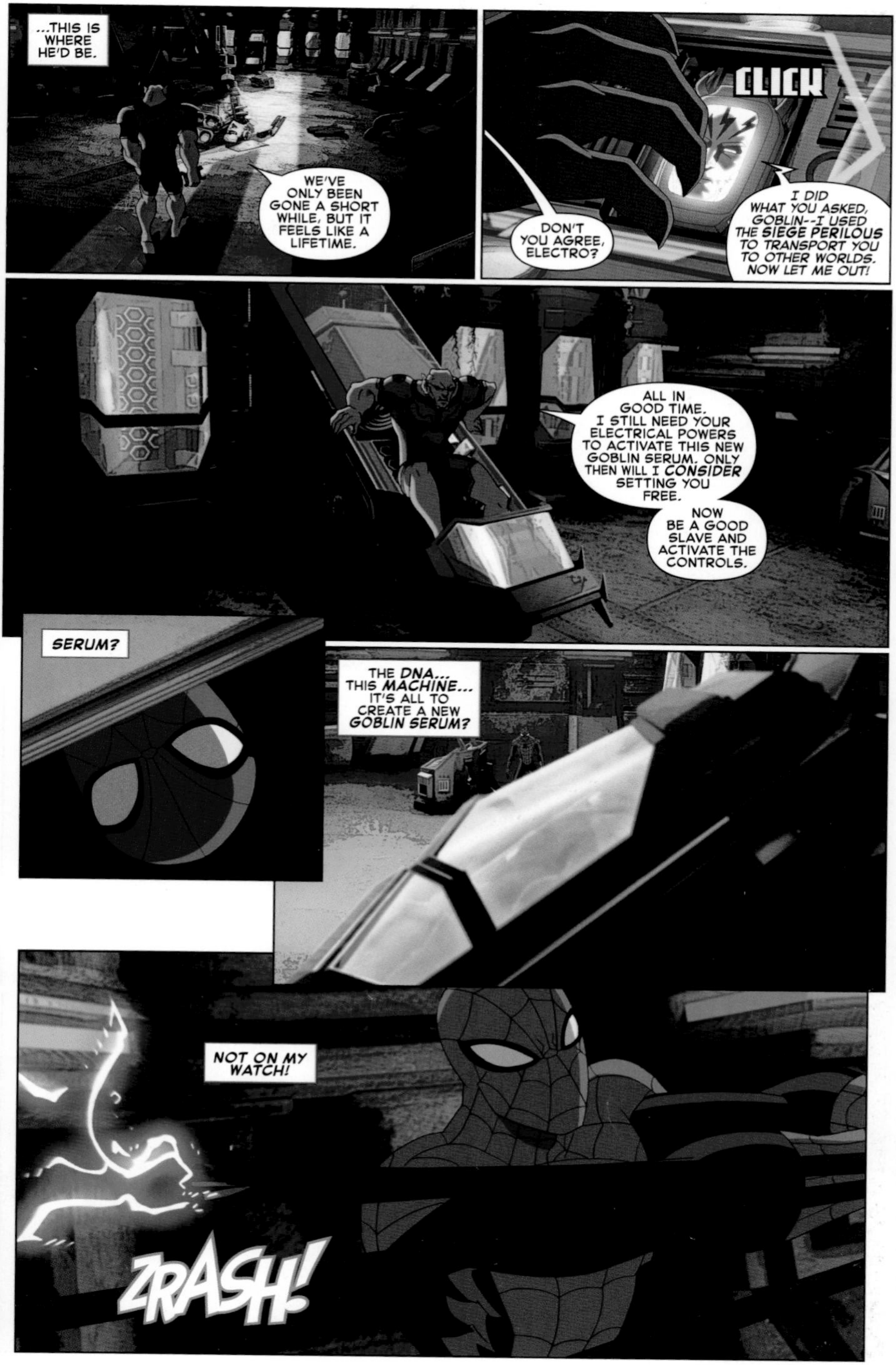
...THIS IS WHERE HE'D BE.
WE'VE ONLY BEEN GONE A SHORT WHILE, BUT IT FEELS LIKE A LIFETIME.
CLICK
DON'T YOU AGREE, ELECTRO?
I DID WHAT YOU ASKED, GOBLIN--I USED THE SIEGE PERILOUS TO TRANSPORT YOU TO OTHER WORLDS. NOW LET ME OUT!
ALL IN GOOD TIME. I STILL NEED YOUR ELECTRICAL POWERS TO ACTIVATE THIS NEW GOBLIN SERUM. ONLY THEN WILL I CONSIDER SETTING YOU FREE.
NOW BE A GOOD SLAVE AND ACTIVATE THE CONTROLS.
SERUM?
THE DNA... THIS MACHINE... IT'S ALL TO CREATE A NEW GOBLIN SERUM?
NOT ON MY WATCH!
ZRASH!

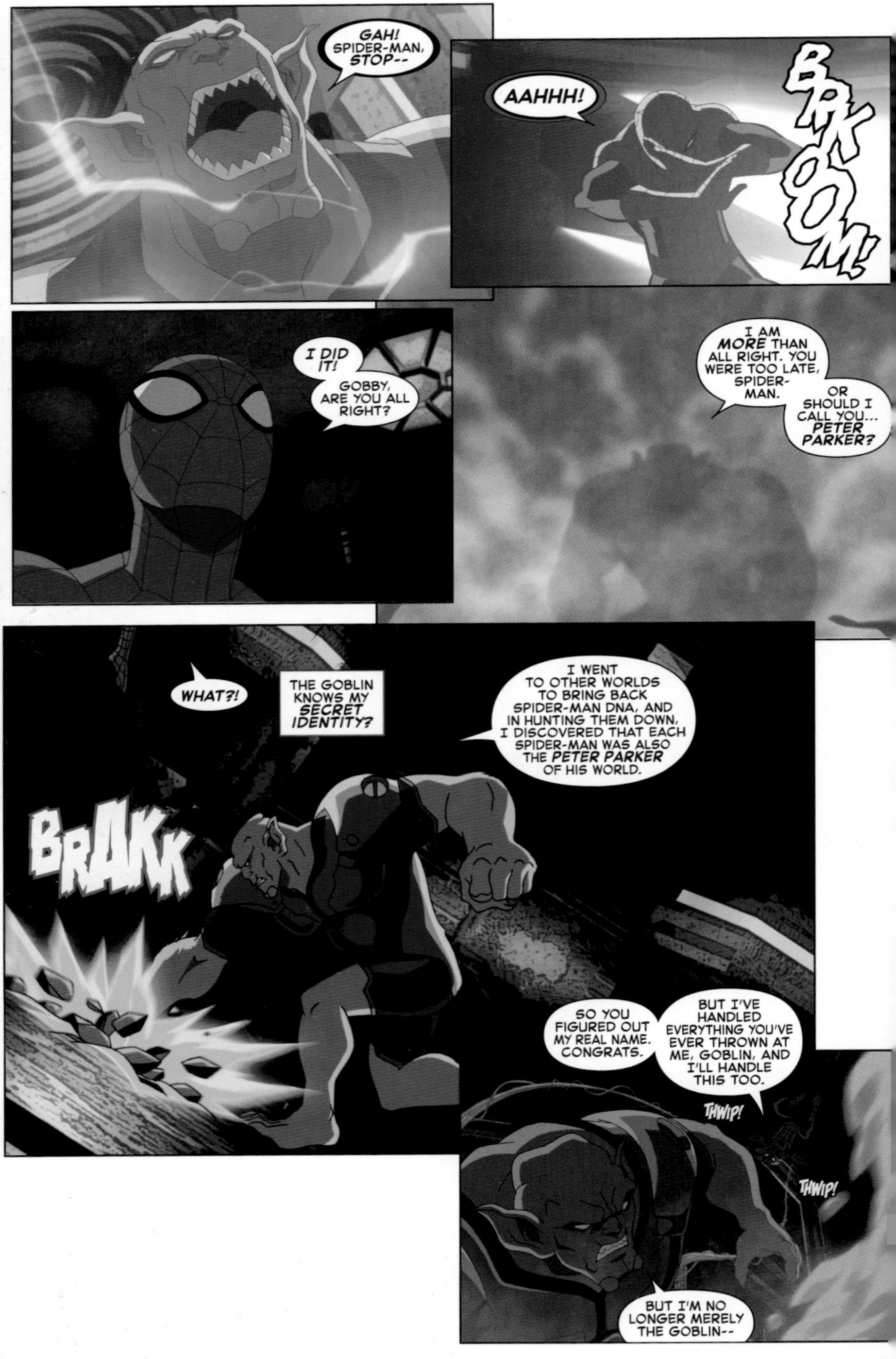
GAH! SPIDER-MAN, STOP--
AAHHH!
BRKOOM!
I DID IT!
GOBBY, ARE YOU ALL RIGHT?
I AM MORE THAN ALL RIGHT. YOU WERE TOO LATE, SPIDER-MAN.
OR SHOULD I CALL YOU... PETER PARKER?
WHAT?!
THE GOBLIN KNOWS MY SECRET IDENTITY?
I WENT TO OTHER WORLDS TO BRING BACK SPIDER-MAN DNA, AND IN HUNTING THEM DOWN, I DISCOVERED THAT EACH SPIDER-MAN WAS ALSO THE PETER PARKER OF HIS WORLD.
BRAKK
SO YOU FIGURED OUT MY REAL NAME. CONGRATS.
BUT I'VE HANDLED EVERYTHING YOU'VE EVER THROWN AT ME, GOBLIN, AND I'LL HANDLE THIS TOO.
THWIP!
THWIP!
BUT I'M NO LONGER MERELY THE GOBLIN--

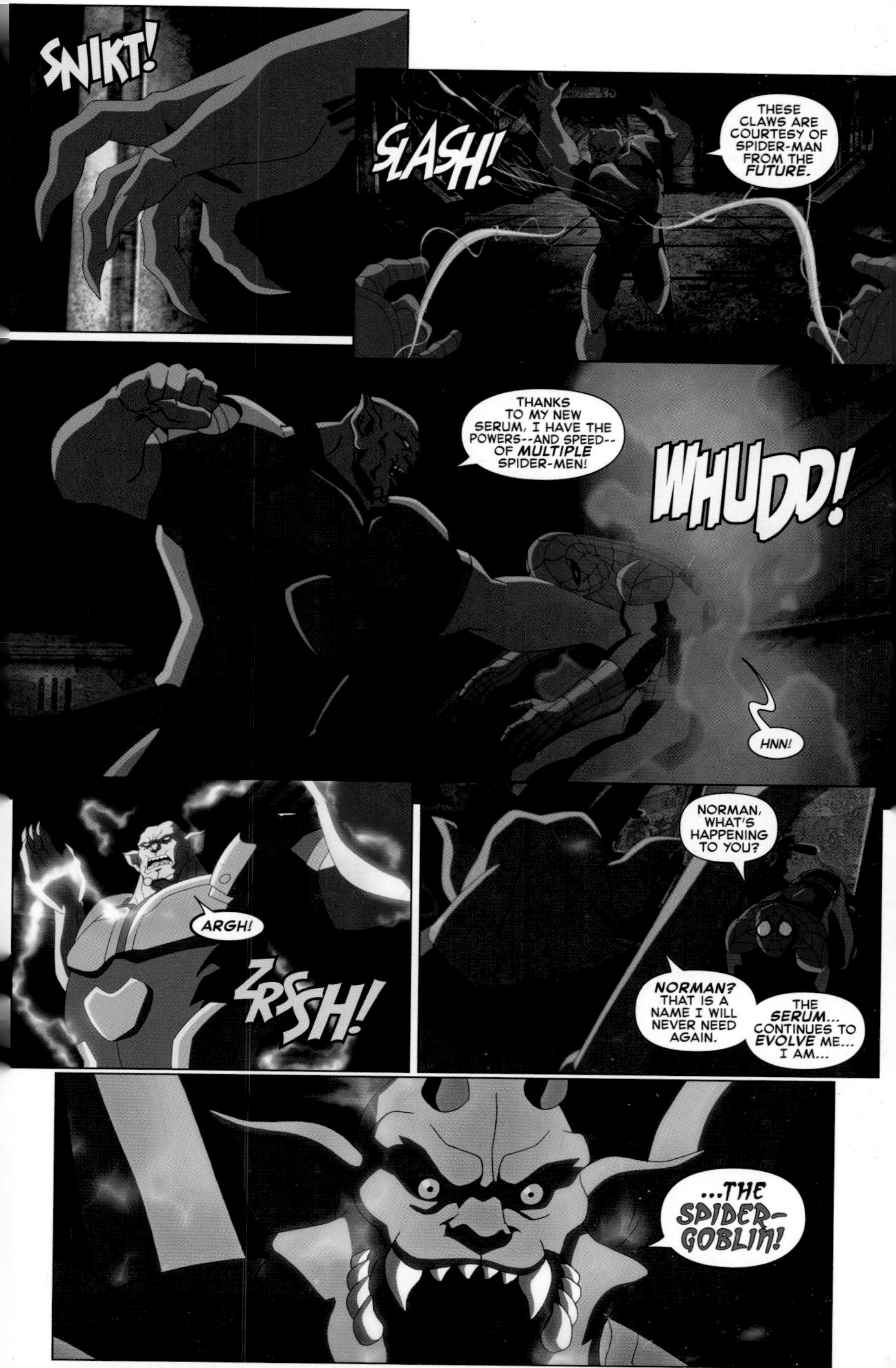

SNIKT!
SLASH!
THESE CLAWS ARE COURTESY OF SPIDER-MAN FROM THE FUTURE.
THANKS TO MY NEW SERUM, I HAVE THE POWERS--AND SPEED--OF MULTIPLE SPIDER-MEN!
WHUDD!
HNN!
ARGH!
ZRSSH!
NORMAN, WHAT'S HAPPENING TO YOU?
NORMAN? THAT IS A NAME I WILL NEVER NEED AGAIN.
THE SERUM... CONTINUES TO EVOLVE ME... I AM...
...THE SPIDER-GOBLIN!

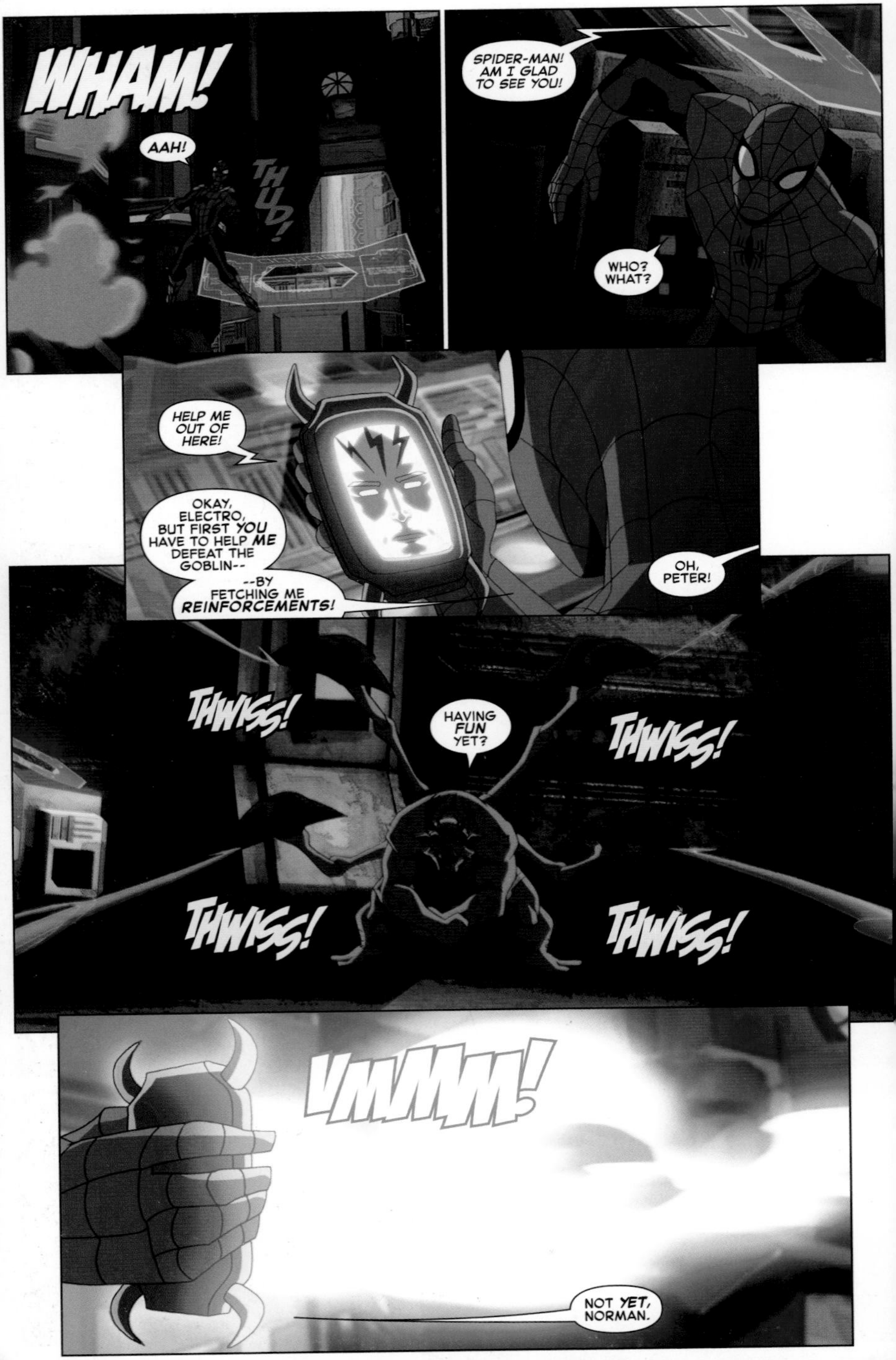
WHAM!
AAH!
THUD!
SPIDER-MAN! AM I GLAD TO SEE YOU!
WHO? WHAT?
HELP ME OUT OF HERE!
OKAY, ELECTRO, BUT FIRST YOU HAVE TO HELP ME DEFEAT THE GOBLIN--
--BY FETCHING ME REINFORCEMENTS!
OH, PETER!
THWISS!
HAVING FUN YET?
THWISS!
THWISS!
THWISS!
VMMMM!
NOT YET, NORMAN.

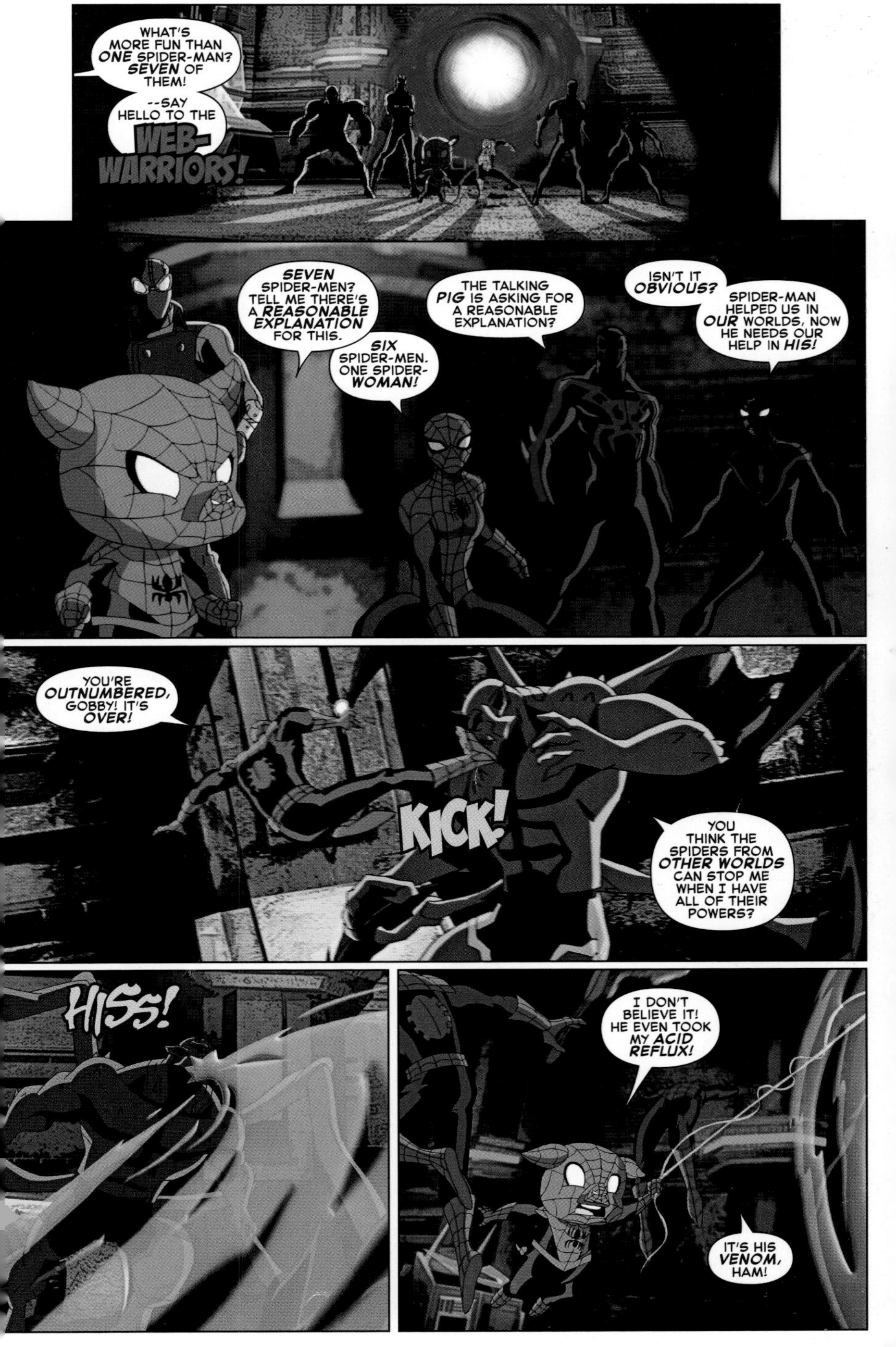
WHAT'S MORE FUN THAN ONE SPIDER-MAN? SEVEN OF THEM!
--SAY HELLO TO THE
WEB-WARRIORS!
SEVEN SPIDER-MEN? TELL ME THERE'S A REASONABLE EXPLANATION FOR THIS.
SIX SPIDER-MEN. ONE SPIDER-WOMAN!
THE TALKING PIG IS ASKING FOR A REASONABLE EXPLANATION?
ISN'T IT OBVIOUS?
SPIDER-MAN HELPED US IN OUR WORLDS, NOW HE NEEDS OUR HELP IN HIS!
YOU'RE OUTNUMBERED, GOBBY! IT'S OVER!
KICK!
YOU THINK THE SPIDERS FROM OTHER WORLDS CAN STOP ME WHEN I HAVE ALL OF THEIR POWERS?
HISS!
I DON'T BELIEVE IT! HE EVEN TOOK MY ACID REFLUX!
IT'S HIS VENOM, HAM!

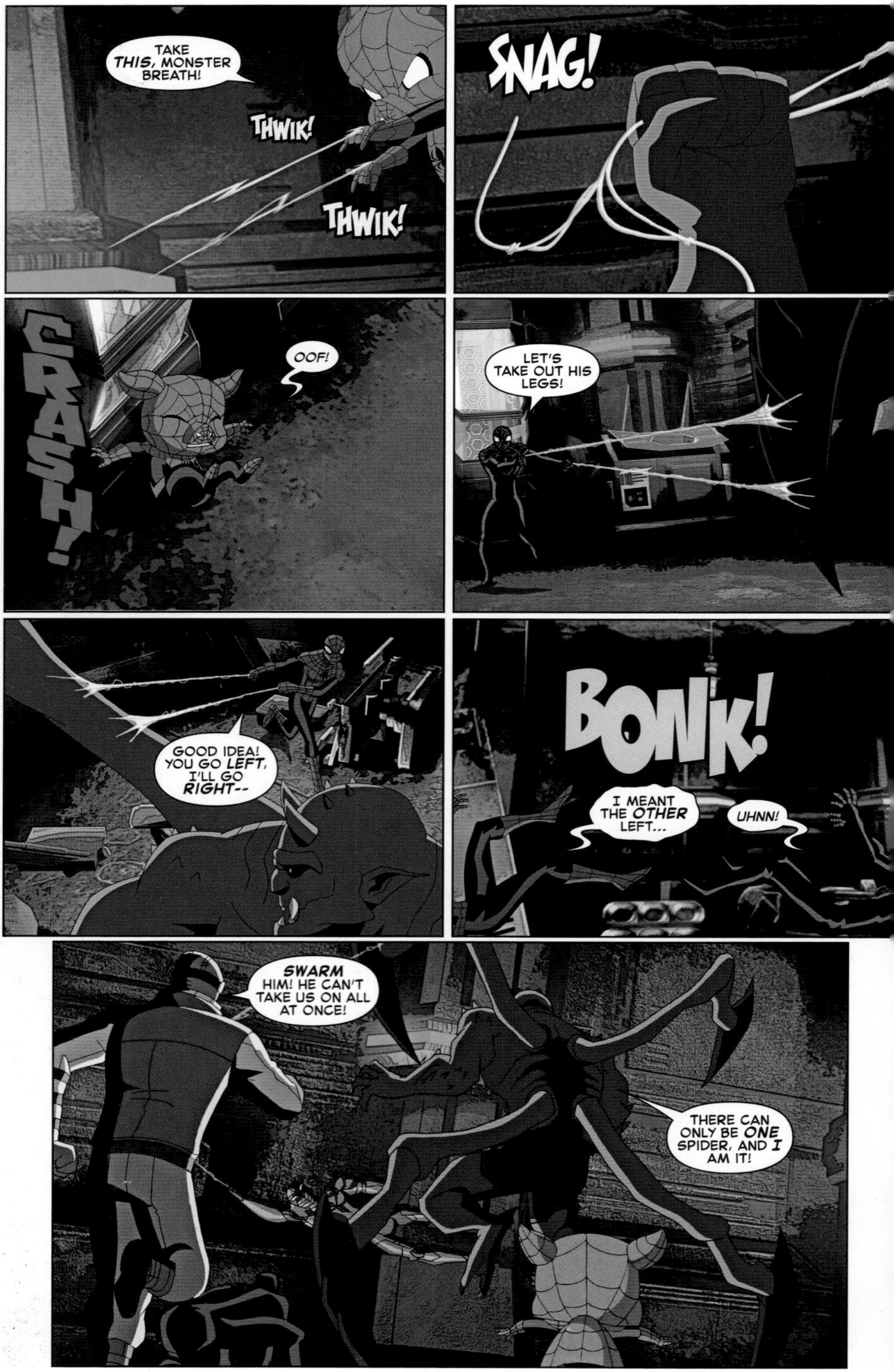
TAKE THIS, MONSTER BREATH!
THWIK!
THWIK!
SNAG!
CRASH!
OOF!
LET'S TAKE OUT HIS LEGS!
GOOD IDEA! YOU GO LEFT, I'LL GO RIGHT--
BONK!
I MEANT THE OTHER LEFT...
UHNN!
SWARM HIM! HE CAN'T TAKE US ON ALL AT ONCE!
THERE CAN ONLY BE ONE SPIDER, AND I AM IT!

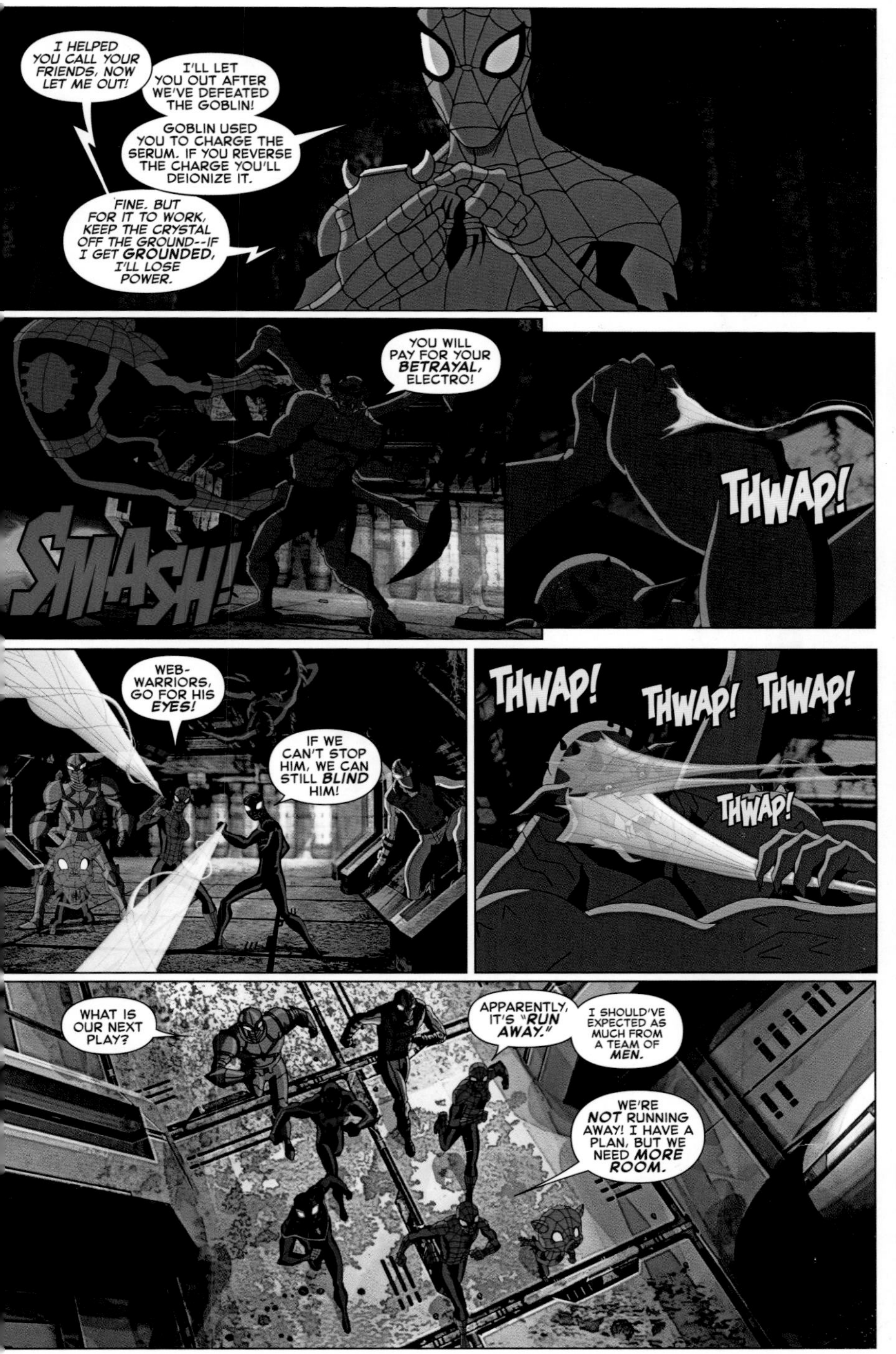
I HELPED YOU CALL YOUR FRIENDS, NOW LET ME OUT!
I'LL LET YOU OUT AFTER WE'VE DEFEATED THE GOBLIN!
GOBLIN USED YOU TO CHARGE THE SERUM. IF YOU REVERSE THE CHARGE YOU'LL DEIONIZE IT.
FINE. BUT FOR IT TO WORK, KEEP THE CRYSTAL OFF THE GROUND--IF I GET GROUNDED, I'LL LOSE POWER.
YOU WILL PAY FOR YOUR BETRAYAL, ELECTRO!
SMASH!
THWAP!
WEB-WARRIORS, GO FOR HIS EYES!
IF WE CAN'T STOP HIM, WE CAN STILL BLIND HIM!
THWAP! THWAP! THWAP!
THWAP!
WHAT IS OUR NEXT PLAY?
APPARENTLY, IT'S "RUN AWAY."
I SHOULD'VE EXPECTED AS MUCH FROM A TEAM OF MEN.
WE'RE NOT RUNNING AWAY! I HAVE A PLAN, BUT WE NEED MORE ROOM.

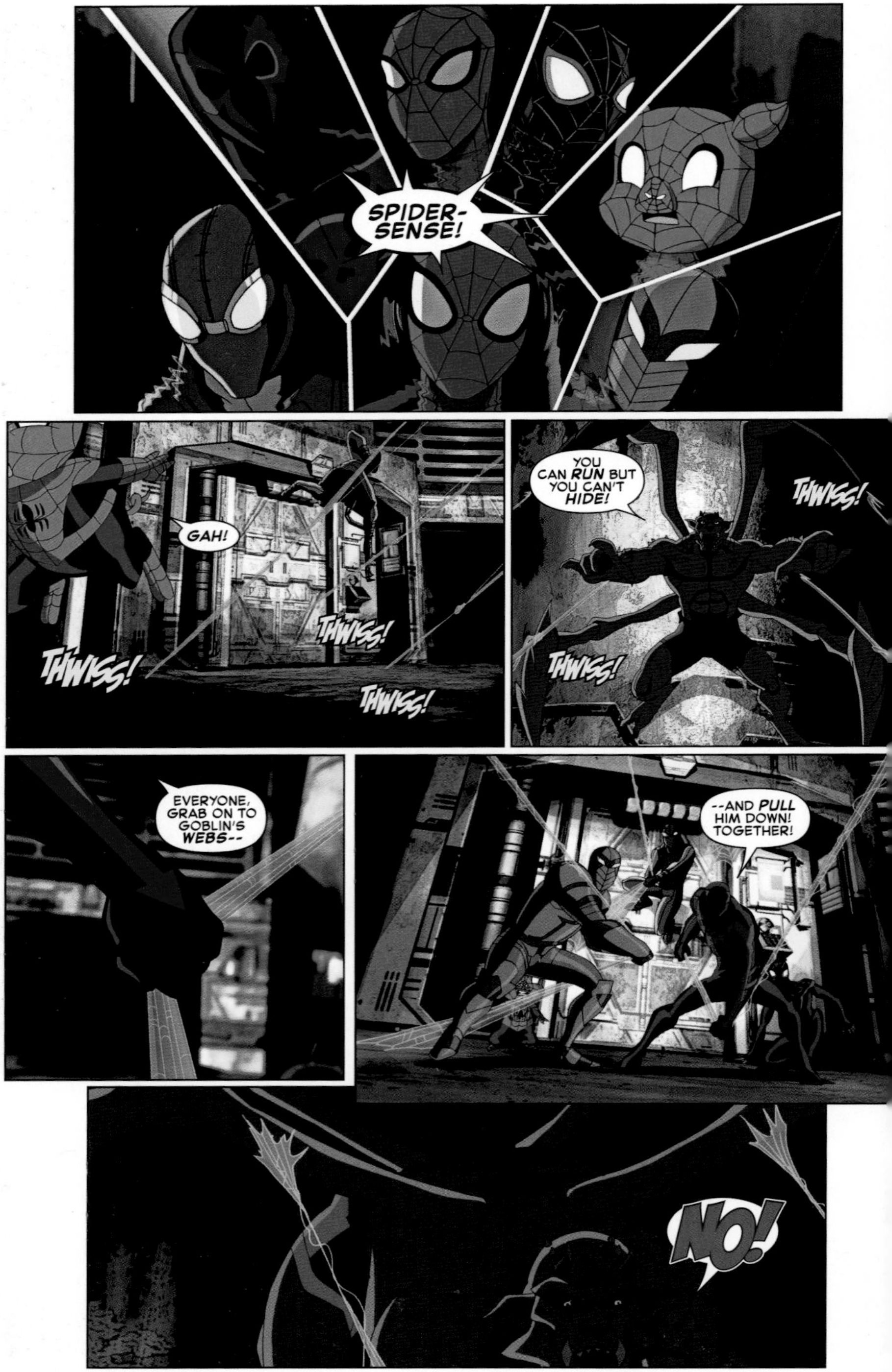
SPIDER-SENSE!
GAH!
THWISS!
THWISS!
THWISS!
YOU CAN RUN BUT YOU CAN'T HIDE!
THWISS!
THWISS!
EVERYONE, GRAB ON TO GOBLIN'S WEBS--
--AND PULL HIM DOWN! TOGETHER!
NO!

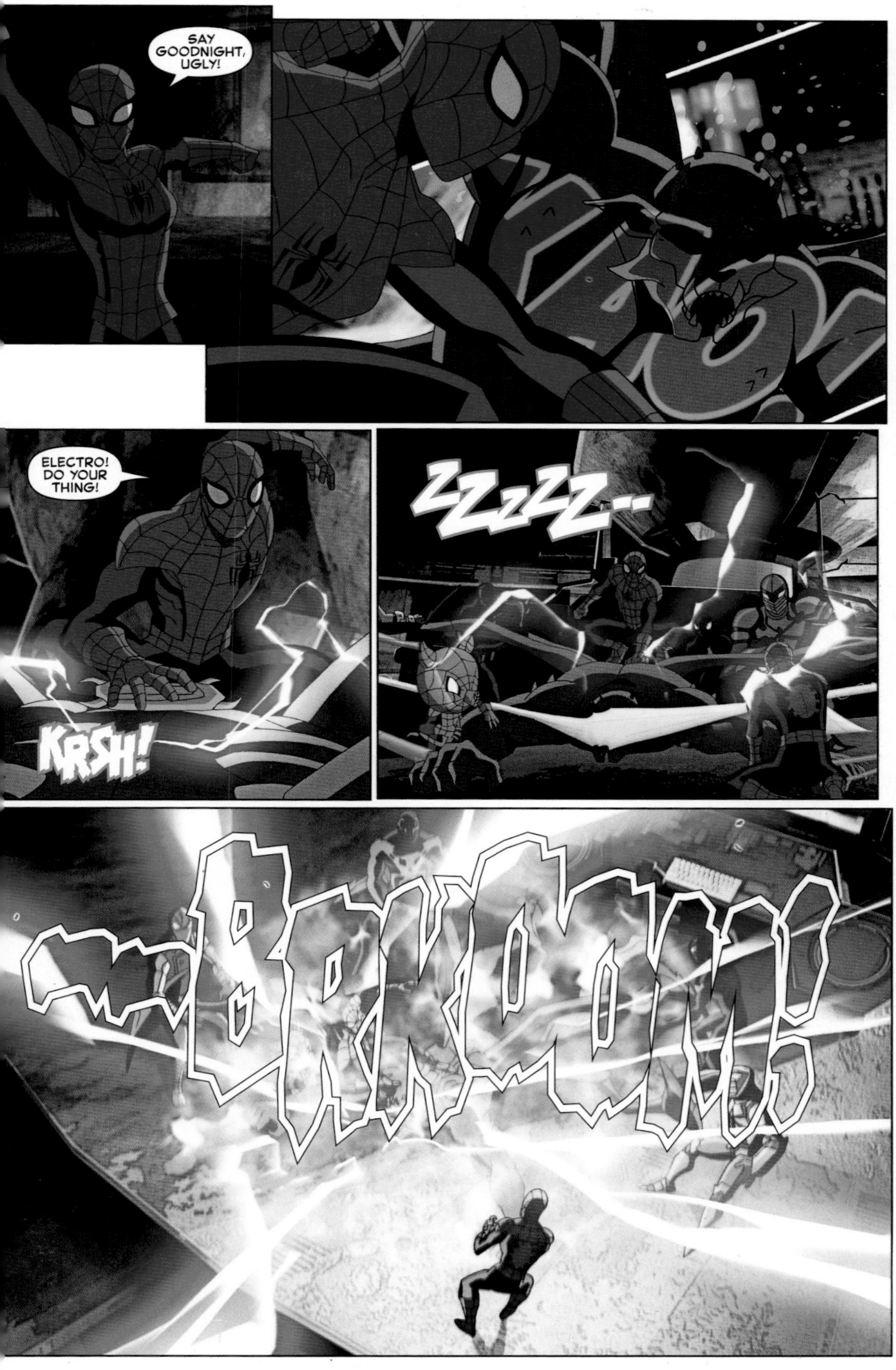
SAY GOODNIGHT, UGLY!
ELECTRO! DO YOUR THING!
KRSH!
ZZZZZZ--

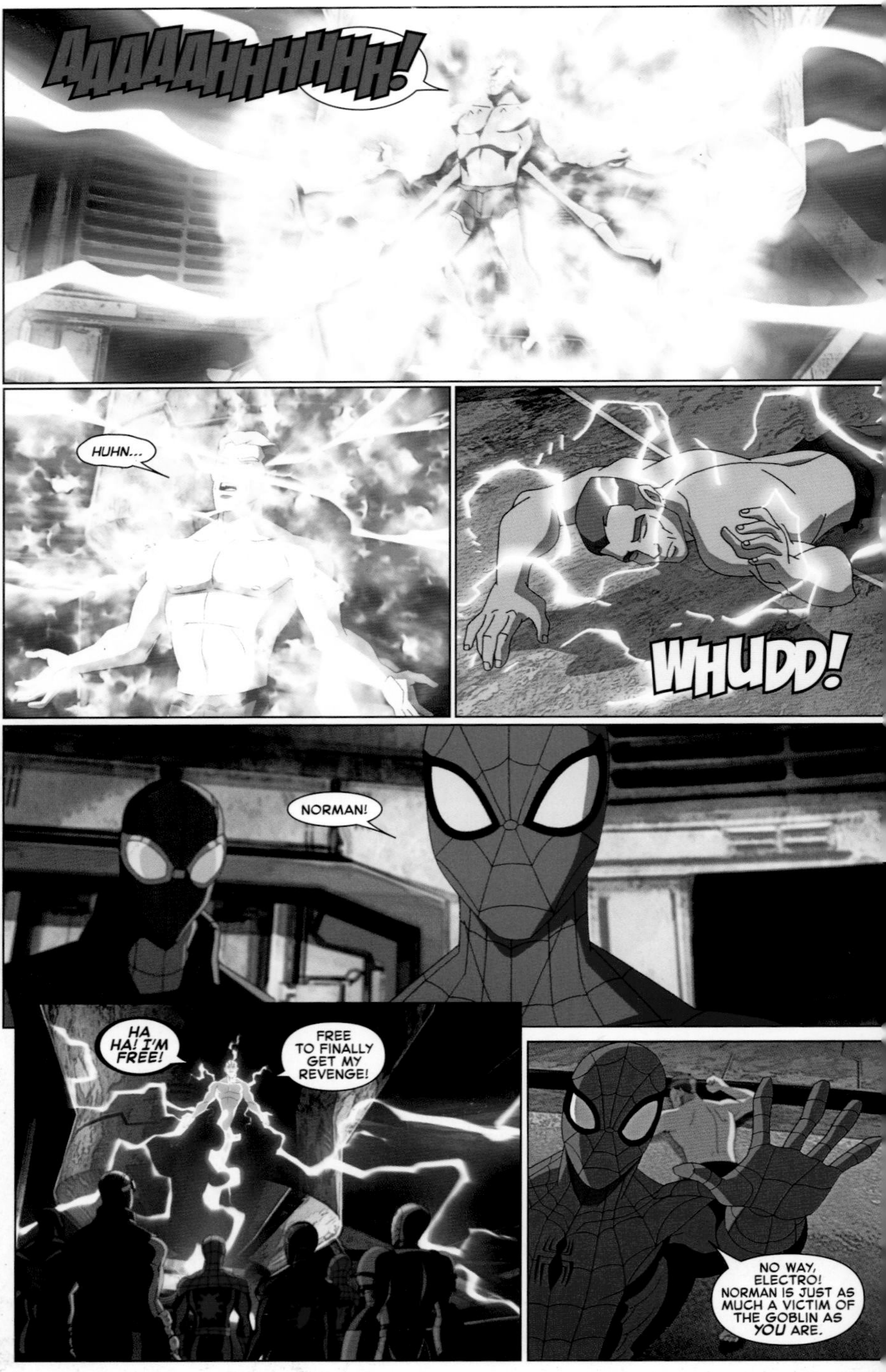
AAAAAHHHHHH!
HUHN...
WHUDD!
NORMAN!
HA HA! I'M FREE!
FREE TO FINALLY GET MY REVENGE!
NO WAY, ELECTRO! NORMAN IS JUST AS MUCH A VICTIM OF THE GOBLIN AS YOU ARE.

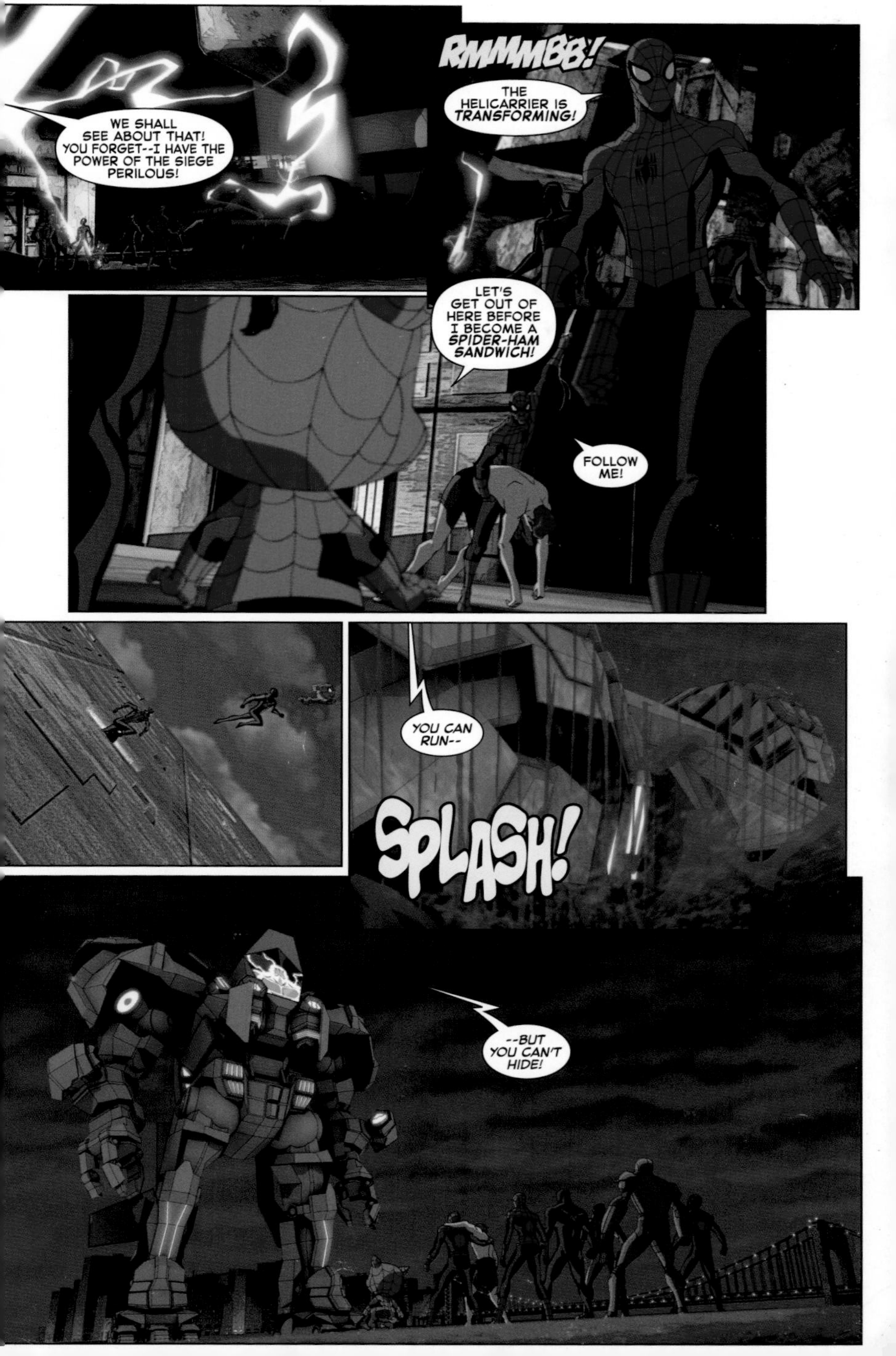

WE SHALL SEE ABOUT THAT! YOU FORGET--I HAVE THE POWER OF THE SIEGE PERILOUS!
RMMMBB!
THE HELICARRIER IS TRANSFORMING!
LET'S GET OUT OF HERE BEFORE I BECOME A SPIDER-HAM SANDWICH!
FOLLOW ME!
YOU CAN RUN--
SPLASH!
--BUT YOU CAN'T HIDE!

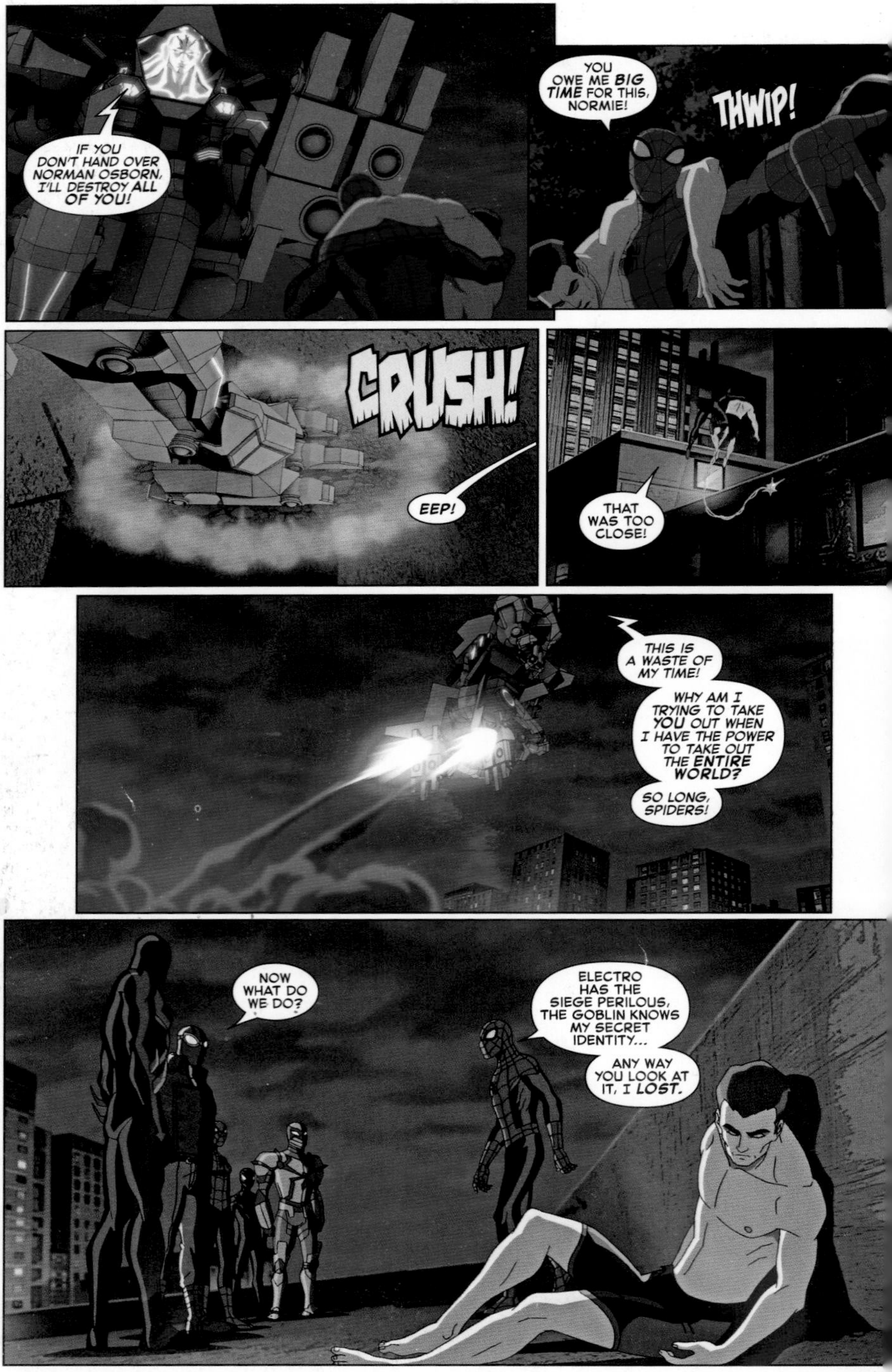
IF YOU DON'T HAND OVER NORMAN OSBORN, I'LL DESTROY ALL OF YOU!
YOU OWE ME BIG TIME FOR THIS, NORMIE!
THWIP!
CRUSH!
EEP!
THAT WAS TOO CLOSE!
THIS IS A WASTE OF MY TIME!
WHY AM I TRYING TO TAKE YOU OUT WHEN I HAVE THE POWER TO TAKE OUT THE ENTIRE WORLD?
SO LONG, SPIDERS!
NOW WHAT DO WE DO?
ELECTRO HAS THE SIEGE PERILOUS, THE GOBLIN KNOWS MY SECRET IDENTITY...
ANY WAY YOU LOOK AT IT, I LOST.

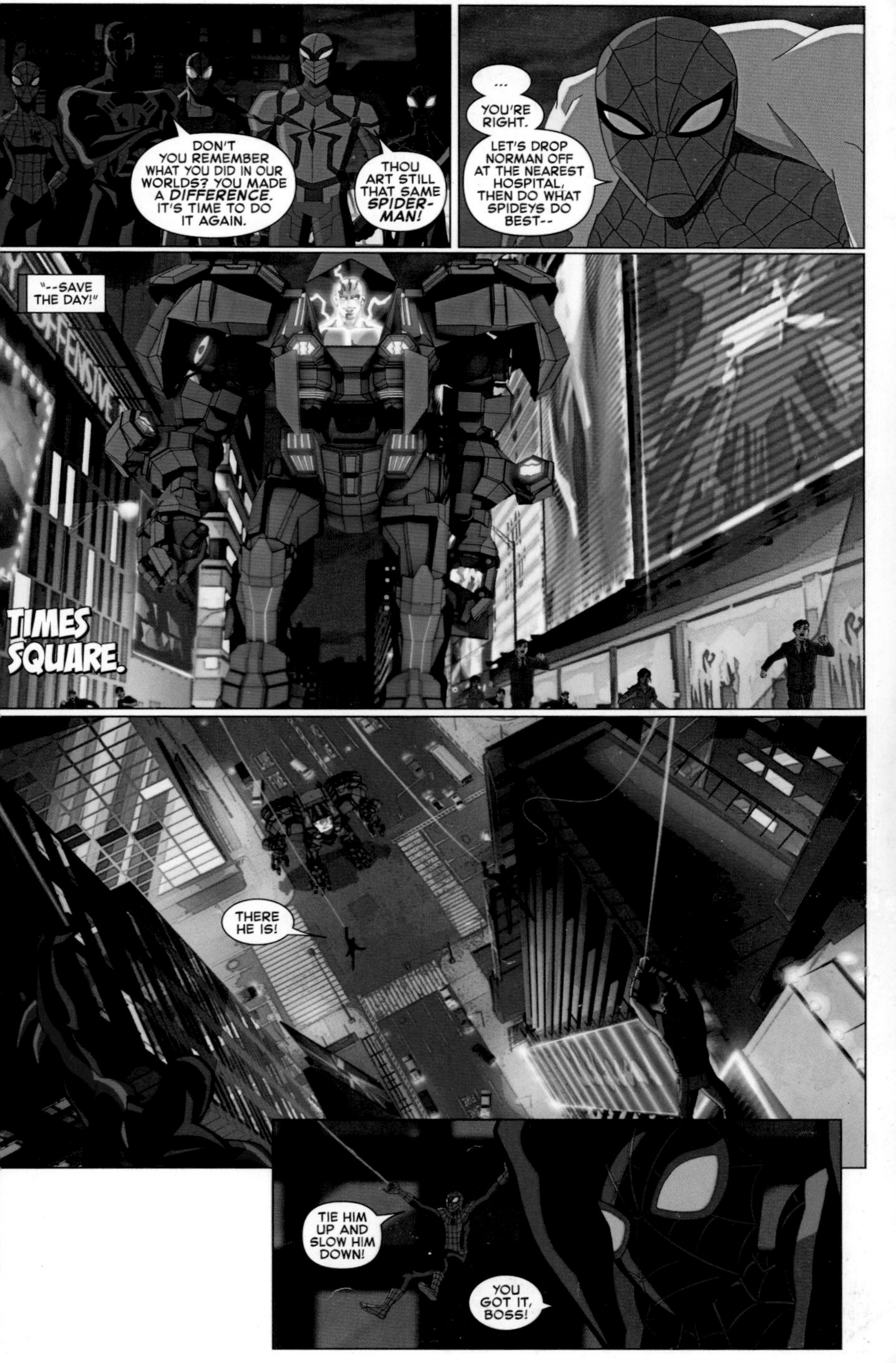
DON'T YOU REMEMBER WHAT YOU DID IN OUR WORLDS? YOU MADE A DIFFERENCE. IT'S TIME TO DO IT AGAIN.
THOU ART STILL THAT SAME SPIDER-MAN!
...
YOU'RE RIGHT.
LET'S DROP NORMAN OFF AT THE NEAREST HOSPITAL, THEN DO WHAT SPIDEYS DO BEST--
"--SAVE THE DAY!"
OFFENSIVE
TIMES SQUARE.
THERE HE IS!
TIE HIM UP AND SLOW HIM DOWN!
YOU GOT IT, BOSS!

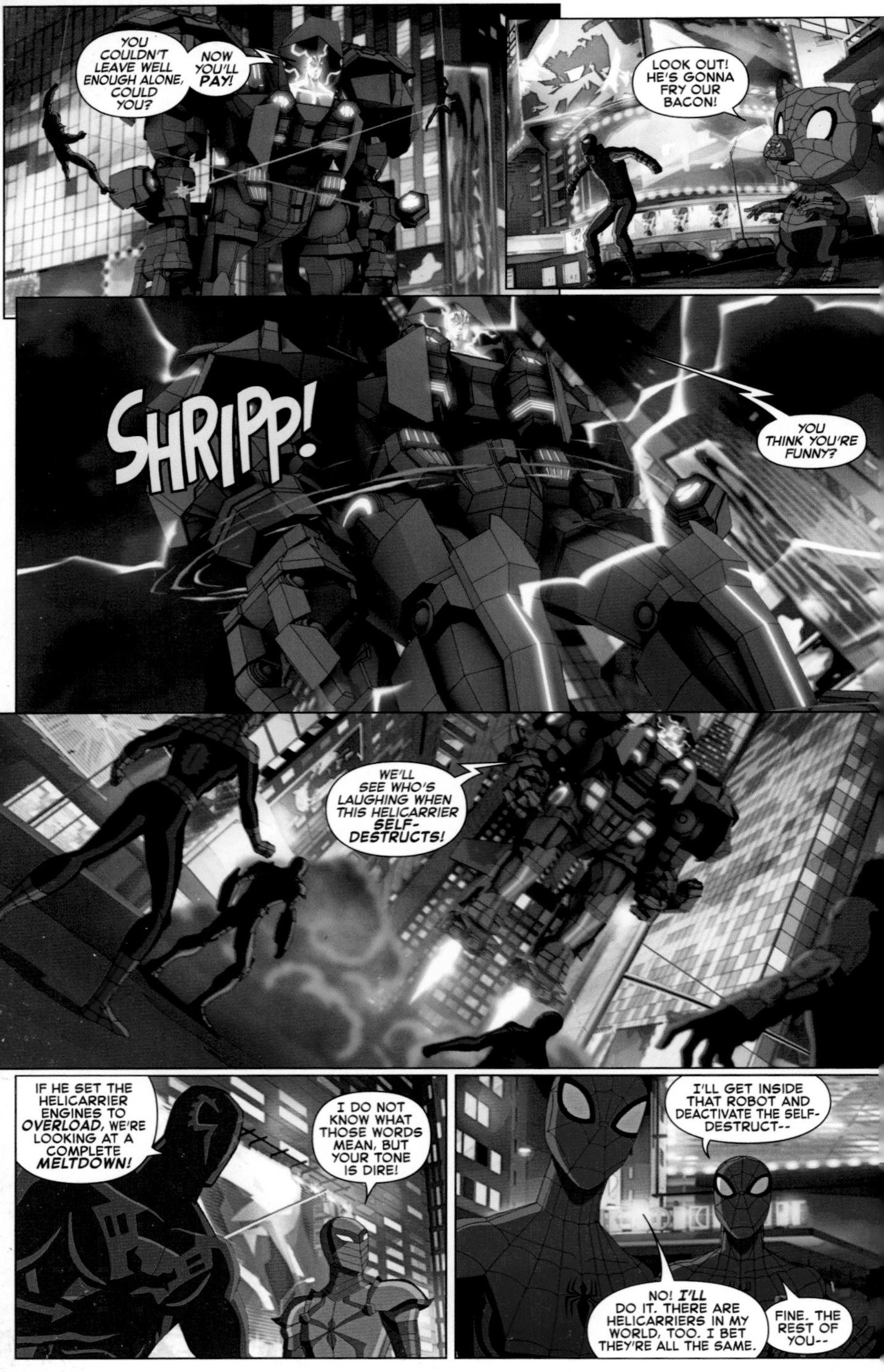
YOU COULDN'T LEAVE WELL ENOUGH ALONE, COULD YOU?
NOW YOU'LL PAY!
LOOK OUT! HE'S GONNA FRY OUR BACON!
SHRIPP!
YOU THINK YOU'RE FUNNY?
WE'LL SEE WHO'S LAUGHING WHEN THIS HELICARRIER SELF-DESTRUCTS!
IF HE SET THE HELICARRIER ENGINES TO OVERLOAD, WE'RE LOOKING AT A COMPLETE MELTDOWN!
I DO NOT KNOW WHAT THOSE WORDS MEAN, BUT YOUR TONE IS DIRE!
I'LL GET INSIDE THAT ROBOT AND DEACTIVATE THE SELF-DESTRUCT--
NO! I'LL DO IT. THERE ARE HELICARRIERS IN MY WORLD, TOO. I BET THEY'RE ALL THE SAME.
FINE. THE REST OF YOU--

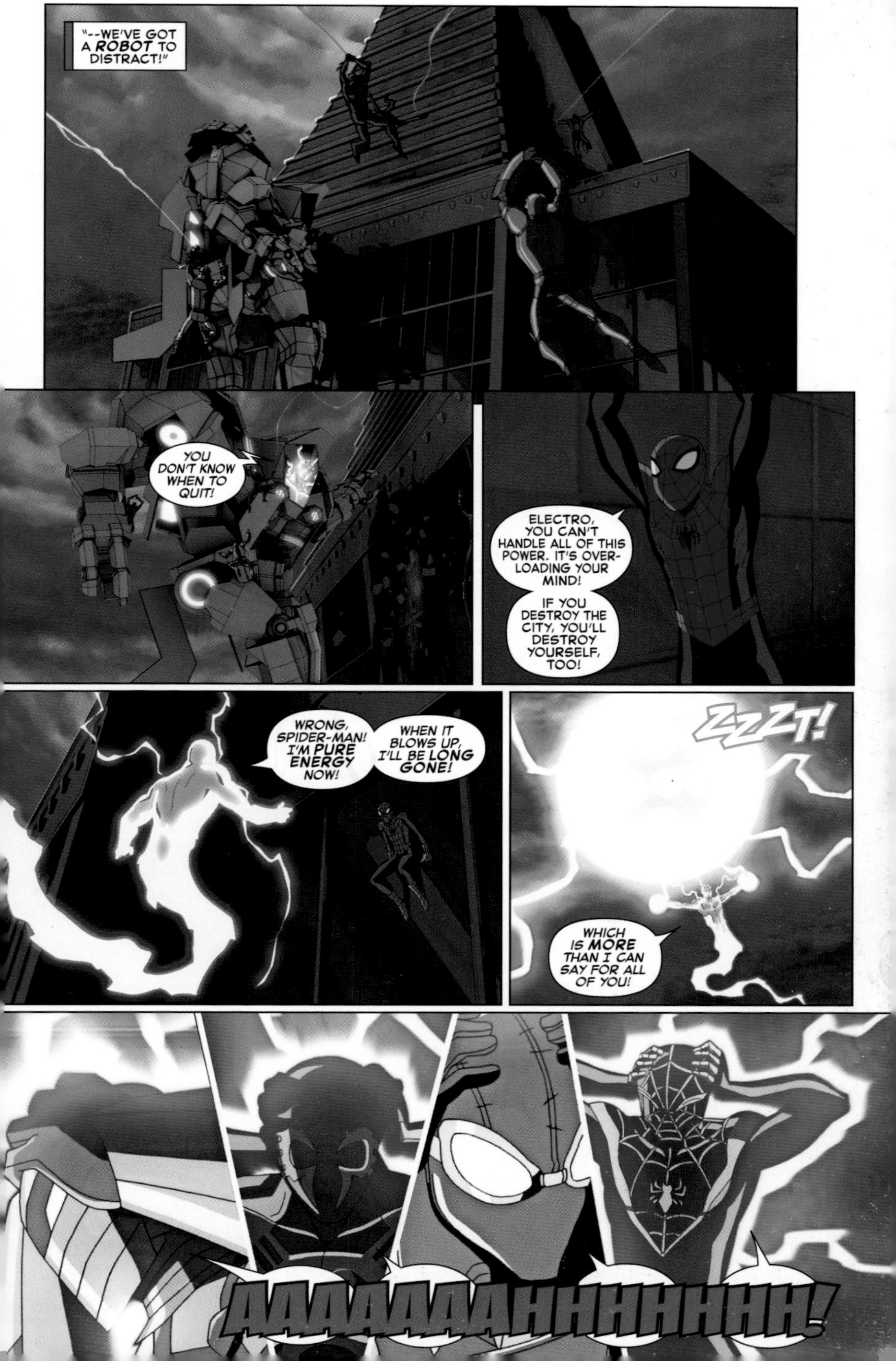
"--WE'VE GOT A ROBOT TO DISTRACT!"
YOU DON'T KNOW WHEN TO QUIT!
ELECTRO, YOU CAN'T HANDLE ALL OF THIS POWER. IT'S OVER-LOADING YOUR MIND!
IF YOU DESTROY THE CITY, YOU'LL DESTROY YOURSELF, TOO!
WRONG, SPIDER-MAN! I'M PURE ENERGY NOW!
WHEN IT BLOWS UP, I'LL BE LONG GONE!
ZZZT!
WHICH IS MORE THAN I CAN SAY FOR ALL OF YOU!
AAAAAAAHHHHHHH!

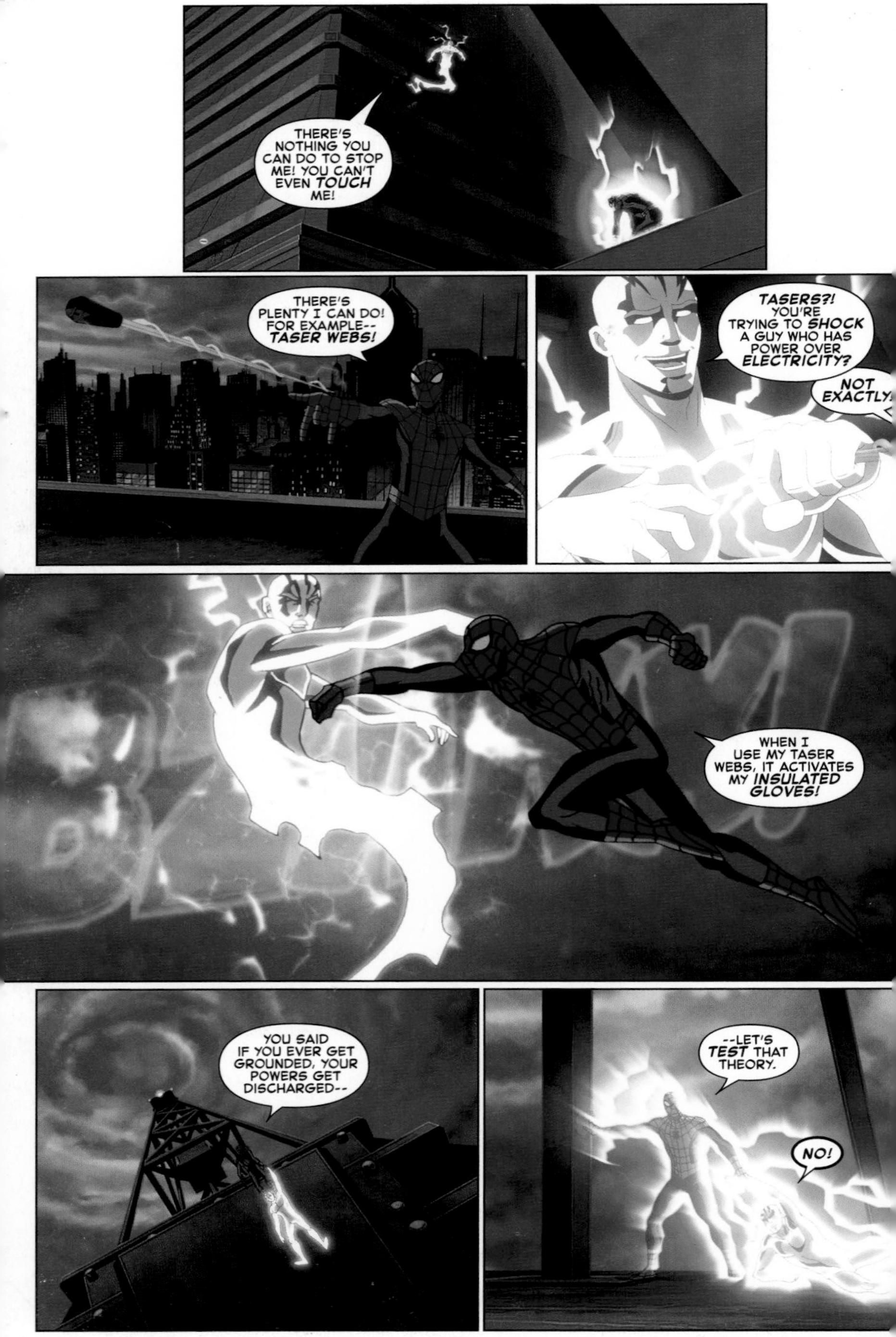
THERE'S NOTHING YOU CAN DO TO STOP ME! YOU CAN'T EVEN TOUCH ME!
THERE'S PLENTY I CAN DO! FOR EXAMPLE-- TASER WEBS!
TASERS?! YOU'RE TRYING TO SHOCK A GUY WHO HAS POWER OVER ELECTRICITY?
NOT EXACTLY.
WHEN I USE MY TASER WEBS, IT ACTIVATES MY INSULATED GLOVES!
YOU SAID IF YOU EVER GET GROUNDED, YOUR POWERS GET DISCHARGED--
--LET'S TEST THAT THEORY.
NO!

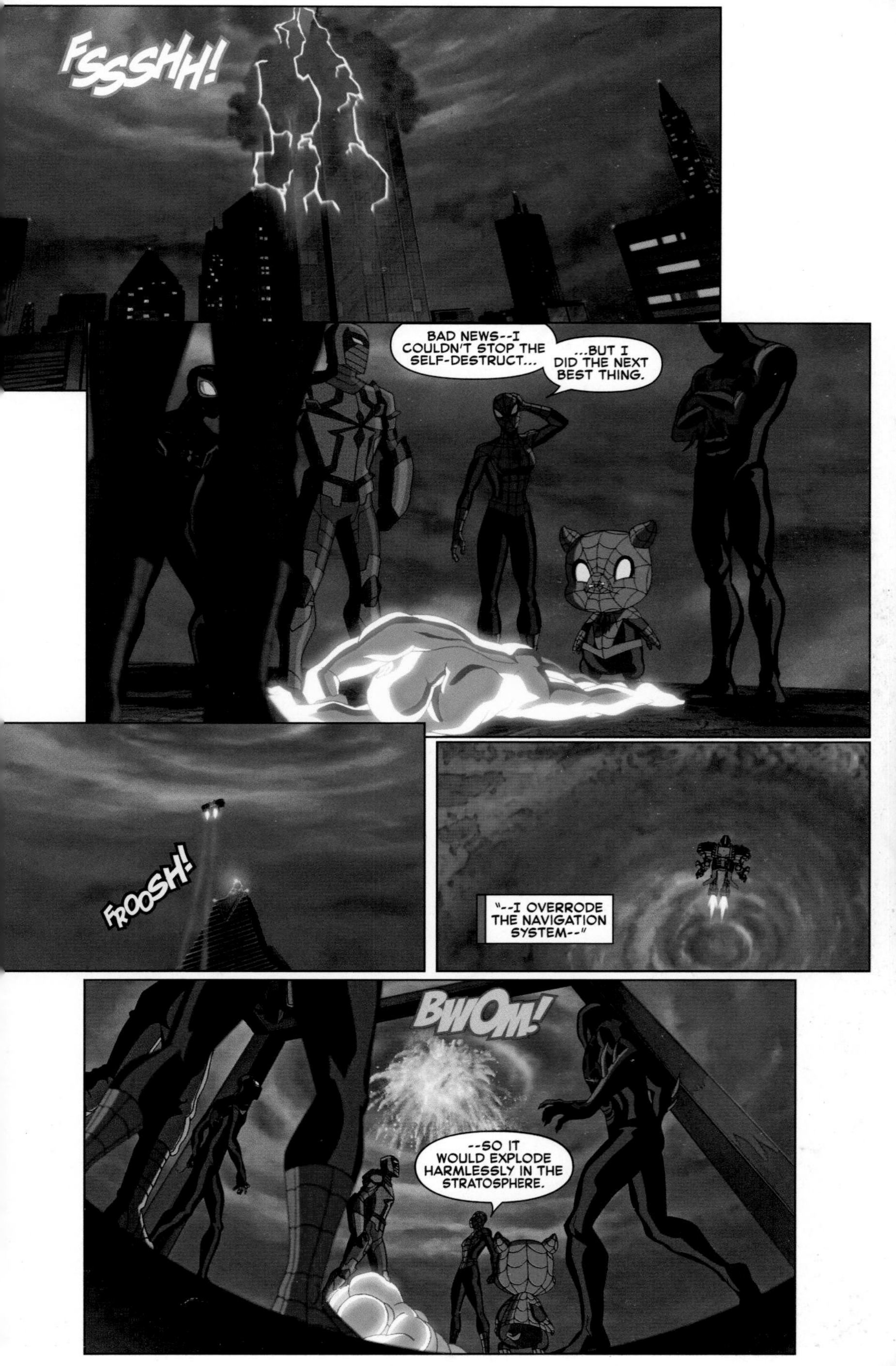
FSSSHH!
BAD NEWS--I COULDN'T STOP THE SELF-DESTRUCT...
...BUT I DID THE NEXT BEST THING.
FROOSH!
"--I OVERRODE THE NAVIGATION SYSTEM--"
BWOM!
--SO IT WOULD EXPLODE HARMLESSLY IN THE STRATOSPHERE.

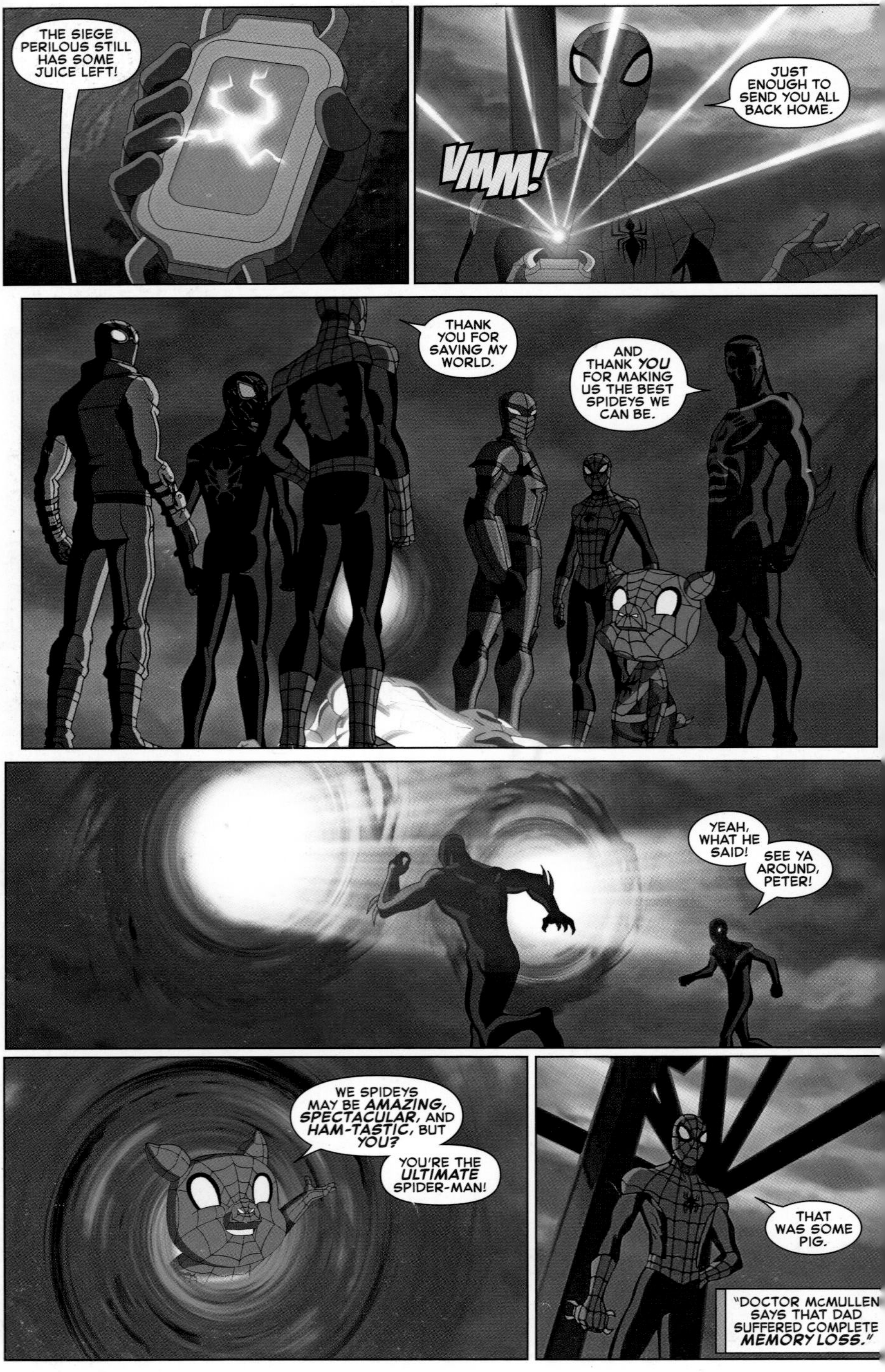
THE SIEGE PERILOUS STILL HAS SOME JUICE LEFT!
VMM!
JUST ENOUGH TO SEND YOU ALL BACK HOME.
THANK YOU FOR SAVING MY WORLD.
AND THANK YOU FOR MAKING US THE BEST SPIDEYS WE CAN BE.
YEAH, WHAT HE SAID!
SEE YA AROUND, PETER!
WE SPIDEYS MAY BE AMAZING, SPECTACULAR, AND HAM-TASTIC, BUT YOU?
YOU'RE THE ULTIMATE SPIDER-MAN!
THAT WAS SOME PIG.
"DOCTOR McMULLEN SAYS THAT DAD SUFFERED COMPLETE MEMORY LOSS."

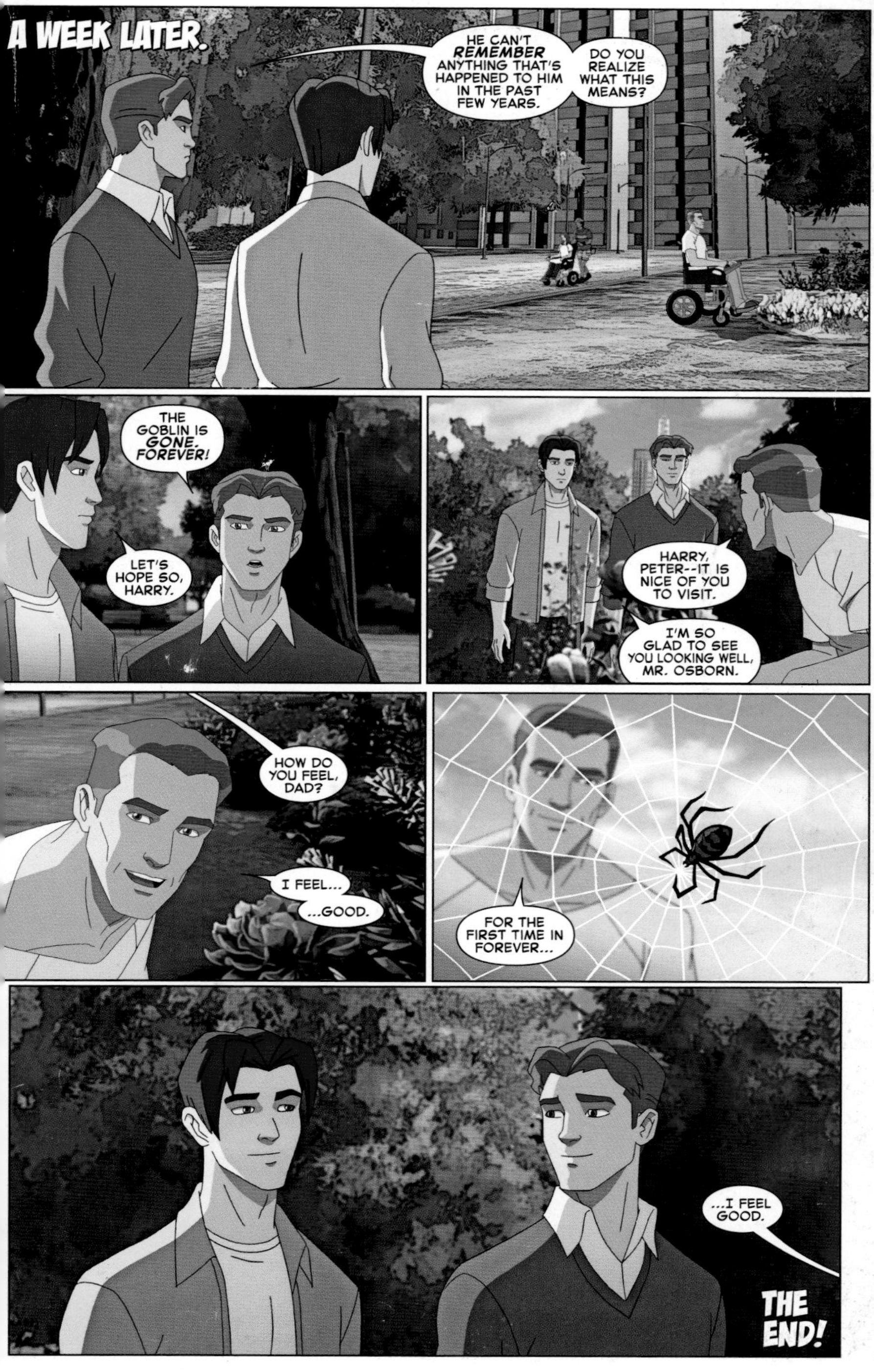

A WEEK LATER.
HE CAN'T *REMEMBER* ANYTHING THAT'S HAPPENED TO HIM IN THE PAST FEW YEARS.
DO YOU REALIZE WHAT THIS MEANS?
THE GOBLIN IS *GONE. FOREVER!*
LET'S HOPE SO, HARRY.
HARRY, PETER--IT IS NICE OF YOU TO VISIT.
I'M SO GLAD TO SEE YOU LOOKING WELL, MR. OSBORN.
HOW DO YOU FEEL, DAD?
I FEEL...
...GOOD.
FOR THE FIRST TIME IN FOREVER...
...I FEEL GOOD.
THE END!

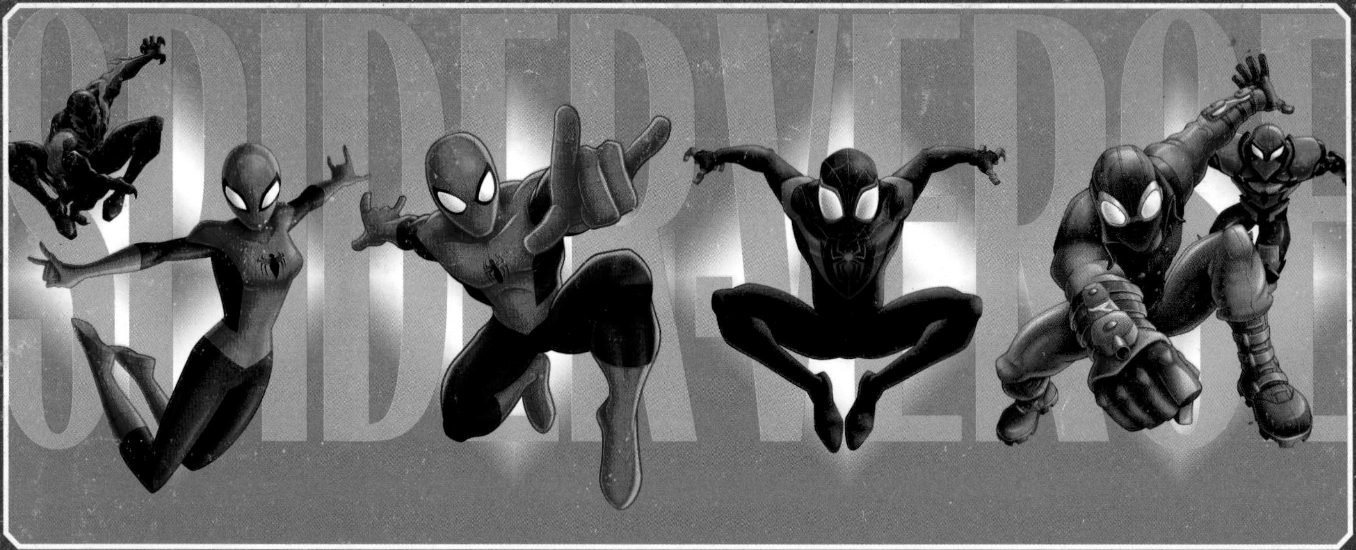

Marvel Universe Ultimate Spider-Man Spider-Verse #1-4 combined covers